Dec 2021

D1055472

Praise for *The Nightmare Thief*

★ "Lesperance has crafted a wonderfully original world...The delightfully descriptive text sets a cozy scene, but there is also real danger and a deliciously disconcerting villain. There is magic and mayhem, horror and hope, and the thread of family and friendship weaving it all together."

—*Booklist*, Starred Review

"A hair-raising, nontraditional horror novel with fantastical elements. Will have universal appeal for children who don't mind a scare."

—*School Library Journal*

"A spine-tingling adventure."

—*Kirkus Reviews*

"Lesperance crafts a resourceful heroine whose loyalty forces her to confront a difficult situation and come out stronger. She also folds a satisfying sense of wonder into the quaint town, balanced with a chilling element of darkness."

—*Publishers Weekly*

Also by Nicole Lesperance

The Wide Starlight
The Nightmare Thief

THE
DREAM
SPIES

Nicole Lesperance

sourcebooks
young readers

Published by Sourcebooks Young Readers, an imprint of Sourcebooks Kids
P.O. Box 4410, Naperville, Illinois 60567-4410
(630) 961-3900
sourcebookskids.com

Cataloging-in-Publication Data is on file with the Library of Congress.

Source of Production: Sheridan Books, Chelsea, Michigan, United States.
Date of Production: November 2021
Run Number: 5023485

Printed and bound in The United States of America.
SB 10 9 8 7 6 5 4 3 2 1

For my sister, Alissa

(who would never ditch me for a smarmy lifeguard).

One

"TU PUES COMME UN PIED DE GORILLE!"

Ignoring Henri, her grandmother Lishta's obnoxious gray parrot, Maren opened the top of the coffee grinder and slid it over to her older sister. It was a warm July day, and a salty breeze wafted in through the open windows of her family's dream shop, tinkling the sea-glass wind chimes her grandmother had recently hung in the center of the room.

"Henri, how would you even know what a gorilla's foot smells like?" Maren's sister, Hallie, rolled her eyes as she added a teaspoon of freshly powdered Astroturf to the coffee grinder. Feeling the tiniest bit glad that Henri had another person to pick on now, Maren broke off three splinters of wood from a piece of an old windmill and added them to the dream mixture.

"I'm sure Henri had a wild and interesting life before he

came to us," said Lishta, looking up from her newspaper to grab a saltine cracker from the plate she was sharing with her beloved bird. "We'll never know where exactly he's been and what he's seen…or sniffed."

"I don't think I *want* to know." Hallie turned to Maren. "Can you grab the putter?"

Maren headed for the closet at the back of the dream shop and rummaged through brooms and mops and rakes and old tennis rackets until she found the golf club. Pulling out a metal file, Hallie dragged it across the head of the club until shiny silver specks dotted the sheet of paper she'd laid underneath.

"What else?" she said as she tipped the putter dust into the coffee grinder.

Maren twisted a green strand of her hair as she pondered. This dream was going to be about mini golfing. But it wasn't just any ordinary golf course. The dreamers could jump in and out of the obstacles if they wanted: take a ride on the windmill's whirling arms, whiz down a triple loop-de-loop slide, climb giant flowers and sit on their swaying tops. So far, Maren and Hallie had concepts for fourteen of the eighteen holes.

"A blue whale," said Maren.

"Ooh, I like that." Hallie's eyes sparkled, which made Maren's heart sparkle.

"You can jump into its mouth and it'll shoot you out its blowhole," continued Maren.

"Yesss," said Hallie, already climbing the ladder. "What do you think, Gran-Gran? Atlantic or Pacific seawater?"

Lishta, absorbed in her newspaper, didn't answer.

"Gran-Gran?" repeated Hallie.

"Hmm?" Lishta pushed her glasses up and squinted at the paper.

"Atlantic or Pacific seawater?"

"For what, dear?"

With a huff, Hallie jumped off the ladder, startling Henri, who flapped his wings and almost knocked over a jar of tiny glass beads before Maren caught it.

"What are you reading?" asked Hallie, peering over Lishta's shoulder.

"An advertisement for a summer camp," said Lishta.

"Don't you think you're a little old for that?" said Hallie.

"Very funny." Lishta poked a knobby finger at Hallie's midsection, causing her to leap backward with a yelp. Maren grabbed another teetering jar before it fell off the shelf.

"Look at this," said her grandmother, spreading the newspaper flat on the counter. An illustrated ad took up the lower half of the page. It had big, cartoony letters, and underneath was a drawing of a lake and some cabins. The sky was full of z's and little thought bubbles with pictures inside: a flying superhero, a smiling cupcake, a kitten wearing sunglasses.

CAMP SHADY SANDS!!

Never in your wildest dreams could you imagine such a perfect summer!!! Nestled on the shaded, sandy shores of Lake Lentille, our camp is literally the stuff of dreams! We offer introductory dream-taking classes for our younger campers and advanced dream-crafting for seasoned dreamers! Plus, each camper will receive their own personal dream package, hand-selected and specially tailored to their individual tastes and wishes!!

DREAM BIG!!! SIGN UP NOW!!!

"That sure is a lot of exclamation points," muttered Hallie.

"Are they actually teaching kids how to make dreams?" said Maren.

Lishta tapped her chin with a pencil. "I wonder who's running this camp."

"TROUPEAU DE VACHES GRINCHEUSES!" shouted Henri.

"That's a good suggestion, Henri," said Lishta, "but it's probably not a herd of grumpy cows."

Maren skimmed through more exclamation-pointed, sales-pitchy text and found the contact info. "It doesn't say. But they have a website."

Hallie already had her phone out, fingers flying across the keypad. "It says here the directors are Calvin and Malvin Peppernot."

"Kelvin and Melvin who?" Lishta adjusted her glasses again.

"Calvin and Malvin." Hallie zoomed in on the photo of two balding men with identical goofy grins. They stood in front of a lake, wearing matching striped shirts, and one of them held a kayak paddle while the other clutched a pillow.

"I've never seen either of them in my life," said Lishta, which was surprising because there weren't many people in the dream industry, and she knew most of them. "Can you make the picture bigger?"

Hallie pinched and zoomed until the left twin's face filled her screen. Freckles dotted his lumpy nose, and the wispy beginnings of a mustache sprouted on his upper lip.

"I've got absolutely no idea who that is," said Lishta, pulling a hairpin from her braid and sticking it in the corner of her mouth.

"Maybe they work for somebody you know?" said Maren.

"Perhaps," said Lishta. "Is there anyone else listed on the website?"

Hallie tapped and scrolled for a while. "Nope."

"Any indication of who's supplying their dreams?" said Lishta.

More tapping and scrolling. "Nope."

"VIENNOISERIES POURRIES," squawked Henri.

"Quite right," murmured Lishta, still chewing on her hairpin. "Something is rotten in the state of Denmark."

"Is the camp in Denmark?" asked Maren.

Hallie laughed. "It's a quote from *Hamlet*, silly."

"Oh." Maren's cheeks went hot. It wasn't her fault they hadn't started studying Shakespeare in school yet.

"It means something's fishy, dear," said Lishta.

"Shady, even," said Hallie, waggling her eyebrows. "Ooh, look, there's going to be a Cleo Montclair exhibition next week." She pointed to the page opposite the ad for the camp. The headline read "Pine Ridge Art Museum Will Showcase Montclair's Magical Monstrosities."

Cleo Montclair was one of Rockpool Bay's most famous former residents, and one of Hallie's very favorite artists. She created giant abstract sculptures that were magically animated, moving in gentle, repetitive patterns that responded to people's emotions. To Maren, they seemed vaguely dangerous, but Hallie had several posters of those magical monstrosities hanging on her side of the room.

The shop phone rang, and they all jumped. Henri let out an outraged screech and flew away to the top of the ladder as Hallie picked up the receiver.

"Hey Mom," she said. "Yeah, I'm taking her in a few minutes." She tipped her chin away from the phone. "Gran-Gran, are you still coming for dinner tonight?"

"Yes, that would be lovely." Lishta stuck the hairpin back into her braid. "What time should I come?"

Hallie listened into the phone. "Maren has dance class until six thirty, so we'll probably eat around seven."

Lishta checked the clocks, one of which read four fifty and the other five ten. "I'd like to make to make a few phone calls first, and then I'll come over."

Ever since the incident with Obscura Gray last year, Lishta and a few other dream shop owners around the country had been keeping an eye on the dream-crafting world, checking in and reporting anything suspicious to each other. She folded up her newspaper as Hallie said goodbye to their mother.

"Should I go put up the Closed sign?" asked Maren.

"Yes, please," said Lishta. "Hallie, dear, could you write down all the contact information for that camp before you go? Especially those directors, Kelvin and Delvin."

"Calvin and Malvin," said Hallie, grabbing a notepad and a pencil.

As Maren made her way through the dim, wonderfully paper-and-ink-smelling typewriter showroom, worry gnawed at her stomach. Dream-making was a traditional art that was passed down through families, not taught at a camp like some fun craft project. More importantly, it was *dangerous* in the wrong hands. She'd seen that firsthand last year with Obscura Gray. Maren shuddered at the memory of the evil ballerina who'd blackmailed her, kidnapped her, and forced her to make nightmares as part of a scheme to brainwash and take over the whole town.

Flipping the Open sign to Closed, Maren whispered the phrase she'd been repeating to herself whenever she started feeling panicky: *Obscura is in jail. You are safe. Obscura is in jail. You are safe.*

It was true. Obscura had been sentenced to ten years. The prison was hundreds of miles away. Still, whenever Maren saw a moth, she flinched, remembering how Obscura had used them to stealthily deliver nightmares.

Back in the dream shop, Lishta was flipping through her address book and Hallie was pouring the contents of the coffee grinder into a jar. Their mini golf dream would have to wait until tomorrow. But that was fine, since they hadn't finished designing the last three holes of the golf course, and it was better not to rush creativity. Especially considering Hallie still needed a lot of downtime so she could continue recovering from her brain injury following the car accident.

"You ready?" said Hallie, fishing her keys out of her sweatshirt pocket. She'd finally been allowed to start driving again last month, and Maren never, ever forgot her duty to look out for hazards.

"Yep." Maren's tap shoes clanked inside her bag as she threw it over her shoulder. "Bye, Gran-Gran!"

Without looking up from her newspaper, Lishta blew her granddaughters a kiss and wiggled her fingers in the air.

Two

Maren's house smelled like an Italian restaurant and a bakery all rolled up in one. The savory aroma of garlic and tomatoes mingled with the yeasty scent of baking bread, and her stomach gurgled so loudly that Hallie heard it and laughed.

"Buonasera, ragazze!" called their dad from the kitchen. Opera music blared, and he sang along in half Italian, half gibberish, adding a dramatic tremolo to his voice.

With a groan, Hallie pulled out her phone and headed down the hallway.

"Aren't you going to hang out with us?" asked Maren.

"In a minute," said Hallie.

Maren's heart sank. She'd spent so much time looking forward to everything she and Hallie would do once she woke up from her coma. They'd spent lots of time together while

Hallie was still in the rehab facility and then recovering at home. But now that Hallie had gone back to school, she'd thrown herself into a social life full of activities and friends and boys…and not Maren.

With a sigh, Maren pulled out a stool at the kitchen island where her dad stood, tossing mushrooms and peppers into a giant salad bowl.

"Lalalalala babababababa ba BAHHH!" he bellowed, and Maren couldn't help but crack up as she reached for a cherry tomato.

"You sound like an injured sheep, hon." Maren's mom wandered in from the living room with an empty tea mug and a book. She kissed the top of her daughter's head and pulled up a stool. "How were things at the shop?"

"Pretty good," said Maren. "We sold four of your new water-skiing potato dream. Hallie was really talking it up to customers."

Her mom beamed. "Excellent."

"But then Gran-Gran found this weird ad in the paper for a summer camp that's all about dreaming. Apparently they're teaching kids how to make dreams."

Her mom's eyebrow lifted. "Who's running that?"

"We don't know," said Maren. "Some guys called Alvin and Galvin."

"Calvin and Malvin," called Hallie from their room.

"Whatever." Maren shrugged. "Gran-Gran wanted to make some calls to find out about them before she came over."

Her mom stole a cherry tomato from the salad, and her dad pretended to smack her hand away. "Hopefully it's all fake and nothing to worry about."

"Hopefully." Maren bit into a yellow pepper. But if the camp was fake, that wasn't great either. She didn't like the idea of anybody spreading false information about dreams. There were enough rumors about their shop floating around town after Obscura had started slipping people their nightmares.

The doorbell rang, and Maren jumped up to open it. There stood Lishta, clutching a bag of cookies and a bouquet of yellow roses from the Green and Fresh grocery store.

"It smells utterly delightful in here," said Lishta, handing the flowers to Maren's mom and taking an exaggerated sniff. "I should come for dinner more often."

"You really should, Ma," said Maren's mom, pulling a vase from the cabinet. Maren's dad set a glass of Lishta's favorite raspberry ginger ale on the island, and she pulled up a stool and took the newspaper from her giant, lumpy purse.

"Did the girls tell you about this?" asked Lishta.

"Yes." Maren's mom scanned the page. "It looks a little fishy, doesn't it? And what's with all those exclamation points?"

"That's what I said." Hallie emerged from the hallway,

having changed into her extra fluffy pajamas and pulled her blond hair up in a messy bun. She stretched and yawned, and her mom gave her a worried look.

"How are you feeling?" Almost a year after the accident, she still asked Hallie this question approximately forty-five times a day.

"I'm fine." Hallie gave her mom a patient smile. "Just tired. I was up until two finishing a book."

And texting her friends, thought Maren with a twinge of jealousy.

Her mother frowned and picked a thread off Hallie's shoulder. "You know you shouldn't be doing that. Your doctors—"

"My doctors said I'm fine," said Hallie, pouring herself a glass of raspberry ginger ale. "If I start feeling bad, I need to rest. But I don't feel bad. And I'll go to bed early tonight, okay?"

"Nine o'clock," said her mom, pointing aggressively at her watch.

Hallie rolled her eyes. "We'll see."

"How did your phone calls go, Gran-Gran? Did you find out anything?" Maren didn't like talking about Hallie's brain injury, and she especially didn't like when her mom harped on it. Hallie was awake; Hallie was fine. It was another phrase she repeated to herself sometimes when she started worrying.

"Everybody watch out!" Maren's dad swung around them with a pot of pasta and dumped it into the sink, sending a huge cloud of steam billowing into his face. Coughing, he flapped a dish towel to clear it. "Let's continue this conversation at the table. Tutti a tavolo!"

Everyone found their seat and began passing around dishes and pouring drinks and jumping up for forgotten Parmesan cheese and salad dressing. Finally, they all had steaming plates of penne with pomodoro sauce and cheesy garlic bread, and the room went silent as they dug in.

"Nothing," blurted out Lishta, setting down her fork. "I found out exactly nothing about that camp or those two young men. Nobody seems to know them."

Maren was tickled by the idea of anyone thinking those balding twins were young.

"So where are they getting their dreams from?" said Maren's dad through a mouthful of pasta.

"That's the thing, isn't it?" Lishta ripped her garlic bread in half, scattering crumbs everywhere. "Where *are* they getting them? You'd need rather a lot of dreams for a whole camp full of children. And nobody's gotten any bulk orders."

"So they must be fake," said Hallie.

"Perhaps," said Lishta. "But that seems like quite a gamble. Obviously the campers would report back to their parents that the dreams didn't work, and then you'd have a lot of angry parents demanding their money back."

"Could be a scam," said Maren. "Maybe they're taking people's money and disappearing before the parents have a chance to get mad?"

"It could be," mused Lishta. "But what if it isn't? What if somebody we don't know is making dreams and providing them to this camp?"

A feathery shiver ran down the back of Maren's neck. A rogue dream maker. Someone with dream magic who wasn't known to the wider dream community. Or somebody who *was* part of the community but had a secret side project. Either way, it made her queasy. Dreams needed to be carefully regulated and controlled so they didn't end up in mind-control schemes like Obscura's. And a camp was a place full of kids all on their own.

"This is potentially too dangerous to ignore," said Lishta, as if she were reading Maren's thoughts. "I'm going there to investigate."

Maren dropped her garlic bread into her salad bowl. "You are? How?"

"I'm going to apply for a job in their dining hall," said Lishta.

Maren's entire family stared, openmouthed, at Lishta.

"You're going to...cook?" said Maren's dad, and Hallie stifled a laugh behind her napkin.

"How hard can it be?" Lishta waved her fork dismissively. "Put some hamburgers on a grill, heat up a pot of soup, give out some cereal."

The last time Maren had slept over at her grandmother's house, Lishta had served crunchy eggs for breakfast. And burnt toast with something vaguely resembling shoe polish spread on top.

"Of course I'll have to go undercover," said Lishta. "But I've got all those wigs at home, and I'm quite looking forward to a makeover."

"Can we come?" said Maren.

Now everyone stared at her instead of Lishta.

"We could sign up as campers and go undercover too," said Maren. "We'd be able to find out a lot more from the kids' perspective."

Summer in Rockpool Bay was fun if you were a tourist, but the crowds everywhere got tedious, and you could only walk on the pier and check out all the attractions so many times before they lost their novelty. With so many hospital bills left to pay, Maren's family hadn't been able to afford a trip anywhere—and probably wouldn't for a very long time.

Hallie clearly felt the same way about getting out of town, because she was practically falling out of her chair. "Can we please go and help Gran-Gran? We could be dream spies!"

"Yesss," hissed Maren.

"Whoa, whoa, whoa," said Maren's dad. "I don't know if that's a good idea."

"Where is this camp?" said her mom.

"It's on Lake Lentille," said Lishta. "In Greenleaf Valley."

"That's not too far," said Maren. Greenleaf Valley was only about a two-hour drive from Rockpool Bay. "Can we go, please-please-please? Gran-Gran will be there to look out for us the whole time!"

"Assuming she even gets the job," said her mother.

"I'm sure she'll be fine," said Hallie. "Come on, aren't you dying to know what's going on there too?"

Her parents exchanged a look.

"The camp starts a week from Saturday, so you've got a bit of time to consider," said Lishta. "I looked it up on the *internet*." She beamed proudly. "And I don't want to step on your toes, parenting-wise, but the fees aren't terribly expensive and the shop's been doing well all summer, so I can pay for them."

"Please!" yelled Maren and Hallie.

Their mother sighed. "We'll think about it."

Under the table, Hallie nudged Maren's foot, and the two shared an excited grin. It wasn't a definite yes, but it was a solid maybe.

Three

By nine o'clock the next morning, Maren and Hallie had weeded the entire flower patch outside their house in a not-very-subtle attempt to convince their parents to let them go to Camp Shady Sands. Hallie hadn't looked at her phone once, and as much as Maren hated yard work, it was almost worth it to have this uninterrupted time with her sister. Pulling off her gardening gloves, she sprawled on the lawn under the shade of an elm tree. Her knees were covered in sweaty dirt, and her legs ached from kneeling.

"How is it this hot already?" Hallie took a gulp from her water bottle and passed it to her.

"I bet Lake Lentille is nice and cool." Maren imagined dunking her entire body into a chilly, clear lake and sighed.

"I bet they have ice cream too," said Hallie.

"When's the last time we went anywhere that wasn't Rockpool Bay or your rehab place?" asked Maren.

Hallie took another swig of water and wiped her chin. "I can't remember. Maybe that trip with Gran-Gran to the cedar forest?"

"I don't know if that counts." Maren scratched her leg, thinking of the dozens of mosquito bites she'd collected along with the dream ingredients. The forest wasn't exactly a destination; it was more of a gathering of trees and bugs.

The front door of their house opened, and their mom stepped out. "Wow, girls, that looks beautiful! Thank you."

"You're welcome," said Hallie.

"So can we go?" said Maren.

Her mom laughed. "Your dad and I had a long talk last night, and we've decided it's okay."

With a whoop, Maren leapt up and started dancing. Hallie jumped up too, but before she could join in, their mom held her hand up like a crossing guard.

"But first, we need to establish a few rules," she said.

Maren's happy dance slowed to a gentle back-and-forth sway.

"Number one," said Maren's mom. "You will listen to your grandmother at all times. No talking back, no negotiating. You will do exactly what she tells you."

"Okay," said Maren and Hallie.

"Number two," said their mom. "You will call me or your dad once a day to check in."

"Okay," said Maren, and Hallie groaned. Their mom threw her a stern look, and Hallie sighed.

"Fine," she grumbled.

"Number three," continued their mom. "You will not, under any circumstances, take any of the dreams at this camp."

"We won't," said Maren.

"Duh," said Hallie. "No one knows who made them or what's in them."

"That's right." Their mom folded her arms over her chest. "I just hope all those other kids will be safe. If you see anything suspicious, report it to Gran-Gran and call me or your dad. Call both of us. If we need to involve the police and shut the camp down, we'll do it."

"But hopefully we won't," said Maren.

"It's probably just a scam," said Hallie. "They're probably just putting beetle legs and Tic Tacs into tea bags and calling them dreams."

Maren shuddered. "I hope they're sterilizing them first."

"Me too," said her mom. "When in doubt, call me—"

"Or Dad," finished Hallie.

"Or both," said their mom. "The camp starts in a week, so

start thinking about your disguises. We might not know who's in charge, but they might know who we are."

"We're not *that* famous in the dream-making world," scoffed Hallie, but Maren's gentle sway turned back into an excited wiggle. She'd been wanting to dye her hair a new color for weeks now, and this was the perfect opportunity. As her mom headed back inside, the wiggle became a hop, then a kick and a spin.

"We're going to Camp Shady Sands!" she sang, grabbing Hallie's hand and whirling her around.

"We're getting out of Rockpool Bay!" Hallie swung Maren into a dip.

More importantly, they were getting out of Rockpool Bay *together*. Without Hallie's friends and potential boyfriends, none of whom ever acknowledged Maren's existence.

A bicycle came wheeling down the sidewalk, but the two sisters didn't stop dancing, not even when the cyclist stopped, dropped his bike to the ground, and joined in.

"Why are we doing this?" said Amos, flinging his leg out and flashing jazz hands.

"Mom's letting us go to camp!" yelled Maren, pounding out eight counts of rocket-fast tap footwork.

Amos tried to copy her moves and managed to get his legs tangled. "Since when do you want to go to camp?"

"Since yesterday!" Hallie shot past in a soaring grand jeté. She'd been a ballet kid until she was eleven and then decided it wasn't for her. As Amos watched her fly across the lawn, his face went a little pink.

"It's a camp where they supposedly give you dreams and teach you to make them," said Maren. "Gran-Gran thinks it's suspicious and we're going to investigate. It starts on Saturday."

"That sounds cool and sketchy all at the same time," said Amos, his grin widening. "Can I come?"

Maren hesitated. On the one hand, this was supposed to be her special time with Hallie. On the other hand, Amos hadn't left Rockpool Bay all summer either. If he went, he'd probably be in a boys' group anyway, which might make it easier for him to investigate different things. And of course Maren hadn't forgotten how helpful he'd been in defeating Obscura Gray.

"Ask your mom," she said. "My grandma said it's not too expensive."

"Awesome," said Amos. "My dad just sent me a check for my birthday, so I can offer to pay for part of it."

Both he and Maren grimaced. Amos's birthday was two months ago.

"Anyway," he continued, picking up his bike from the ground, "I bet my mom will let me spend it on camp. I'm on my way to meet her at the nursing home right now for my grandpa's birthday party."

"Don't go yet," said Maren. "I made something for you." She dashed back into the house and pulled a waxed paper bag from her backpack. Inside were three sachets of a brand-new dream she'd made the day before, inspired by a graphic novel series she and Amos had both read in elementary school.

"Oh wow," he said, opening the packet and peering inside. "Is this what I think it is?"

"Yep," said Maren. "It's mostly based on book one, but I also added the spaceship from book two and the talking toilet from book three."

"Awesome. I wish it was bedtime already," said Amos.

"Let me know what you think after you take it," said Maren. "I might still add a few more things, and I'm not sure there's enough powdered sock lint."

To most people this would have been a turnoff, but Amos laughed. "From *your* socks?"

"I'll never tell." Maren attempted a wink that ended up more like a scrunchy, two-eyed blink. "But don't worry, they were clean, and I also sterilized them."

Amos stuck the dream packet in his pocket and climbed back on his bike. "I'll text you as soon as I know about camp, and I'll give you a full report on the dream tomorrow."

"Sounds good," said Maren. "Tell your grandpa I said happy birthday."

She watched Amos ride away down the street, and then with a quick hop-shuffle, Maren went inside to start planning her disguise for Camp Shady Sands.

Four

Maren stood in the shower, watching a worryingly large amount of brown water swirl down the drain.

"How long am I supposed to keep rinsing this?" she called to Hallie, who stood at the sink wearing plastic gloves and putting the final touches on her own gloopy, dye-coated hair, which was currently the color of a traffic cone.

"Until the water runs clear," said Hallie. "But hurry up because I need to rinse mine too."

Maren rinsed and wrung her hair, but it still leaked brown everywhere, so she added shampoo a few more times until finally the water turned the color of a puddle on a moderately clean street. The shower was running out of hot water, so she turned off the tap before Hallie freaked out. Then she gingerly wrapped her hair in one towel and her goose-bumpy body in another.

"Is my scalp supposed to feel all tingly and weird?" she asked.

"Probably," said Hallie. "Now can you please leave so I can get in the shower?"

Trailing droplets of faintly brown water, Maren headed to her room and got dressed with the towel still on her head. The nerves jangling around her body were more than just worry about her hair. She'd felt jangly ever since Hallie's accident. Maybe even before that, to be honest.

From the bathroom, she heard the shower shut off, then rustling and the roar of the blow-dryer. Hallie sang loudly over the roar. Despite everything that'd happened to her last year, she never seemed traumatized or worried. Then again, Hallie hadn't been kidnapped. Maren kept expecting her own nerves to go away now that everything was safe again, but they hadn't. Not all the time, anyway. And they had a nasty habit of sneaking up on her when she least expected it, for the smallest of reasons. Sometimes for no reason at all.

The door swung open, and Maren almost fell off her bed. There stood her sister, wrapped in her robe with a gloriously blazing mane of flame-colored hair.

"You don't look like a traffic cone at all!" Maren said.

Hallie laughed and swung her hair over one shoulder. "I guess it's kind of cool."

"Kind of?" Maren touched her sister's silky hair. "It's gorgeous. You should keep it this way."

"We'll see." Hallie lifted the edge of Maren's towel and peered underneath. "Ready to find out what yours looks like?"

"No." Maren ducked away, but Hallie grabbed the end of her towel, untwisting until it fell off.

"Ooh," said Hallie.

"Ooh, pretty, or ooh, you look like a troll?" squeaked Maren.

"It's super dramatic," said Hallie. "Come on, let's dry it."

She made Maren face away from the mirror as she wafted the blow-dryer at her head, and Maren resisted the urge to peek. The strands of hair flying past her face were almost black, so different from her usual Kool-Aid colors.

"Am I going to look like that girl from *The Addams Family*?" she yelled over the blow-dryer's roar.

"Is that a bad thing?" yelled Hallie.

Maren wasn't sure. Finally, her sister turned her around, and Maren blinked at her reflection. She did look a tiny bit like Wednesday Addams...if Wednesday had blue eyes and rounder cheeks.

"You look sooo good," squealed Hallie.

Maren set her mouth in a straight line and folded her arms across her chest. "I...like it," she said, narrowing her eyes and nodding slowly.

"Me too." Hallie gave her shoulders a squeeze, and Maren leaned into her for a few seconds. It still felt like a miracle that she'd gotten her sister back.

"You're going to need a cool new name for your alias," said Hallie. "Something dark and mysterious, like Raven or Draconia."

"Or Monday," said Maren. "That's like Wednesday but worse."

Hallie snorted. "What's Amos doing for his disguise?"

"Not sure yet," said Maren. Amos had texted her the night before, letting her know that he was allowed to go to Camp Shady Sands as long as Lishta kept an eye on him. This had set off another round of happy dancing from Maren, though not from Hallie, who had been busy texting some boy from her biology class.

From out in the living room came the ding of the doorbell, and Hallie jumped, clutching her bathrobe tight around her. "Can you get that while I get dressed?"

"Sure." Maren brushed a dark curtain of hair over one eye and skulked dramatically to the door. She hoped it wasn't that boy from Hallie's biology class. But when she opened the door, a short woman wearing black sunglasses and a red jumpsuit stood on the steps. On top of her curly bluish wig perched a smug-looking green bird.

"Gran-Gran!" Maren stepped back to let her grand-mother inside. "How was the interview? And what did you do to Henri?"

"Good, good," said Lishta. "They offered me the job on the spot. Your hair looks ravishing, by the way."

Maren's heart leapt, and jitters filled her stomach. This was really happening.

"BONJOUR, CROTTE DE NEZ!" yelled green Henri, launching off Lishta's head and whizzing over to the arm of a chair.

Lishta gave her parrot a stern look. "Excuse me?"

"GUTEN TAG, POPEL!" It didn't sound like French, but Maren wasn't sure what language Henri was now speaking.

"How did you get him that color?" she asked.

"I brought him over to Mr. Alfredo's Splendid Salon," said Lishta. "I was a little concerned that hair dye might not work on feathers or that it might be unhealthy for birds. But Mr. Alfredo did something with his styling magic. I'm not quite sure what, but he assures me it's bird-safe and will wear off in a few weeks' time."

"SCHÖNER VOGEL," squawked Henri. "SCHÖNER SCHÖNER VOGEL."

Hallie emerged from the bedroom. "Love your jumpsuit,

Gran-Gran." She let Lishta ooh and aah over her gleaming orange hair for a minute before jabbing her thumb at Henri. "Why's he calling himself pretty in German?"

Lishta beamed. "This, my dear girls, is Heinrich."

"GUTEN TAG, HÄSSLICHE ROSINEN," yelled the bird.

Hallie narrowed her eyes. "Did he just call us...ugly raisins?"

"It's possible." Lishta waved a hand dismissively. "My German is a little rusty."

"Are you seriously bringing him with us to Camp Shady Sands?" Maren wasn't sure this was the best idea, considering Henri was the exact opposite of stealthy.

"I certainly am," said Lishta. "Hen—Heinrich will be an essential member of our team, able to slip unnoticed into all kinds of places to eavesdrop."

Hallie ruffled Henri's chest feathers with her knuckle. "Can we call him Heinie?"

Henri snapped at her finger and she snatched it away.

"How was the interview?" Maren filled the kettle with water and pulled Lishta's favorite peppermint tea from the cupboard.

"Fine," said Lishta. "I only met the head of dining services. A sweet young woman. She didn't seem to know much about the dreams, though I didn't press her too firmly."

"And she didn't ask you about your cooking skills?" asked Hallie.

"She asked how I felt about heating up large quantities of frozen things, and I told her I was an expert at that!"

Maren agreed. That was probably Lishta's one solid cooking skill.

"What does the camp look like?" she asked.

Her grandmother shrugged. "Rather unspectacular, to be honest. Cabins, canoes, trees, you get the idea. But I'm sure they'll fancy things up before opening day."

"Did you see any dream stuff?" said Maren.

"Not a single sachet," said Lishta. "It's all very curious. But I did have to sign a few forms that seemed a bit suspicious. Including a nondisclosure agreement."

"A nondis-what?" said Maren.

"Nondisclosure," said Lishta. "Otherwise known as an NDA. It means I've legally agreed not to tell anyone anything that goes on there."

"And if she does, they can sue her," added Hallie.

"Is that normal for a summer camp?" said Maren.

"Is what normal for a summer camp?" Maren's dad swung through the screen door at the back of the kitchen. "Wow, I'm digging this Gothic look, Mare-bear. And Hallie, you could be twins with that little mermaid. What's her name, Arianne?"

"Ariel." Hallie looked horrified, which made Maren laugh. He had a point.

"Maybe you should use that for your alias," she joked, but Hallie pulled out her phone to take a selfie, then started tapping away on her screen.

"And who is this utterly stunning creature?" Maren's dad clasped his hands over his heart and squinted dramatically at the parrot. "Henri? Is that you?"

Henri let out an irritated screech, hopped over to a potholder, and tossed it on the floor.

"Are you staying for dinner, Lishta?" Maren's dad picked up the potholder and flapped it at Henri, who squawked a stream of what Maren assumed were German swears, then launched into the air and landed on Lishta's curly wig.

"No, thank you," said Lishta. "I want to get everything ready at the shop before we go. My cousin Claudette is coming down from Quebec to take care of things while I'm away."

"And Mom's going to help too, right?" said Maren.

"She is." Lishta beamed. "I can't wait to see what dreams she makes while we're away."

Maren was struck by a sudden, strong wish for her mother to come to Camp Shady Sands too. But who brought their mom to camp? That would definitely look suspicious. Anyway, it was just a ridiculous camp run by silly people who didn't seem to know how dreams actually worked.

"Henri and I need to get going now," said Lishta. "We just wanted to come over and share the good news. And Henri wanted to show you his new look."

Henri opened his beak and made a long, wet fart noise that made Maren and her dad laugh. Lishta rolled her eyes.

"Pack your bags," she said. "Don't forget lots of pajamas! That's what everybody wears at Camp Shady Sands."

"We won't," murmured Hallie, not looking up from her screen.

As her grandmother's yellow VW Beetle backed out of the driveway, Maren waved and tried not to worry. This was going to be a fun adventure, she told herself.

But what if something bad happens? said a tiny voice in the back of her brain.

"Shh," she whispered, then went to her room to find her pajamas.

Five

"Hello, campers!" A young woman wearing a unicorn onesie waved from the camp's registration table, which sat in a grassy clearing nestled in pine-scented woods. Faded cabins and larger wooden structures ringed the edges of the clearing. Through the trees on the left lay a sandy beach, with a long dock extending into the sparkling lake and small boats tied up along its sides. Beside the registration table was a hand-painted blue sign that read Welcome to Camp Shady Sands, where all your dreams come true!!!!

"Oh my God, why?" whispered Hallie, and Maren edged closer to her sister. She felt awkward in pajamas and slippers in the middle of the day, but the camp website said everybody wore them at Camp Shady Sands. Maren had brought a few sets of summertime short sets in shades of black and gray to match her new, dark personality, and Hallie had opted for vivid prints and florals to offset her hair.

"I'm Judy, the head counselor," said the onesie-clad woman, stretching her hand across the table to fist-bump Maren's mom. "It's so *dreamy* to meet you!"

"Great to meet you too." Maren's mom returned the fist bump with a strained smile. "These are my daughters, Zoe and Vesper Finch. They're thrilled to be here."

"*So* thrilled," Maren also fist-bumped the head counselor, who looked a bit sweaty in her onesie under the sweltering sun.

"We think dreams are super-duper cool," said Hallie, which was laying it on a bit thick, but Judy's smile widened even further until the gums around her teeth were visible. She consulted her clipboard.

"Zoe, you're in Bunk Three, and Vesper, you're in lucky Bunk Seven! When you get to your cabins, you'll find your personalized dream packages on your beds. Feel free to look through them, but remember, *no taking any dreeeaaams*"—she sang the last few words—"until we go through all the rules at tonight's Dreamboree!"

Maren wondered what a "Dreamboree" was. But at least they were being responsible and making rules for the dreams. She couldn't wait to see what her personalized dream package looked like.

"Evan!" Judy called out to a floppy-haired teenage boy wearing red shorts and a lifeguard T-shirt. "Can you help these new dreamers find their cabins?"

"We're not new dreamers," muttered Maren as the boy flashed a grin—to Hallie specifically—and veered in their direction.

"Hello, ladies," he said, again mostly just to Hallie, whose cheeks went a little pink.

Great, thought Maren. They'd only just arrived, and already somebody was distracting Hallie away from her. Plus, whenever somebody referred to girls as "ladies" in that tone, it made Maren feel squirmy and gross.

"What bunk?" said Evan the lifeguard, grabbing Hallie's giant duffel bag and hoisting it over his shoulder like it weighed nothing. He completely ignored Maren's wheelie suitcase, which didn't surprise her.

"My sister's in seven," said Hallie, "and I'm in three."

"Awesome," said Evan with another grin that made Maren want to throw him in the lake.

"Girls," said Maren's mom. "A quick word before you head off to your cabins?"

Hallie rolled her eyes, but let her mother pull her and Maren a few paces away from Judy and Evan.

"Be very careful," whispered Maren's mom. "Look after each other. Call me every night before you go to bed."

"We already promised we would," groaned Hallie.

"No, you won't!" trilled Judy.

Maren's mom's eyebrow lifted. "Excuse me?"

"There's no cell reception at Camp Shaaaady Sands," Judy sang, then coughed and cleared her throat. "And no Wi-Fi. Or computers. But you're welcome to write all the letters you want!"

Maren's mother's polite grin was starting to look more like a grimace, and for a second Maren was afraid she wasn't going to let them stay. But then she gave a quick nod. "All right. Thank you, Judy."

"No problemo!" said Judy.

Maren's mom turned so she shielded her daughters from the eavesdropping Judy, whose fleece unicorn horn had started wilting over her forehead. "I want you both to keep your phones charged, just in case," she whispered.

"They're not going to work if there's no service," said Hallie.

"Better safe than sorry," said their mom. "I don't know what I was thinking, letting you do this."

"You can't change your mind now," whined Hallie.

"Yeah, come on, Mom," said Maren. Even though she still felt like she had bats flapping around in her stomach, her curiosity was winning out.

"Anyway, Gran-Gran's here to keep an eye on us," said Hallie. "I'm sure they have phones for the staff to use. She can keep you updated on everything, and we promise to check in with her every day."

"Twice a day," said their mom.

"Three times," said Maren.

Her mother sighed. "Your dad isn't going to like this."

"He'll be fine." Hallie's feet were already dancing back toward the sleazily smiling, floppy-haired boy holding her duffel bag. Maren's urge to throw him in the lake was just as strong as ever.

"Remember to take care of yourself," said their mom, grabbing her oldest daughter and planting a kiss on her forehead. "Take lots of breaks. And lots of naps." Her voice dropped to a whisper. "But no dreams."

"Got it!" Hallie leapt away, and Maren's mom heaved the heavy kind of sigh she used to do all the time after the accident.

"She's going to be fine." Maren fought the urge to hold her mom's hand because that would be embarrassing. "We're both going to be fine."

"I know," said her mom with another gusty sigh. "And I'm so proud of you girls for helping out here."

"Come on!" called Hallie, grabbing the handle of Maren's suitcase and following Evan as he started across the clearing with her own bag. Loneliness hit Maren like a chilly blast of wind. She just didn't know how to be interesting enough to keep Hallie's attention.

"Bye, Mom." She crash-hugged her mother so hard it made her gasp.

"Bye, sweetie," said her mom with a laugh. "I love you."

"Love you too." Before she had a chance to change her mind and get back in the car, Maren dashed off after her sister.

Six

LUCKY BUNK SEVEN WAS A blue cabin tucked in a copse of prickly pines. A short flight of stairs led to a covered porch crowded with cozy chairs and couches. Waving goodbye to her sister, who barely noticed she was leaving, Maren took a deep breath and climbed the steps. This was it. She was on her own.

"*You can do this*," she muttered. "*You are safe. Obscura is in jail. You are safe.*"

As the door swung open, Maren sucked in her breath. She'd been expecting a rustic room, maybe with some dusty bunk beds and a lantern or two. Instead she found a bright, airy space that smelled of lavender and mint. There were two rows of beds with gauzy canopies that hung from the ceiling and trailed all the way down to the floor. Each canopy was a different color, each dotted with silver stars and moons. Quiet, new-agey music played in the background.

"Hello?" called Maren.

From beneath a mauve canopy came a giggle, and then the fabric swung open and a girl's face poked out. She gave Maren an up-and-down appraisal, wrinkled her nose, and then the canopy swung shut. A whispered conversation under the canopy ensued, followed by another girl's laughter.

Maren tugged on her black pajama bottoms and shrank a little. Maybe this Wednesday Addams makeover wasn't the greatest idea after all.

"Hello and welcome!" called a bubbly voice from the back of the cabin, and a young woman in bright yellow summertime pajamas bounced down the aisle between the beds. "My name is Kendall, and I'm so lucky because I get to be the counselor for lucky Bunk Seven!"

"I'm Vesper," said Maren, fist-bumping Kendall's tiny hand. The counselor looked like a gymnast or one of those cheerleaders who were always getting tossed into the air. Judging from her giant smile, which showed the top and bottom rows of her teeth, Maren guessed cheerleader.

"Isn't a vesper like a moped or something?" A different girl's face poked out from under the mauve canopy, wearing the same wrinkly-nosed expression as her friend.

"That's a Vespa, genius," said a voice directly behind Maren. She whirled around and discovered a tall girl in regular, non-pajama shorts and a tank top who'd just come in. Her brown hair had been dip-dyed pink from her ears down to her shoulders, and Maren felt a sharp pang of longing for her old hair.

"It's basically the same thing," said a voice from under the canopy, and both girls giggled. The pink-haired girl rolled her eyes.

"Ignore them," she said.

"Thanks," murmured Maren as the girl slipped past, heading for the large shared bathroom at the back of the cabin.

"Peyton and Maddie, let's make sure to be extra welcoming to all of our new bunkmates," said Kendall with a frowny pout. "Vesper, your bed is right over there." She pointed to a forest green canopy at the end of the row, thankfully on the other side of the room from the mean girls. "And your dream package is on your pillow. Feel free to look through it, but don't take anything until we've gone over all the rules at the Dreamboree!"

"I won't," said Maren, wondering what this counselor knew about dreams and what the rules were. She wheeled her suitcase over to the bed and ducked under the canopy. The bed's coverlet was the same shade of dark green, and propped on top of two overstuffed pillows was a fancy gift basket, all tied up in gauze and ribbons.

A little reading light on a string hung from the center of the canopy. Maren clicked it on and began unpacking her dream package. First was a rolled-up scroll of paper, tied with yet more ribbon.

Dearest Vesper!

We are so pleased to welcome you to Camp Shady Sands!!!!!! Where all your dreams really will come true!! Here is your personal dream package, which contains a selection of our most spectacular, exquisite, and magnificent dreams, based on the preferences you indicated in your camp application form!! But don't worry, this is only a start!!! There are loads more where these came from! We can't wait to start dreaming with you!!!!!!!!!!!!

Yours dreamily!
Camp Shady Sands
Co-Directors Malvin and
Calvin Peppernot

Hallie was going to get an eye twitch from all those

exclamation points, Maren thought as she dug into the basket and began pulling out little cellophane bags full of dream sachets, each tied with a different colored ribbon and a handwritten tag. She shivered with anticipation as she read the descriptions of all these foreign dreams crafted by someone she'd never met.

Flying: an exhilarating experience, said the first packet in elegant cursive writing. Of course—it was the most popular kind of dream. They probably gave that one to everybody. Maren pulled out a sachet, carefully holding it by its edges, and sniffed. But instead of the familiar scent of tree pollen and dragonfly wings, this one smelled like feathers—some kind of hawk, if Maren wasn't mistaken—and something rubbery that was probably balloon. There was no hint of anything that smelled like dreamsalt.

"Interesting," she whispered, digging out the next cellophane bag, labeled *Snorkeling with mermaids: a fantasy/adventure experience.* Whoever had labeled these packages didn't share the same deep love of exclamation points as the person who wrote the official camp communications—presumably Calvin or Malvin Peppernot.

More campers trickled in as Maren shuffled through the little bags of dreams: *Tango on Mars, Singing alphabet soup, Everything is made of candy, Step inside a painting.* There were some extremely creative concepts, things she wished she'd thought of, and Maren wondered if they really worked. She ached to test them out. There wasn't a single nightmare in the dream package, and she hoped that was the case for everyone.

At the bottom of the dream basket was a red T-shirt that said CAMP SHADY SANDS! on the front and a matching baseball cap that said DREAMER! Maren wondered if she should put them on, but nobody else was wearing theirs, which was a relief. Every so often, she poked her head out to smile and wave at new people coming in, just in case those two girls were being unfriendly to everyone. Most of the campers looked nervous but excited, and most didn't seem to know each other. The bed next to Maren's, which had a sky blue canopy, remained empty. She hoped that was because it already belonged to the pink-haired girl.

"All right, dreamers!" called Kendall, clapping her hands. "It's time for your first Camp Shady Sands Dreamboree! You'll get to meet our directors and we'll tell you all about dreaming and how it works and all kinds of other cool stuff. Come on! Grab your hats!"

The red "Dreamer!" hat did not work at all with Maren's new dark personality. Or her old personality, for that matter. Heaving a sigh, she crammed it onto her head and climbed out from under her canopy. Girls stood beside each bed, except for the one next to Maren's, all wearing their red baseball caps and nervous smiles. Even the two mean girls, who wore matching silky green pajamas and looked like they might be related, seemed excited.

"Is everybody ready?" called Kendall, and Maren cheered along with her bunkmates. She couldn't help but grin as she followed Kendall's bouncing ponytail down the steps and into a chattering stream of campers, all headed toward the clearing. It was impossible not to get swept up in the excitement, especially about something she was already so passionate about. She hoped—really, deeply hoped—that whoever was in charge of this place knew what they were doing.

⁓

"I can't wait to dream about winning the World Series tonight!" Maren heard one kid say.

"I'm going to snuggle so many koalas," said somebody else.

"I'm going to *turn into* a koala," said a girl.

"You're going to have to eat eucalyptus leaves!"

"So what? Maybe they're delicious."

Maren itched to take the dreams too, especially the one about dancing the tango on Mars. Maybe if this place ended up being legitimate, Lishta would let her try it.

As they flooded across the big clearing at the center of

Camp Shady Sands, the campers veered left and passed the mess hall, which was a long, gray-shingled structure. Maren craned her neck, trying to catch a glimpse of Lishta inside, but the windows were dark. She followed the crowd around a bend, down a short path, and into another clearing where the ground sloped down in a big semicircle, creating a natural amphitheater with a stage at the bottom of the hill. It was empty, aside from a set of huge speakers. Along the sloping hill, logs had been set as benches, propped in place with rocks.

Maren joined her bunkmates on a log, sitting as far as possible from Peyton and Maddie, who were stealing glances at somebody else and whispering. There was no sign of the pink-haired girl. Three logs ahead, Hallie sat chatting with two other girls and, unfortunately, Evan the lifeguard. Amos was nowhere to be seen, but he'd had a soccer game that afternoon, so it was possible he hadn't arrived yet. Maren tucked her knees up under her chin and sighed. Everything was okay. She was safe.

The two girls to her left were passing dream sachets back and forth.

"What'd you get?" Maren asked, nudging the black-haired girl, who wore orange pajamas with smiling popsicles printed on them.

"A whole bunch of stuff," she said, splaying her hand open so Maren could look at the jumble of sachets. "Ice-skating at the North Pole, swimming with mermaids, queen of the universe…"

"You shouldn't hold them like that for too long," said Maren. "It's hot out, and if you sweat they might start to leak."

The other girl, a redhead in silver pajamas that matched her silver braces, squinted at Maren. "What do you mean, leak?"

Maren caught herself. She was supposed to be a regular kid, not a dream expert. "Oh, um, my mom bought some dreams a while ago, and the lady at the store told us to keep them in the package and not get them wet. Because they might leak? Or something?"

"Leak where?" said the dark-haired girl. "We're not even sleeping, so why does it matter?"

"I…don't really know," stammered Maren. "That's just what I heard. Anyway, I got swimming with mermaids too. It sounds really cool."

"I got one about the dentist," said the redhead, running her tongue over her braces.

Maren stiffened. That sounded suspiciously like a nightmare. "Cool," she said, trying to sound mildly curious. "I don't think I got that one. What did the label say?"

"The dentist gives you rainbow teeth with different fruit flavors," said the girl, and Maren relaxed a little. "I'm Emma, by the way."

"Ma—Vesper," said Maren. "Nice to meet you."

"This is Anika," said Emma, and the girl with the popsi-cle pajamas smiled.

Maren was about to ask where they were from when a piercing microphone screech filled the amphitheater and everyone clutched their ears.

"HELLOOO CAMP SHADY SANDS!" yelled a man's voice.

"Hello, Malvin and Calvin!" yelled all the counselors, jumping to their feet and gesturing for the campers to do the same. Maren joined her bunkmates in cheering for the two identical middle-aged men in matching dinosaur onesies who were dancing around the stage like international pop stars.

"Welcome, welcome, *welcome!*" yelled the second man in a slightly more nasal version of the first man's voice. These were clearly the people responsible for the exclamation points on all the camp communications. The crowd's cheers became a roar, and the two men stood still, arms outspread, soaking up the adoration until it died to a murmur.

"It is *so dreamy* to see you all!" said the first man. "I'm Malvin, and this is my brother Calvin."

There were several whoops from the counselors, and a smattering of applause from the campers.

"Who's ready to start dreaming?" shouted Calvin. The

smattering of applause turned to raucous cheers as he swerved around his brother and raced to the other side of the stage, crouching to give the kids in the front row fist bumps.

"So are we, because dreams are the coolest!" said Malvin, or at least Maren thought it was Malvin. It was getting hard to tell who was who with all of their bobbing and weaving and spinning.

"Who are these guys?" she muttered to Anika.

"Haven't you seen them on FlipFlop?" said Anika. "They have, like, millions of followers."

"*Had*," corrected Emma. "They took their account down last week. The last video was just a screen that said 'See you next week' with like four hundred exclamation points. And now here we are!" She wiggled with excitement, clutching her fistful of dreams to her chest.

"My mom won't let me have a FlipFlop account," said Maren. She wondered how she, Hallie, and Lishta had missed that in their research. Well, she knew how Lishta had missed it, but Hallie was an internet sleuthing expert.

"How did you find out about this place then?" asked Anika.

"An ad in the newspaper," said Maren, and both girls looked at her like she'd grown an extra head. "Actually, my grandmother found it."

She wondered why the ad hadn't mentioned the fact that

Calvin and Malvin were FlipFlop-famous or why searching Camp Shady Sands hadn't led to their account. Something about all of this wasn't adding up.

"We've got all kinds of fabulous activities planned for the next two weeks," said Malvin or Calvin. "You all got your starter packs, right?" He cupped his hand next to his ear and received a loud chorus of yeses. "Excellent! You can start taking those right after dinner tonight."

"Whichever ones you like," said his brother. "For the first few days, you'll want to get a feel for the dreams, see which ones you like, which ones you don't. Write a list of all your favorite stuff in each dream in your dream journal, because you're also going to learn how to make those puppies!"

"We're making puppies?" whispered Emma.

"No, we're making dreams. It's just an expression. Now shh!" hissed Anika.

A gentle, metallic tinkling sound came from behind Maren, and she turned to see a young woman drifting down the aisle. She wore black lace-up boots and a floaty black garment that was somewhere between a dress and a nightgown. Her loose, silver braid had clearly been dyed that color. She smelled of incense and herbs and something else, some imperceptible scent that Lishta's dream shop also had but Maren had never been able to find the source of. Maren's skin went shivery.

"Who's *that*?" whispered Anika.

"Must be a counselor," said Emma. "She looks cool."

Maren had to agree. Ignoring the stares of the campers, the woman found a seat and focused her attention on Malvin and Calvin. If anybody in this place actually knew about dreams, it was her, thought Maren.

"Now let's go over some of the rules before you get started with those amazing dreams!" said Malvin or Calvin.

Maren nodded. This was good. Rules were important, especially considering how many kids might be tempted to give each other dreams without knowing what they were or how they worked.

"Rule number one: If you're planning to dream outside, make sure to wear sunblock!" said Calvin or Malvin. "You'll get a nasty burn if you sleep in the sun too long."

"Even better, use a sun lounger under an umbrella!" said his brother.

This wasn't quite what Maren had in mind. Hopefully they'd get to the serious rule about consenting to dreams soon.

"Rule number two: If you're dreaming anywhere near the water, make sure to use a safety harness," said Malvin or Calvin. "You'll find buckets of them all over the beach. Attach yourself to your lounger or the dock or something heavy!"

"And no dreaming in the canoes or kayaks," said Calvin or Malvin. "Even with safety harnesses, they could tip over."

"It's just not safe!" said Malvin or Calvin.

Maren huffed. Who would intentionally put themself to sleep in a canoe?

"Next rule!" said Calvin or Malvin. "Tomorrow morning, you all need to go check out our awesomesauce dream shack!"

That wasn't even a rule, thought Maren. It was more of a directive.

"What's a dream shack?" called one of the boy counselors, who had clearly been instructed to ask the question.

Malvin or Calvin strode to the edge of the stage and pointed double finger-guns at the counselor. "Excellent question, my dreamy friend!"

Maren bit down on her lip to keep from groaning.

"The dream shack," continued the camp co-director, "is a little building on the beach, right beside the dock. How many of you already spotted it?"

About half the audience raised their hands, including Hallie, and Maren felt foolish for not having noticed it.

"Excellent," said the other camp co-director. "The dream shack is where you get your dreams. You've all got a great starter pack, but once you're ready for the next level, that's where you go to buy the *even cooler* dreams."

"But how do we buy them if we can't use money?" called a girl counselor who had also clearly been instructed to ask this question.

"So glad you asked!" sang Calvin or Malvin. "They're free! Take as many as you want!"

Maren's eyebrows lifted so high they almost joined her hair.

"Mix and match! Share them with your friends! At Camp Shady Sands, we believe in teamwork AND dreamwork!" Malvin and Calvin hopped around the stage like dinosaur-kangaroos, pumping their fists. "Remember, everybody, there's no 'I' in dream!"

A hysterical peep of a laugh squeezed out from between Maren's clenched lips, and she covered it up with a cough. This was utterly absurd. There was no way either of those silly men had any idea how dreams worked or what to do with them. They'd given no information on which dreams were best for certain personalities, how long they should last, or what to do if they didn't work as expected. And they hadn't even touched on the rule about never giving them to people without their consent. In fact, it sounded like they might even *encourage* it.

Calvin or Malvin stopped and pointed into the crowd at a boy who'd raised his hand. "Young man?"

"Uh, I just had a question about...different kinds of dreams?" The boy dipped his head so the brim of his hat hid his blushing face. Beside him, a green-haired Amos flashed Maren a grin and a wave. She returned the wave, but not the grin. This Dreamboree made her stomach hurt. Amos's hair did look nice in that froggy shade of green, though.

"Do you have...nightmares too?" asked the blushing boy.

"Good lord, no!" said Malvin or Calvin, and his brother did an exaggerated shudder. "At Camp Shady Sands, we don't believe in bad dreams."

Maren waited for him to explain how campers might accidentally have nightmares on their own, even if they didn't specifically take any. Maybe he'd explain how eraser dreams worked, or calming dreams. But the twins simply spun on their heels and dragged a big cardboard box out from the back of the stage.

"Who wants some more dreams?" they called, grabbing fistfuls of sachets and tossing them into the audience. "Life-sized sandcastles! Talking wombats! Flying sailboats!"

Maren gawped. Those dreams weren't labeled, and there was no way of knowing which was which. What if somebody had a phobia of wombats and that dream turned into a night-mare? Kids were jumping out of their seats, crawling around to pick up sachets off the ground. Those dreams might have just absorbed dirt and grass, ingredients that could change their entire storyline.

Three rows ahead, Hallie turned around, and her eyes found Maren's.

"O. M. G," she mouthed.

Maren nodded. If those dreams were real, this was bad.

Seven

MAREN LAY IN HER BED, listening to the sounds of dreaming campers. One girl was muttering about pandas, another kept laughing, and a third was making various birdcalls. The dream sachets were real. Someone here knew what they were doing. Maren's head swirled with all the possibilities as well as the dangers, but for now everyone seemed safe. There were no signs of nightmares, but she was prepared to wake her bunkmates if necessary.

The pink-haired girl had returned and slipped into the bed beside hers a few minutes after lights-out. For some reason, Kendall hadn't seemed bothered by her late arrival. Maren itched to talk to her, but her eyes kept drifting shut. The air was stuffy, especially under her canopy, and everything smelled of bug repellent. It had been a long day full of weird surprises, and she longed to sleep, but she wanted to wait a little while longer, just to make sure everyone was okay.

She'd been hoping to speak to Lishta at dinnertime, but the first night's meal hadn't been served in the mess hall where Lishta worked. Instead, everyone roasted hot dogs over a campfire, which meant that everyone ate half-charred, half-cold hot dogs. At least there'd been lots of potato chips, though her stomach gurgled and whined now, needing some regular food. With a groan, she kicked off her sweaty blankets and flopped back on her pillow.

"Hey," came a whisper from the bed beside hers. "You awake?"

"Yeah," whispered Maren, poking her head out to find the pink-haired girl peering at her in the dark. "How come you are too?"

The girl grimaced. "Not sleepy, I guess."

"Don't you want to try your dreams?" asked Maren.

The girl scoffed. "They don't work on me."

A very small percentage of people were immune to dreams. No matter what kind they took, nothing happened, even the worst nightmares in the shop. Lishta always gave those people a full refund and a gift certificate to Mr. Alfredo's Splendid Salon to make up for their disappointment.

"Why are you at this camp, then?" whispered Maren.

"My grandma works here," said the girl.

Maren nearly blurted out that hers did too, but caught herself.

"I'm Ivy, by the way," said the girl.

"Vesper," said Maren.

"I know," said Ivy. "Remember the whole scooter thing?"

Maren's cheeks went hot. Of course she did. "What does your grandmother do here?"

"She works in the shack on the beach, selling the dreams. I didn't want to come here, because what's even the point? But my mom's in Chile doing research for the summer and I'm staying with my grandma and she just got this new job, so here I am." Ivy made a sad trombone noise.

"That stinks," said Maren, though Ivy was definitely dodging a bullet by not taking dreams that had been picked out of the dirt. She desperately wanted to know more about Ivy's grandmother, whether she was an actual dream seller or had just been hired to run the shack, but she didn't want to let on just how much she knew about dreams. Not until she got to know Ivy better.

"How come you're not taking your dreams either?" asked Ivy.

"Oh, um, I was just about to take one," said Maren. "I

couldn't decide which one to start with. They all look so good, it's a lot of pressure."

Ivy paused. "I guess."

"You must feel so left out," said Maren.

"It's no big deal," said Ivy. "And it's only for two weeks. I'll survive."

Suddenly, two weeks felt like an eternity. Maren felt a pang of longing for her mother, for her own bed, for Lishta's calm shop where dreams were treated responsibly and carefully. But Maren had a job to do here, and that was more important than feeling uncomfortable or lonely.

"Anyway," continued Ivy. "I'm a lucid dreamer, so I can do whatever I want in my dreams anyway."

"Wow, that's cool," said Maren. Lucid dreaming was a fascinating skill that some people had, where they were able to figure out mid-dream that they were dreaming and then interact with and change their dreamworld however they wanted. "How long have you been doing that?"

Ivy shrugged. "A couple of years."

"I'd love to learn how to do it," said Maren.

"It's not that hard," said Ivy. "You just have to practice."

Maren decided not to mention the fact that she'd tried a few times but couldn't manage it. "Well I'm here if you ever want to vent about stuff. Or just hang out."

Ivy stifled a yawn. "Thanks. G'night."

"Goodnight." Maren ducked back under her canopy, crinkled the cellophane wrapping of her dream basket, and pretended to drift off into a dream-filled sleep.

Eight

THE NEXT MORNING, A BLEARY and tousled Maren joined her bunkmates as they headed to the mess hall for breakfast. Ivy had disappeared again, probably gone to eat with her grandmother. Maren wished she could eat with her grandmother too.

"That was even cooler than I expected," said Emma, who skipped down the path.

"I can still feel the wind in my wings when I close my eyes." Anika held her arms out, shut her eyes, and let out a hawk-like screech.

"Take me out to the ball game," sang a girl behind them.

"Take me out with the crowd," added another girl, who must have taken the same baseball dream.

Clearly the dreams were real and working perfectly, so even though Malvin and Calvin didn't know what they were talking about, somebody did. Maren couldn't wait to tell Lishta, and she wondered if her grandmother might let her try one or two dreams, just to see how they compared to the ones in their shop.

The campers filed into the mess hall, and Maren blinked for a minute in the brightness. The wide room was crowded and filled with rows of tables, and the smell of eggs was overwhelming. Maren's eyes watered as she searched for her sister or Amos in the jumble of kids. No sign of either one of them. But then she spotted Lishta behind a counter, wearing a hairnet over her blue wig and dishing out floppy bacon with a pair of tongs.

Maren wanted to run over and throw her arms around the old woman, but she grabbed a tray and joined the line with her group. She took two pieces of pre-buttered toast, said a polite "No, thank you" to the lady giving out watery scrambled eggs, and slid her tray agonizingly closer to Lishta.

"We've got lake time after this," said Emma. "I hope that means we get to take dreams next to the lake, not have to go swimming or canoeing."

Maren murmured her agreement and finally pushed her tray up to the bacon station, but the serving dish was empty, and Lishta was gone. Maren's stomach sank.

"Keep moving!" someone behind her yelled.

"I'm waiting for bacon," she yelled back. Emma and Anika picked up their trays and skirted around her, heading for the juice.

"We'll save you a seat," said Anika.

Come on, Gran-Gran, thought Maren as loudly as she could. From the back of the kitchen came a clattering clang and Lishta's voice yelling a string of almost-swears, like *shooty-toot* and *fudgesicles*. Maren drummed her fingers on her tray and aimed a steely stare at the boys bunching up in line behind her.

"Just go around me if you don't want bacon," she said, but they were more interested in playing bumper cars with each other's trays than listening to her. Finally, Lishta emerged with a steaming tray of bacon, and Maren smiled so hard her face hurt.

"Hello, dearie!" said Lishta. "Sorry to keep you waiting."

"That's okay," said Maren, sliding her tray closer so Lishta could put two droopy slabs on her plate.

"Meet me in the ladies' room in five minutes," muttered her grandmother without moving her lips, and Maren gave a quick nod. She grabbed some watery juice and silverware, then joined Emma and Anika at the end of a table.

"These eggs taste like feet," said Anika, dragging her fork through the watery yellow pile on her plate.

"They smell like feet too," said Emma, nibbling on a slice of toast.

"Take me out to the ball game!" sang a boy at the next table over.

Maren prodded her floppy bacon. It seemed impossible, but apparently Lishta wasn't the worst cook here. She fit right in. Suddenly, half-cooked hot dogs didn't seem so bad after all.

"Tomorrow I'm having cereal," she said. "They can't possibly mess that up."

Anika jabbed her thumb at a big cereal dispenser filled with brown and green flakes. "Wanna bet?"

"You'd think if they were so great at making dreams, they'd be better at making food, wouldn't you?" said Emma.

"They're probably not making the dreams," scoffed Maren.

Emma and Anika both looked up from their gloppy breakfasts. "What do you mean?" asked Anika. "Why wouldn't they?"

"Oh, uh, I don't know," said Maren, frantically backpedaling. "I thought I read somewhere that they shipped them in."

Anika cocked her head. "From where?"

That was the million-dollar question.

"Who knows?" said Maren. "Anyway, I bet making dreams is way different from making food. I'll be right back."

Tossing her crumpled napkin next to her sad bacon, Maren headed toward the sign that read RESTROOMS in the hall beside the kitchen area. She passed a table full of girls a couple of years older than her. Every single one of them wore her hair in two French braids, and they were all sulkily and silently pushing their food around, casting suspicious glances at each other. At least three other kids were quietly singing "Take Me Out to the Ball Game" as they ate.

The ladies' room was empty when Maren poked her head inside. With a sigh, she turned on the tap and made a face at her tired reflection in the mirror. Even though she'd already made a few friends, she couldn't believe how lonely and unsettled she felt.

"I wish I was home," she whispered.

The door swung open, making her jump a foot into the air. But it was Lishta, red-faced and sweaty with her wig and hairnet askew. She checked under all the stall doors to make sure they were really alone, then turned to Maren with outstretched arms.

"Darling!" she whisper-yelled, pulling her granddaughter into a bacon-and-egg-scented hug and planting a kiss on top of her head. "It feels like it's been ages!"

It really did. Maren's throat went tight, which was silly because she'd literally seen her grandmother a couple of days ago, and her mother just yesterday.

"Your sister came in about half an hour ago," said Lishta.

Another pang of longing hit Maren, this time for her sister, which was even sillier because Hallie was right here at camp, even if she couldn't see her all the time. Or talk to her.

"Are you all right, dear?" asked Lishta, tucking her finger under Maren's chin.

"Yeah," said Maren, forcing a smile. "What did Hallie say?"

"Well, she told me about the dream throwing," Lishta's lips pursed. "Like it was some sort of parade." She sighed heavily. "Those two co-directors are imbeciles who've got no idea what they're doing. But somebody here does."

"Yes, that's exactly what I was going to say," said Maren. "The dreams seem to work perfectly." Lishta threw her a sharp look. "Not that I've tried them, I swear!"

"I believe you, sweetheart," said Lishta, tugging her wig straight and grimacing at her reflection. "I haven't met all of the other staff members yet. I wonder if one of them is making or buying the dreams, or if it's someone who's staying entirely behind the scenes."

"There's a girl in my bunk whose grandmother works at the dream shack," said Maren. "I don't know her that well yet, but I'll see what I can find out."

"That sounds marvelous," said Lishta. "The dream shack just opened yesterday, and we had a food services training session until ten at night. I'll try to get over there later, and in the meantime, if you can take a look, I'll see what I can find out from my new friends in the cafeter—"

The door flew open, and in marched Peyton and Maddie, wrinkling their noses at the smell. Lishta snatched up a wad of paper towels and pretended to dry her hands while Maren turned on the tap and studied her forehead in the mirror. "Hi," she said nonchalantly.

"Hey, scooter girl," said Peyton, and Maddie made a motorcycle noise. They both laughed as they shut themselves into stalls, and then one of them started humming "Take Me Out to the Ball Game." Silently, Lishta rolled her eyes and stuck out her tongue.

"Bye," Maren mouthed at her, and Lishta headed back to the cafeteria. After giving her grandmother a head start, Maren left the bathroom. The cafeteria crowd was thinning out, and Kendall and the rest of her bunkmates stood in a clump near the entrance.

"Are you ready for lake time?" called Kendall.

"I sure am," said Maren. It was time to do some sleuthing.

Nine

THE LAKE WAS, IN A word, beautiful. Crystal blue water lapped at the sandy beach, and leafy maple trees and tall pines provided just the right amount of shade along the edges. Everything smelled fresh and sharp and summery, and Maren couldn't help putting a little skip-hop in her step as her group descended a short flight of wooden stairs to the beach.

A dock stretched out into the sun-dappled water, with canoes and kayaks tied up along its sides. On the dock, several kids lay fast asleep on cushions, tethered with yellow safety harnesses around their waists. A boy was yelling about pinball, and a girl's legs wheeled like she was riding a bike. Maren felt a twinge of worry, but they looked safe enough, and Evan the lifeguard sat in a chair at the end of the dock, keeping an eye on them and the non-dreaming swimmers.

There was still no sign of Hallie or Amos, and Maren fought off a wave of nerves. Everything at camp was fine so far, aside from the wild misuse of dream sachets. They were just busy with their own groups.

Beside the dock, nestled under the trees, sat a low building with a canopy-shaded open front. Kendall beckoned for the girls to follow as she headed toward it, and Maren's heart leapt as she spotted a row of bins full of all different kinds of sachets. Yes, it was irresponsible how they treated dreams at this place, but there were *just so many* of them, and the range of smells wafting off the bins was intoxicating. Maren closed her eyes and inhaled deeply. Peppermint and rubber and cotton and brine and fresh-baked bread. Rose pollen and marjoram and jet fuel and pencil shavings. Someone definitely knew what they were doing.

"Howdy, campers!" An old woman wearing a tiger-print blouse, a pair of gold lamé pants, and a green visor waved with both hands from inside the building. She looked like she'd just returned from a weekend in Atlantic City.

"Go on, don't be shy little mice! The dreams aren't gonna bite you!" The woman threw her head back and gave a roaring belly laugh that made Maren smile. Her bunkmates descended on the bins of dreams with a chorus of oohs and aahs.

"Grab a bag!" said the woman. "Fill it up! I'm Carmella, and I'll be taking care of all your dreamy needs while you're here."

Carmella didn't seem to care that the girls were digging through the bins with their bare hands, which was not only bad for the dreams but also unsanitary. Maren sidled up to the counter and scanned the labels on the bins. A few were familiar:

Everything is candy
Tango on Mars
Queen of the universe

Many were new and intriguing:

All the teachers turn into statues
Painting with sharks
Art museum comes to life
Giant feet

And some Maren desperately wished she were allowed to try:

Surfing with Vincent van Gogh
Magic crayons
Pirate ship captain

She wondered why there were so many dreams about

painting and drawing and museums. Whoever created them all must really love art. Maybe they *were* an artist.

"Dive in!" Carmella nudged Maren with her elbow and handed her a cellophane bag. She smelled of powdery perfume, and her platinum hair was gray at the roots.

"Thanks," said Maren. "Do you have a scoop or something for the dreams?"

Carmella tossed her head back and crowed with laughter. "There's always one in the bunch."

"One?" Maren stiffened. One person who knew about dreams? One person sent there to spy?

Carmella clapped her on the back and pointed to a pair of metal tongs on the counter. "One germophobe. Try not to think about it too much, honey. You'll be fine."

Maren wanted to point out that the tongs looked sharp and might tear the dream sachets, but she held her tongue. It was becoming clear that Carmella was no dream expert either. She gave Maren an appraising look and then dug her hand into a bin marked *All kinds of floating*.

"You look like you could use a nice, relaxing dream," she said.

It was true. But Maren would find it a lot easier to relax if she weren't watching someone plunge their arm up to the elbow in a bunch of dream sachets.

"They're extra strong at the bottom," promised Carmella, which was absurd, but Maren nodded enthusiastically. She held her bag open and squeaked out a perky "Thanks!" as Carmella deposited three crushed sachets inside

"No problem, hon," said Carmella, wiping her hand on the side of her gold pants. Lishta was going to have a heart attack when she saw this place.

"You sure know a lot about dreams," said Maren, casually perusing the nearby bins.

"I've been reading up and testing them out ever since I got offered this job last month," said Carmella. "But the more I learn, the more I think I've got a natural inclination for them. You know, like a sixth sense?"

Maren nodded, though she absolutely did not think this woman had a sixth sense for dreams. "Do you know where these came from?"

Carmella gave her a funny look.

"I'm just wondering how to get more when I go home from camp," said Maren quickly. "Can I buy them on the internet?"

"Oh no, hon," said Carmella. "You need to buy them from a reputable place. From someone who really *understands* how it works."

"That makes sense," said Maren. "Well, thanks for the floating dreams. I can't wait to try them."

"You're welcome." Carmella headed for the counter, where two older girls were waiting to ask a question. Maren chose a few more dreams at random and tried to eavesdrop, but Kendall was clapping her hands and yelling.

"Come on, girls! Time to test out those dreams!"

As her bunkmates rushed off to the umbrella-shaded loungers along the beach and began planning which dreams to take first, Maren kicked off her slippers and waded into the blissfully cool lake. She'd gotten progressively sweatier in her black pajamas, even though they were shorts, and she wished she'd chosen a more heat-friendly disguise.

A splash hit the backs of her legs, and she turned to find Ivy grinning at her.

"How was dream shopping?" asked the pink-haired girl.

"It was fun," lied Maren. "Your grandma is super nice."

Ivy laughed. "She's got terrible taste in clothing, but she's pretty fun. I stay with her every summer while my mom travels for work."

"Do you miss your mom, with her being gone the whole summer?" said Maren.

Ivy huffed. "She's a professor, and she's always super busy even when she's home."

"I'm sorry," said Maren, who remembered how lonely

74

she'd felt when her mom was working double shifts and preoccupied with Hallie's coma.

"It's totally fine," said Ivy, kicking another splash across the shimmery water. "Aren't you going to try out your new dreams?"

"I guess," said Maren, squeezing the packet she'd picked out at the shack. "It feels weird to take them out here instead of in my bed though. What if I talked in my sleep or drooled everywhere?"

Ivy rolled her eyes. "You wouldn't be the only one."

"True." Maren sighed. "I don't know, I just don't feel like it right now."

"Me neither," said Ivy, and they both laughed. "Do you want to go exploring?"

"Do you mean the camp or the woods?" said Maren.

"The camp. There are some off-limits areas, and my grandma won't let me go in them, but I'm dying to find out what's there. Aren't you?"

Maren folded up her packet of new dreams and stuffed it into her pocket. "Absolutely."

Ten

MAREN AND IVY SNUCK ALONG the edge of the beach, keeping close to the trees until they reached the end of the sand and found a sign that read No Campers Beyond This Point!!!! Casting a quick glance over their shoulders to make sure no counselors or lifeguards were watching, the girls slipped past the sign. The shore here was narrower, the dirt crowded with tree roots and dead leaves, and it was easier to take off their footwear and wade through the water. Maren swatted at a fly, then a mosquito, wishing she'd put on more bug spray. At least she had her EpiPen, just in case.

"So this lucid dreaming thing," she said as they waded. "Do you have any tips for a newbie?"

"Sure!" said Ivy. "The main trick to controlling your dreams is knowing you're dreaming. Once that part clicks in your brain, you can start making stuff happen instead of being at the mercy of whatever your subconscious is making up."

Or whatever dream you've taken, thought Maren. "But how do you know you're dreaming? Most of the time, even as this ridiculous stuff is happening to me, like talking hamsters or flying over skyscrapers, my brain just accepts it as normal."

"You have to train yourself," said Ivy, tapping her finger to her temple. "And one way to do that is to practice something called a reality check. You get into the habit of asking yourself 'Am I dreaming?' regularly when you're awake, and when you ask yourself, you also do something like look at your watch."

"Um, okay?" Maren couldn't see exactly where this was going.

"Every day, you have to ask yourself a bunch of times, 'Am I dreaming?'" continued Ivy. "Eventually that routine will stick and you'll start doing it in your dreams too. And when you look at your watch while you're dreaming, it's not going to look the same as it usually does. The numbers will be all wrong or the dial will spin backward, because dreaming minds can't handle logical things like letters and numbers. And that's going to be your tip-off that you're dreaming."

"But I don't wear a watch," said Maren, still fuzzy on the concept.

"It doesn't have to be a watch," said Ivy. "But that's one of the easier ones to use. You could look at the clock on your phone. No matter what it is, when you look at that thing and it's not like how it usually is when you're awake, that's your signal that you're dreaming. And that's when the magic happens. You can do anything you want! I've punched monsters in the face and flown on the backs of dragons and done way more cool stuff than those dreams my grandma is peddling."

Maren bristled at the insinuation that store-bought dreams were inferior, but she kept her tone light. "I guess nobody would bother coming to camps like this if they could already do whatever they wanted in their dreams." Nobody would bother with her family's dream shop either. It was a good thing lucid dreaming wasn't as easy as Ivy made it out to be.

"Probably not," said Ivy.

They rounded a bend and a little inlet opened up with a rotting, abandoned boathouse on its tiny beach. A flock of green and black ducks drifted along the water's edge, quacking pleasantly. As the girls approached, they swam away, leaving one slightly disheveled-looking green duck behind.

"QVACK!" it called.

Maren stumbled and soaked one leg of her shorts. That wasn't a duck. It was Henri.

"QVACK QVACK! ICH BIN EIN KLEINES ENTLEIN."

"Oh no," she muttered, shielding her face with one hand and backing away. If Henri spotted her and came over, she had no idea how she'd explain why she knew a parrot that was pretending to be a duck.

"Is that duck speaking German?" said Ivy.

"No idea," said Maren.

"I think that's a...parrot? With an identity crisis?" said Ivy. "I had a German au pair when I was little, and I'm pretty sure it just said, 'I'm a little duckling.'"

"Super weird," said Maren, thinking frantically. "Ouch! I just stepped on something sharp and I think I'm bleeding. Can we go back?"

Henri cocked his head and hopped closer. "MAREN PARTRIDGE IS IN THE STARLIGHT THEATER!"

"Oh no, oh no, oh no," whispered Maren, turning and dramatically hobble-wading in the other direction.

"Are you okay?" called Ivy, hurrying to catch up.

"Yeah, I just...my foot, it's killing me and I want to get back to the beach so I can look at it."

"Hold it up and let me see," said Ivy.

"TU ES UN—VERSCHWITZTER BUSFAHRER," screeched Henri, remembering midsentence what language he was supposed to be speaking.

"I'm a sweaty bus driver? Really?" Ivy spun back toward the parrot, but Maren grabbed her arm.

"Please, can we just go?" she begged.

"Yeah, of course," said Ivy. "Sorry. Do you want to lean on me to walk?"

"No, but thanks." Maren wondered if she should try to actually step on something sharp so Ivy wouldn't catch her lying, but decided against it. The last thing she needed was stitches.

"AUF WIEDERSEHEN, KAMEL-FURZ!" yelled Henri.

"No, *you're* a camel fart," muttered Ivy, but she didn't turn back. When they finally reached the camp's beach, Maren sat on a rock and pretended to inspect the bottom of her foot.

"No blood," said Ivy. "That's a good sign."

"Yeah," said Maren. "Wow, I thought for sure it was worse than this." She felt bad lying to her brand-new friend, who seemed genuinely cool. She wished she could tell Ivy about her secret mission, but considering who Ivy's grandmother was, it just wasn't a good idea. "Do you want to keep exploring? Looks like Kendall is out for a while." She pointed to their counselor, dozing on a blanket under a tree with a trail of drool slipping down her chin.

"Sure," said Ivy. "Are you sure your foot will be okay?"

"I think it'll be fine with my slipper on," said Maren, testing it out and smiling. "Much better."

As they crossed the hot sand, Maren spotted Hallie on a lounge chair, hands folded over her stomach and the brim of her baseball hat tipped low. As she neared her sister, a familiar sensation of dread filled Maren's gut. The way Hallie was lying, perfectly still and flat on her back, was too similar to how she'd looked when she was in a coma. Swallowing a sour mouthful of nerves, Maren nudged her sister's foot with her shin as she passed. The right corner of Hallie's mouth twitched, and she flashed a stealthy thumbs-up.

Tap-dancing in sand was impossible, especially while wearing slippers, so Maren did a tiny, jazzy leap and hurried after Ivy.

"Miss Ivy Fowler, I see you!" called a voice from inside the dream shack as the girls crept toward the staircase that led back to the main part of camp.

Ivy swore under her breath. "Hi, Grammy!" she called.

Carmella's head poked around the side of the shed.

"Where are you girls headed? And why aren't you dreaming, Vesper? Don't tell me you're still afraid of those germs, sweetheart."

Maren faltered for a second, then held up her foot and winced. "I was trying to find a good dreaming spot, but then I stepped on something sharp. Ivy's taking me to the, um, what do you call it here? The nurse's office? The medical tent?"

Ivy stifled a giggle.

"The health center?" said Carmella.

"Right!" said Maren. "The health center. It's not bleeding, but I think there's a huge splinter stuck in my toe."

Carmella's face turned a little green. Maren slid her foot out of her slipper. "Want to see?"

"No!" yelped Carmella. "Ahem, no, thank you. Ivy darlin', you go ahead and take her to the health center. They'll take care of it...I mean, you. Good luck!"

With another visible shudder, Carmella disappeared into the shack again, and Ivy gave Maren a conspiratorial grin. The girls dashed up the steps and headed for the clearing at the center of camp, Maren adding a tiny fake hobble to her run.

"Hey!" A green-haired kid shot out of a cluster of boys.

Maren tripped over the back of Ivy's heel. "Oh, hi…"

"Fred," supplied Amos with a slight waggle of his eyebrows.

"Ivy, this is my friend Fred," said Maren. "He goes to my school."

Ivy barely looked at Amos. "Hey."

"We were just on our way to check out—" Maren started, but Ivy cut her a look that could instantly wilt flowers, "the health center, because I hurt my foot."

"Are you all right?" Amos's eyes filled with worry. "Do you want me to come?"

Ivy shook her head almost imperceptibly.

"No, I'm fine," said Maren. "I probably just need some antiseptic and a Band-Aid. No big deal. You don't need to come. I'll find you later, okay?"

His face fell. "Sure."

Maren hated ditching her best friend, but she couldn't bring him along without looking suspicious to Ivy or potentially risking their mission. She mouthed a silent "sorry" at him, and he nodded before jogging away to catch up with his group.

"I can't believe you almost told him where we were going," said Ivy.

"Sorry," said Maren. "But he wouldn't have told on us."

"Maybe." Ivy pursed her lips. "You never know who you can trust."

Very true, thought Maren.

Eleven

"This way," called Ivy, swerving down a path that led in the opposite direction from the campers' bunks. "This is where all the non-counselor staff stay."

Lishta probably lived here too. Maren wasn't sure how her grandmother would feel about her sneaking around with another camper. It wasn't the best idea, but as long as she kept the purpose of her mission secret, it was probably fine.

The buildings along this path were more cottages than cabins. They sat tucked under big willow trees, all with little gardens in front and some covered in trailing ivy. It looked like a village where elves or fairy folk might live, and Maren wondered how long the camp had been around and who'd built it. It was quiet out here, her footsteps muffled by the soft dirt of the path. Birds sang high in the trees, and the air felt cooler.

To their right was a cluster of blue cottages in a meadow full of violets. One of the doors banged open, and Maren and Ivy ducked behind a tree. A short woman in a hairnet emerged and headed the opposite way down the path. That must be where the lunch ladies lived. Maren wondered if they each got their own cottage or whether they had to share.

"This way," said Ivy again, beckoning for her to follow around the back of a yellow cottage with two rosebushes on either side of its door. Maren thought longingly of the Green and Fresh grocery store in Rockpool Bay, and she missed home—especially her parents.

You'll see them in thirteen days, she told herself. *It's going to be fine. You can do this.*

She crept behind the yellow cottage with Ivy, where they found a little cement patio with an umbrella table and a few old chairs. As Ivy moved a chair aside, its metal legs made a toe-curling screech, and Maren leapt backward, stumbling over a potted plant.

"Watch out or you might hurt your foot," said Ivy, and Maren wondered if she knew she'd been faking this whole time. Unfazed, Ivy tested the back door to see if it was open (it wasn't) and then looked under the doormat and inside the barbecue for a key.

"You didn't say we were breaking and entering," hissed Maren.

"Relax," said Ivy. "I just wanted to see if we could enter without breaking."

"Do you know whose house this is?" whispered Maren.

"It's Calvin and Malvin's," said Ivy.

Maren gulped. This was an excellent place to snoop—probably the best place. But she hadn't expected to jump into the deep end quite so quickly with her snooping. She'd planned to do a little reconnaissance around the camp, pick up some general information, learn a few things here and there, then ramp up to the bigger stuff once she knew what she was doing. If she got caught in the co-directors' house on her second day of camp, it'd blow her cover and possibly get her and Hallie sent home.

Ivy dragged a chair over to a window and climbed up. "Whoa," she said.

Maren rushed over and climbed up beside her new friend. The dim bedroom inside was cluttered with boxes and bins and bags, most of them closed but a few ripped open at the top. Tiny dream sachets were visible. Maren wondered why the twins were keeping the dreams here, rather than at the shack on the beach, but maybe there wasn't enough storage room. On the table directly underneath the window, papers lay scattered. Most looked like invoices or bills, but a handwritten note poked out from under an envelope, signed with a dramatic, illegible flourish.

Maren tipped her head and stood on tiptoe, trying to read the rest of the note. The chair teetered, and she clung to the windowsill. Ivy yelped and nearly fell off.

"Sorry." Maren wrenched her neck as far sideways as she could, smooshed her nose against the window, and finally made out the last few lines of the letter.

...for the campers once they've returned. I appreciate your cooperation and your loyalty. The payment will be deposited into your account as soon as the mission is complete.

Sincerely,

S R

"What does it say?" asked Ivy.

"Something about the campers returning," said Maren. "And a mi—"

"*You* have a really dreamy day too!" called a goofy man's voice on the other side of the house. Both girls froze. The man began to whistle.

"It's Malvin or Calvin," hissed Maren, grabbing Ivy and dragging her into the bushes behind the patio. The two girls crouched under the damp leaves, barely daring to breathe as the whistling came closer. The front door of the house slammed.

A mosquito whined in Maren's ear; another crawled up her leg. She longed to slap them off, but had to settle for a useless, slow swipe. The bugs returned three seconds later, bringing friends. And then she heard it. A low hum.

Maybe it's a fly, she thought. But flies didn't hum like that. They buzzed. Bees hummed. The humming stopped, and she let her breath out, but then it was back again, somewhere behind her head, and Maren squeezed back tears as she remembered how Obscura's killer moth bee had hovered in that exact spot when she was forcing her to make nightmares.

After what felt like an entire lifetime, the humming faded again, and the front door of the yellow cottage slammed. Maren wiped her damp palms on her shorts.

"We need to get out of here right now," she whispered. "Let's stay in the bushes and go that way."

The shrubs continued all the way to the edge of the lot, then merged in a big leafy jumble with a hedge that bordered the path. Maren crawled through the plants, their branches pulling at her hair and scratching her skin. Sweat dripped down her nose and plopped into the dirt. She cursed her ridiculous all-black outfit, she cursed the humidity and the bugs, and she cursed herself for getting dragged into such an un-sneaky stealth mission. By the time they finally emerged from the hedge, both girls were covered in dirt and scrapes.

"You've got leaves in your hair," said Ivy.

"So do you," said Maren, looking all around in case the bee had followed them.

Ivy let out a shaky laugh. "I can't believe we made it out of there."

Even though the bee was gone, Maren's legs still trembled "We need a plan if we're going to do something like that again."

Ivy waved her hand airily. "Plans, shmlans. So what did that note say?"

Maren tried to hide her irritation. Of course this was just a joke to Ivy. She wasn't here undercover with half her family. "It said something about a payment going into an account once the mission is completed."

Ivy froze. "A mission? What kind of mission?"

"It didn't say." Maren's stomach churned at the realization that there really was something serious going on. Something that involved payments and secrecy.

"Did you see who it was from?" asked Ivy.

"Just an S with a scribble," said Maren.

Ivy's face clouded over for the briefest second, but then

she rolled her eyes. "It's probably some publicity stunt for FlipFlop."

"Maybe," said Maren, "but I heard they closed their acc—"

"Girls? What are you doing out here?" One of the lunch ladies stood outside a blue cottage, still wearing her hairnet.

"Sorry, we got a little turned around," said Maren. "Is this not where the nurse's…um, I mean the medical tent…er, medical center is?"

"The health center?" said the lunch lady. "No, it's over on the other side of the mess hall. You know, the big blue building that says Health Center on the front of it."

"Oh!" Maren forced a silly laugh. "How did we miss that?" She jabbed Ivy in the ribs, and her friend let out an equally silly laugh that threatened to turn Maren's fake laughter into a hysterical giggling fit. Judging from Ivy's watery eyes, she was having a hard time holding it in too. Something about this situation being deeply unfunny made it even funnier.

"Thank you!" the girls called as they ran back down the path toward the health center.

Twelve

MAREN AND IVY MADE IT back to the beach just as Kendall sat up in her lounge chair, yawning and stretching her arms.

"Wow, that was so great!" she said, slipping her feet back into her slippers. "Did you *love* your dreams?"

"Yeah," said Maren.

"Totally," muttered Ivy. "Is it lunchtime yet?"

Kendall checked her watch. "It sure is! Wow, time flies when you're having a flying dream!"

It was a cheesy joke, but Maren couldn't help but smile anyway. Flying dreams really were incredible the first time you took one. Any time you took one, really. She scanned the lakefront for the girls from her bunk. Most of them were awake or just waking up, some on loungers and others on the dock. The dreamsalt—or whatever the sleeping agent was in these dreams—must have been carefully dosed so that all the dreams all lasted the same amount of time.

"Take me out to the ball game," sang a girl wearing orange and pink flowered pajamas.

"Bunk Seven girls!" called Kendall. "Whooo's hungry?"

"Me!" called a girl named Sadie.

"Me too," said a girl called Brianne. "I want a—"

"Turkey sandwich," said five other girls at the same time as her.

Everyone went silent for a moment, then burst out laughing.

"Are you guys making fun of me?" said Brianne.

"How could they have known what you were going to say?" said the girl next to her, rubbing her arms and shivering as she stared at the other girls.

"This is creepy," said Ivy, backing slowly away from the group.

"Well, I really do want one," sniffed Peyton.

"Me too," said Maddie.

"Hey, no worries, everyone!" Kendall beamed her toothy smile. "They've got plenty of turkey sandwiches at the mess hall!"

Maren hung back as her bunkmates got ready to leave. It wasn't normal for everybody to wake up from different dreams all wanting the same thing. And she was sure most of them had taken wildly different dreams, judging from their conversations right before they all went to sleep. Something very strange was going on. She needed to talk to Lishta.

"Um, Kendall?" Anika came jogging up, her forehead creased with worry. "I can't get Emma to wake up."

For the first time since camp had started, Kendall's giant grin disappeared.

"Where is she?" demanded Maren, and Anika pointed to a lone figure lying on a cushion on the dock, legs kicking. Maren dashed over, Kendall and Anika trailing behind her, and crouched beside the red-haired girl.

"Emma? Can you hear me?" she said.

"Take that! And that! Ha!" yelled Emma, whipping her arm out in a karate chop that narrowly missed Maren's face.

"Emmie, it's time to wake up," said Kendall, nudging Emma's shoulder.

"Don't call me Emmie!" yelled Emma, swinging her foot up to face level and almost knocking their counselor over the side of the dock. She must be a dancer or a gymnast, Maren thought, to be that flexible. Or maybe she really did know karate.

"Sorry," said Kendall. "Emma, sweetie, it's time for lunch. Aren't you hungry?"

A pause. A loud stomach gurgle.

"Yes." Emma's eyes snapped open. "I want a turkey sandwich." Everybody laughed except for Maren.

"Are you okay?" Maren asked, unbuckling Emma's safety harness and helping her to sit up.

"Yeah," said Emma, rubbing her eyes. "That was weird. I could hear you guys talking, but I couldn't get out of the dream. I just kept bungeeing up and down, fending off my competitors. I was totally winning, by the way."

"That *is* weird," said Maren. She'd heard of this kind of thing happening if the dosage of dreamsalt was too high. That was why they were so careful at Lishta's shop. But unless somebody was using an ingredient like whispering dust, there was no explanation for the mass turkey sandwich cravings.

"I'm so glad you're awake!" Kendall's bright voice had a frantic edge to it. "Vesper, thanks so much for helping. Now let's go get some lunch!"

Maren's stomach fluttered as Kendall joined the other girls, who were all chattering about turkey sandwiches. Emma linked arms with Anika, and Maren followed close behind to make sure she was all right, but she seemed perfectly lively and recovered from the dream. As they reached the steps, Maren realized with a twinge of disappointment that Ivy was gone. Her new friend had snuck off without her.

Twenty minutes later, Maren sat nibbling the crust of the soggiest peanut butter and jelly sandwich she'd ever seen, in the middle of utter pandemonium. At least half the campers at Camp Shady Sands had woken up from their morning dreams with an irresistible urge for a turkey sandwich, and there weren't enough to go around.

"Settle down and get in line, kids!" yelled a lunch lady with her hair falling out of her hairnet and a giant blob of mustard on her cheek. "We're making more sandwiches as fast as we can!"

"We want them now!" yelled a gang of boys.

"Calm down and wait your turn," yelled Amos, throwing Maren a sympathetic look. The poor cafeteria workers were running ragged. Maren kept trying to catch Lishta's eye so they could talk, but her grandmother was so busy dashing around waving bread and turkey and condiments that she hadn't noticed her.

A tiny girl from the youngest group of campers finally got to the front of the line and squealed with glee when she received her sandwich. But then an older boy swooped in, grabbed it off her tray, and dashed outside. With a shriek, the girl threw her tray and sat down in the middle of the floor, sobbing.

"Howdy, y'all!" Carmella swept through the door with a magazine tucked under her arm. "My goodness, what's all this fuss about?"

"I NEED MY TURKEY SANDWICH!" wailed the little girl.

"Hush now," said Carmella, rushing over. "I'm sure we can find you one, sweetheart."

This was definitely not normal. Maren cut the sandwich line, ignoring the shouts and curses of the waiting campers, and waved to Lishta.

"Take me out with the crowd!" sang a boy. "Buy me some peanuts and Cracker Jack."

"You're out of toilet paper in the ladies' room!" Maren called, hoping Lishta would catch her hint.

"I'll be right there," called Lishta, frantically slathering mayonnaise on a soggy slice of white bread. "Try and hold it for just a"—she glanced up, realized who she was speaking to, and gave a curt nod—"minute!"

"Where's my sandwich?" yelled a boy.

"Try saying please!" snapped Maren. "They're going as fast as they can." With that, she spun around and headed for the restroom.

Several minutes later, an exhausted Lishta burst through the door, clutching several rolls of toilet paper. "I'm so sorry, dear, but I need to get right back to the kitchen. I don't know what's come over all of these children!"

"I think it's the dreams," said Maren. "There's something weird going on. And this girl from my bunk—"

The door swung open, and two older girls stomped in, ranting about how annoying it was that they'd only been allowed one turkey sandwich each. Lishta waited until they were in their stalls, then leaned in to whisper in Maren's ear.

"I'm sorry, but I have to get back. Can you write down everything that's happened on a paper towel and leave it under the cereal dispenser?" She pulled a pen from her apron pocket, handed it to Maren, and dashed away with a quickly blown kiss.

Feeling small and abandoned, Maren took a paper towel, locked herself in a stall, and started scribbling. The pen kept tearing holes in the paper towel, but she managed to get most of the information down. Then she flushed, washed her hands, and returned to the chaos.

It had only gotten worse. Kids were openly fighting over sandwiches, a boy had climbed over the counter and was making his own, and a counselor crouched in the corner, delightedly stuffing turkey into his mouth. At least five kids were singing about baseball, and Carmella was dashing around like a headless chicken, trying to calm everyone down and failing miserably. Amos's group had left, and Maren made a mental note to find him that afternoon and pull him aside to talk.

Invisible in the pandemonium, she slipped over to the cereal dispenser, which was filled with little brown nuggets that looked suspiciously like cat treats. She slid her paper towel under the dispenser, then headed back to her table, but it was empty.

"Out here!" Through the open doorway, Anika waved. She pointed to Emma and Ivy, who sat under a tree, passing around two bags of cheese puffs.

"Phew," said Maren as she joined them under the tree. "It's like the Wild West in there."

"I know, right?" said Emma. "I'm glad I got my turkey sandwich though."

Maren leaned in close to Ivy. "Did you tell your grandmother about Emma not being able to wake up?"

Ivy nodded. "She said she's never heard of that happening before, but she's going to stop selling the bungee-jumping karate dream just to be safe."

She's never heard of it happening before because she doesn't actually know anything about dreams, thought Maren. "So, this turkey sandwich thing," she said. "Don't you think it's a little weird that everybody woke up wanting one?"

"I didn't want one," said Anika.

"But lots of other people did," said Maren. "And what

about everybody singing that baseball song? Maybe that's caused by the dreams too?"

Ivy stopped chewing. "Could dreams do that?"

"Maybe if it was somebody's *mission* to make them do that." Maren lifted her eyebrows meaningfully.

Ivy gulped hard, looking a little green. "People are probably just getting that song stuck in their head because everybody's singing it. I don't think you can blame my grandma for that."

"No!" Maren said quickly. "Of course not. But Ivy, you said she didn't really know anything about dreams, and I'm just worried she might not realize if something was wrong with them."

"She would never do anything to hurt the campers," Ivy said, looking hurt herself.

"I didn't mean it like that," said Maren.

"Hey," said Anika, stuffing a handful of cheese puffs into her mouth. "Let's not worry about it, okay? Guess what we've got next!"

"What?" said Maren and Ivy at the same time.

"Dream-crafting workshop." Anika licked orange powder off her fingertips. "With that weird-looking lady with the silver hair."

"Oh great," deadpanned Ivy, but Maren sat up straighter. This day had just gotten even more interesting.

Thirteen

Tucked in a shady grove of weeping willows, the dream-crafting workshop was in a lavender-colored building with a flat roof and dark windows. As Maren stepped inside, the scent of incense tickled her nose and made her want to sneeze. The room was dim, and the air was slightly smoky. Several sets of wind chimes hung from the ceiling, and the sound of water trickling over stone came from some hidden place.

All along the back wall were shelves that reminded Maren of Lishta's shop—if someone with a deep passion for organizing had taken it over. There were separate rows for the bottles, jars, bins, and boxes, each item carefully labeled and set in a perfectly straight line. On one of the bottom shelves sat a little white machine with STERI-TIZE printed on the front. In the center of the room stood a long counter, empty except for an eyedropper, a set of measuring spoons, and a blender.

Behind the counter stood the young woman with silver hair who Maren had spotted at the Dreamboree the night before. Today she wore a deep purple nightgown, a long, beaded necklace, and a golden bracelet that wound all the way up to her elbow. Her hair hung in waves around her shoulders, and her eyes were lined with pale blue. On anyone else, it would have looked cheesy. On her, it was mesmerizing.

"Welcome," she called in a voice that was as silvery as her hair. "Come in, come in."

Murmuring among themselves, the girls drifted inside, and Maren shut the door behind them. Underneath the cloying incense, it smelled like a real dream shop. Her feet did a quick, delighted *fah-lap heel toe heel step*, even though she was supposed to be investigating, not getting caught up in the glamour of this place.

"My name is Thalia Mandrake," said the woman, beckoning them closer. "And I'm here to teach you the subtle art of dream-crafting."

A couple of girls laughed awkwardly, and Peyton and Maddie started whispering. Someone started humming the baseball song. Thalia turned to the rows of shelves and pulled down two boxes, two jars, and a bottle.

"Crafting a dream is a bit like baking," she said, setting the items in a straight line on the counter. "Mix the right ingredients, in the right quantities, in the right order, and you'll get something lovely."

So far, this woman sounded legitimate. Maren wondered if she might be the only person at this whole camp who actually understood dreams.

"But if you get your quantities wrong," continued Thalia, "or if you add the wrong ingredient, even in a tiny dose, poof!" Rings flashed on her fingers as she made an exploding gesture with her hand. "The whole thing falls flat. Or worse, you end up with a *nightmare.*" Her voice dropped low on the last word, and a hush fell over the girls.

"What if you wanted a nightmare?" said a girl from the back of the group.

Thalia's blue-ringed eyes flashed. "That isn't something you'll learn from me—or from anyone at Camp Shady Sands. Nightmares are very tricky and potentially very dangerous."

This woman really did know her stuff. Maren rested her elbows on the counter and surveyed the ingredients Thalia had chosen. Lavender, brick dust, old-fashioned pen nibs, apple seeds, a bottle of ink, and a little scrap of paper. Maren wasn't familiar with the combination, but she could guess where it was going.

"Let's try putting these together," said Thalia, pulling the tops off the containers. "What do the ingredients make you think of?" She held up a pen nib, a corner of paper, and an apple seed.

"School!" called out a couple of girls.

"Old-fashioned school," said Ivy.

Thalia smiled at her. "You have a good eye for detail. Constructing a dream is all about taking the associations your brain makes and building them out with tiny details."

Maren's foot tap-tap-tapped. This was exactly right.

"So, let's introduce lavender," Thalia said, tipping the ingredients into the blender and reaching for another jar. "Who or what might smell like lavender?"

"An eye pillow!" called out Maddie.

"A teacher," said Ivy.

Thalia gave her another approving smile. It was a shame Ivy had such a knack for dreams but couldn't take them. Maybe it was the lucid dreaming that made her so knowledgeable. Maren wished she could show off a bit too, because a tiny part of her really wanted to be friends with this cool new teacher.

"Who wants to dream about school anyway?" said Peyton, and Maddie giggled.

"Ah, but this isn't just any ordinary school. Where's the

fun in that?" Thalia gestured at the wall of ingredients behind her. "What makes this school unique?"

"It's a wizarding school!" someone said.

"A circus school," said someone else.

"A school for Victorian cats!" The words flew out of Maren's mouth before she could stop them. Apparently she missed the dream shop cat, Artax, more than she realized.

"Weirdo," muttered Peyton.

But Thalia burst out laughing, and her laugh was a beautiful, glittery thing. "I love it! One of the best things about dreams is that they can be literally anything you want."

It was one of Maren's favorite parts too. She felt warm all the way down to the tips of her toes as the teacher whirled around, purple dress swirling, to face the shelves. "Let's see, cat hair and..."

Add some whiskers too, thought Maren.

"Whiskers!"

Despite her efforts to remain impartial on her spy mission, Maren already loved this teacher.

Thalia grabbed an armload of ingredients and set them on the table. "All right. We've got cat hair and whiskers, mouse fur, a pinch of chalk dust, just a smidge of powdered tuna, and gold foil stars—because of course the dreamer is going to do very well in Victorian cat school."

Maren wanted to take this dream so badly it hurt. Maybe Lishta would make an exception for a dream she'd watched being crafted. If not, she'd make it the instant she got back to her own dream shop.

"Now remember, everything has been sterilized ahead of time," said Thalia as she added ingredients to the blender. "Nobody wants to put unsterilized mouse fur in their mouth, right?"

The blender's crunchy, roaring whir drowned out the campers' disgusted responses. Several girls pressed their hands over their ears, but Maren was used to this part, even though they used a hand-cranked coffee grinder at her shop. She wondered how electric-powered blades would affect the dream's texture.

As the blender ran, Thalia pulled out a box full of little mesh pouches. They looked more like cheesecloth than the sachets Lishta used, and they didn't resemble the dreams that had been in Maren's starter pack or the ones at the dream shack. She leaned in closer.

Thalia switched off the blender and dipped a long-handled spoon inside. "Now let's measure out a little bit of the dream mixture into each sachet. About a quarter of a teaspoon."

And then the dreamsalt or whatever the sleeping agent is, thought Maren. But Thalia finished filling all the sachets and pulled out a spool of thread with a needle stuck in the top.

"Just a few quick stitches with dissolvable thread, and that's it!" she said, threading the needle and flashing it through the first sachet with the quick ease of a seasoned seamstress. "I like to let them sit for a few days to percolate, but you can start using them anytime, really."

"What about the…" Maren pressed her lips together and gulped the words back down.

"What about the what?" Thalia picked up the next sachet and sewed it shut in three seconds flat. She really did look like she knew what she was doing, but how could she forget the magical part? Without dreamsalt or something like it, those dreams would just leave the gross taste of cat hair and mouse fur and chalk in somebody's mouth. Thalia hadn't even blown on the dreams, though Maren was certain that only worked for members of her own family—and they still needed to add dreamsalt.

"Those are…all the ingredients?" squeaked Maren.

Thalia gave her a funny look. "That's it."

Maren's heart sank down to her knees. She'd been so hopeful that this beautiful, impossibly cool woman was a real dream-crafter like her. But Thalia was just pretending—like everyone else at Camp Shady Sands.

"Can I have one?" asked Peyton, apparently forgetting that only weirdos liked Victorian cat dreams.

"Me too," said Maddie.

"Me too!" yelled all the other campers.

"Of course," said Thalia, needle flashing as she whipped up more dreams and slid them across the table, one by one. "You all helped invent this dream, after all. I hope you love it."

They wouldn't. Maren sighed. Somebody was making real dreams for this camp, but it wasn't Thalia Mandrake.

Fourteen

"Everybody, pick a spot!" Kendall swept aside a gauzy curtain, revealing a covered deck that overlooked the sparkling lake. Multicolored hammocks hung throughout the space, swaying gently in the breeze. Squealing with delight, Maren's bunkmates ran to claim their places, everyone jostling to get the hammocks closest to the lake. It looked like a gorgeous way to spend a hot afternoon, and Maren longed to climb into a hammock, take a minty calming dream, and float away for an hour or so. But she had work to do.

Unfortunately, Ivy was gone again. This would have to be a solo mission. Maren waited until everybody was nestled in their hammocks and Kendall was gently snoring before sliding off her slippers and rolling out of her hammock. Her bare feet hit the boards with a quiet thump, and she waited for a few seconds before tiptoeing to the exit.

The center of the camp was deserted, though the beach was packed with sleeping campers. Ivy was probably in the dream shack, hanging out with her grandmother, and Maren felt a twinge of jealousy. She wished she could talk to Lishta somewhere outside of a smelly public restroom without having to whisper.

"Hey, Ma-Vesper!"

Maren swung around and spotted Hallie and two girls from her group emerging from the shack. She beckoned for Hallie to come over, and one of the girls said something under her breath. The other girl laughed, but Hallie rolled her eyes and jogged up the steps.

"What's going on?" she said.

"What did that girl just say?" Maren narrowed her eyes at Hallie's friends, who were busy waving at Evan, the lifeguard.

"Don't worry about it," said Hallie. "Is everything okay?"

"Yes," said Maren. "But I have a bunch of stuff to tell you. Can we go somewhere to talk?"

Hallie glanced back at her friends, who were already heading down the dock. "I can't right now."

"Are you kidding me?" said Maren. "You'd honestly ditch me to hang out with some slimy boy?"

"He's not slimy," said Hallie. "And besides, that's not why

I can't come. I have a couple of things to do. How about we meet up in half an hour?"

It sounded like a fishy excuse, but Maren nodded anyway. "If you walk down the beach past that 'No campers beyond this point' sign and keep going, there's a boathouse. Meet me there in thirty minutes, and don't be late, because I have to get back to my group."

"Got it. See you then." Hallie gave her arm a quick squeeze, then dashed off to join her friends. The way Evan watched her run down the dock made Maren think of a hungry person at an all-you-can-eat buffet.

"Do your job and watch the swimmers," she muttered, trying to ignore the sting of Hallie blowing her off. Thank goodness Amos and Lishta were here, because Hallie was turning out to be no help at all. Part of Maren felt bad blaming her sister, who'd had no social life or even spoken to a boy for months because of her coma, but a bigger part of her resented Hallie for not taking this seriously enough.

After heading across the field, Maren skirted along the backs of the buildings. Behind the mess hall stood a dumpster filled with buzzing flies. She held her nose as she peered through the grubby window, but the kitchen was dark and silent. Maybe the lunch ladies got to take naps and dreams in the afternoon too.

As she passed a white building with the word LAUNDRY over the door, a stack of boxes in the window caught Maren's eye. She slowed, peered over her shoulder to make sure nobody was looking, and ducked inside the building.

A huge pile of towels and sheets lay beside a row of washing machines and dryers. The air was steamy and smelled comfortingly of fabric softener. Maren inhaled deeply and wished she were home, tucked in a freshly laundered bed, her parents watching TV in the living room. But she was here, not there, and she had a mission.

Trying to stay away from the window and out of sight, Maren edged closer to the boxes. *Moonbeam Illusions,* they all said in cursive script with a little crescent moon design underneath. It sounded and looked like the name of a dream company. Maren eased the top box off the pile. It was light, which was another good sign.

Sniff sniff.

She froze, clutching the box to her chest. The sound was coming from inside the room, from somewhere near the washing machines.

Sniff.

It wasn't a washer or a dryer. It wasn't a mouse.

"H—Henri?" whispered Maren.

"AAAAAA-CHOOOOOO!" yelled the pile of laundry,

and Maren dropped the box. She cast about for a weapon and grabbed a heavy jug of laundry detergent.

"Who's there?" she said, winding back and aiming the jug at the laundry pile. "Come out now!"

"Maren?" The pile wiggled and shifted, and Amos's tousled head appeared.

Maren dropped the jug and dug Amos out. "What are you doing in here?"

He blinked sheepishly and wiped his nose on the back of his hand. "Hiding?"

"But why?"

"I was throwing Frisbees with my group over near the parking lot, and this lady pulled up in a truck and unloaded those." Amos pointed to the Moonbeam Illusions boxes. "I thought she looked suspicious, so I followed her here, and I was about to open the boxes when Calvin and Malvin came in and I had to dive into the laundry pile."

"What did they do?" asked Maren.

"They counted the boxes and then tried to do some math to figure out if something was going to be enough for the next phase," said Amos.

Maren's skin went cold and crawly.

"They're really bad at math," said Amos. "They had to use a calculator to multiply five by one thousand."

Maren eyed the boxes. "So there are five thousand dreams in there." That was a lot for a camp of this size, especially considering how many dreams they already had. "What did the lady look like?"

"I don't know, kind of old?" Amos wiped his nose on a stray towel, and Maren cringed.

"How old? Like Gran-Gran old or like our moms old?"

Amos pondered. "Maybe a little older than our moms?"

"And she wasn't anybody you've seen at camp before?" said Maren. "What was she wearing?"

"I dunno, normal clothes?" said Amos. "She had really bright red glasses."

"And she just dropped off a bunch of boxes in the laundry room and left?" said Maren.

"I think so," said Amos. "She definitely knew her way around the camp."

Casting a glance out the window, Maren pulled the tape partway off the box and squeezed her hand inside. Sure enough, it was full of dreams—she'd know the feel of them anywhere. She pulled out a handful of white sachets.

"I wonder how they know which ones are which?" she said, turning to the box to see if it was labeled. But the only thing printed on it was the Moonbeam Illusions logo and a string of letters and numbers. Maren pulled out her phone and took a photo, then took quick snaps of all the other boxes, which had different letter-number combinations printed on them. Then she checked the time.

"Come on," she said. "We have to go meet Hallie."

Amos's eyes went wide as bus wheels, and Maren groaned. She didn't begrudge Amos his feelings, but things would be a lot easier if everybody could stop crushing on her sister.

Fifteen

As she and Amos made their way through the muggy, bramble-filled woods, Maren's entire body itched. Her scratches were covered in scratches, and all she could think of was diving into that cool blue lake. Just as they reached the edge of the forest by the boathouse, a croaking voice rang out.

"DU RIECHST NACH HAMSTERFÜßEN!"

Amos threw out an arm to stop Maren, clocking her in the stomach. "There's somebody in there!"

With a sigh, Maren waved off a swarm of mosquitoes. "It's just Henri. Or should I say, Heinrich." She pointed to the green bird perched on the roof of the crumbling structure.

"What exactly is he spying on all the way out here?" said Amos.

"I don't know," said Maren. "Gran-Gran is in charge of him. I mean, as much as anybody's ever in charge of Henri."

"RENIFLEUSE DE FROMAGE!" yelled Henri.

"I have no idea what you're saying," said Maren.

"He called you a cheese sniffer," said Amos.

"Awesome," said Maren. "At any rate, you need to stop yelling before somebody hears you, Henri."

The parrot hopped left and right and made a disgruntled, quieter squawk.

"That's better," said Maren, peering inside the boathouse. Waves lapped at the front of the building, but the inside was dry, and the back wall was lined with wide shelves that had probably once held canoes and kayaks.

Amos skirted past her, his sneakers squelching in the mud, and swept an armful of cobwebs as thick as yarn off the lower shelf. "There's no such thing as haunted boathouses, right?" he said, wiping his hands on his shorts and peering up into the rafters, where things rustled and stirred.

"Definitely not," said Maren, although she'd never seen a boathouse this creepy before. Even though there was only a gentle breeze outside, the rotten timbers of the structure creaked and groaned. The shadows leapt and twisted, and it was at least ten degrees colder inside than outside. Maren shivered. The ingredients from this place would make an epic nightmare, and she wished she'd brought some containers to collect bits and pieces.

"Hello?" called Hallie from outside.

"SACRE BLEU!" yelled Henri.

Maren and Amos trudged out to the beach, and there was Hallie, surrounded by a flock of ducks that quacked hello to Henri and swam over to join him.

"Hey Amos," said Hallie.

"Hey, uh, hi, what's up?" said Amos, and Maren rolled her eyes so hard it hurt. Quickly, she got Hallie up to speed on what she and Amos had found, and then she told them both about the letter she'd spotted in the co-directors' cabin, as well as Thalia Mandrake's dream-crafting workshop.

"Her ingredients are completely legitimate, and she seemed like she knew how to make dreams, but then she didn't use any sleeping agent," said Maren. "So it was just a little bag of all the right ingredients that didn't work."

"That's weird," said Hallie. "Do you think she didn't know or she purposely left it out?"

"That's the million-dollar question," said Maren.

"Gran-Gran told me not to trust anybody here," said Hallie. "Even the people who seem totally clueless."

That was good advice. Maren had been writing off a lot of seemingly clueless people lately. "What was so important at the beach that you couldn't meet me until now?" She tried and failed to keep the petty tone out of her voice.

"I've been asking Carmella about her dreams," said Hallie. "I told her I want to be a dream seller like her when I grow up, and I asked her to teach me everything she knows."

"That was bold," said Amos, and Maren agreed. Hallie's plan had the potential to go very wrong if she asked too many questions.

"You wouldn't believe the nonsense she was spouting," said Hallie. "She actually told me they're more potent if you put essential oils on them."

Maren gagged. Essential oils weren't supposed to go in your mouth, and they'd definitely change the dream's structure. She hoped Carmella wasn't adding that to the sachets she was selling.

"I saw Gran-Gran at lunch and gave her all the dreams I've collected," continued Hallie. "She's analyzing them back in her cottage, but she has a roommate so she has to be sneaky."

"QVACK QVACK!" Waddling in an exaggerated imitation of the ducks' gait, Henri was busy leading them in a circle in what seemed to be some kind of weird bird game.

"Heinie, did you manage to do anything besides make friends today?" asked Hallie.

Henri puffed up his feathers until he was twice his normal

size. "The plane tickets are here," he said in a perfect imitation of a man's goofy voice. "Let's make sure we're ready."

Maren, Hallie, and Amos exchanged stunned looks.

"Have you been spying on Calvin and Malvin?" asked Hallie.

"WAFFELHOSEN!" shrieked the bird, so loudly Maren's ear started ringing.

"QUACK!" said one of the ducks.

"Ugh," said Maren. "Did you at least tell Gran-Gran what you heard?"

Henri let out a big, wet dropping and flew away to the boathouse roof. Maren sighed. She didn't know why she ever expected anything with Henri to be simple. Plane tickets and payments were an interesting development, though. Clearly it had something to do with that letter she'd seen in the co-directors' cottage.

"We need to get back to camp soon," said Maren.

"Let's hope everybody's over the sandwich thing," said Hallie, and Maren nodded, but she had a sneaking suspicion that turkey sandwiches were only the beginning.

Sixteen

IN THE GRASSY CLEARING, MAREN spotted a cluster of her bunkmates, rubbing their eyes and yawning, and jogged over to join them. A bonfire was already crackling, and pajama-clad counselors were busy adding wood to build it up. Beside the fire stood a long table piled with hot dogs, buns, and chip bags.

"There you are!" said Kendall, straightening her crooked ponytail.

"Sorry," said Maren. "I woke up early and had a million bug bites so I went back to the cabin to get more bug spray." A mosquito whined in her ear, and she desperately wished she'd actually stopped and put more bug spray on.

"That's a *great* idea." Kendall's eyes brightened as she unzipped a pouch on her mini backpack and pulled out a spray bottle. "Who else needs bug spray?"

Maren edged as close as she could while Kendall sprayed the other girls down, hoping to catch some of the dregs. So far, nobody was raving about turkey sandwiches or any other kind of food. They all seemed perfectly normal after the latest dream session.

"Did that cat school dream work on you?" said Emma, who had a faint crosshatch pattern on her cheek from the hammock.

"Uh, kind of?" said Maren.

"It didn't for me," said Emma, "but Anika swears it did for her."

"It was so funny!" Anika coughed and waved away a cloud of bug spray as Maren tried to waft it onto herself. "We were jumping all over the desks, catching mice in our teeth. And the mice had little calligraphy mustaches."

"*I* got a gold star," said Peyton.

Interesting, thought Maren. Even though the dream had no technical way of working, talking about it—and expecting it to work—must have influenced some of the girls' subconscious. A placebo effect, she remembered from school. It didn't make Thalia Mandrake any more of an expert, but it was fascinating nonetheless.

Maren waited in line for her hot dog, bun, chips, and long stick, and then tried to squeeze through the mob of campers all jostling to cook their dinners over the fire. One of the lunch ladies was doling out paper bowls of beans to go with the hot dogs, and Maren drifted closer to peer inside the pot. The bubbling sauce was bluish-brown and smelled like egg salad.

"Over here!" Ivy waved from a spot across the fire, and Maren hurried to join her.

"Where've you been?" Maren asked as Ivy nudged some kids sideways to make space for her.

"With my grandma," said Ivy. "I told her how frustrating it is to have to sit around and watch everybody else take dreams, and she said I can help run the shack when it's dream time."

"Lucky." Maren's hot dog began to sizzle as she held it over the flickering flames, and her stomach gurgled.

"I think she feels bad for dragging me here," said Ivy. "But not bad enough to let me go home."

"You don't really want to go home, do you?" said Maren. "I mean, it's kind of nice here even if you're not dreaming. You can swim or take the boats out or do arts and crafts. It's got to be better than sitting around your house without your mom or anybody else." She thought of the months when Hallie had been in the hospital and she'd been alone, and how awful it was.

"Excuse me!" called a voice from behind them. "Excuse me! I said, *excuse* me."

A blond girl in red pajamas elbowed her way through the crowd. "Excuse me!" she kept yelling. "Sorry, can you please move? I'm going to miss it."

"Going to miss what?" called a laughing boy.

"My train." The girl tugged on something invisible behind her. More kids started laughing, but Maren's body went cold. The girl's eyes were shut tight. She was sleepwalking and dreaming at the same time.

"Hold this," Maren gave her hot dog stick to Ivy and tried to push through the crowd, but even more people had arrived and it was jammed. "Excuse me!" she yelled.

"Are you late for your train too?" said the obnoxious boy.

"It's not funny," said Maren. "Somebody grab her before she gets too close to the fire. She's sleepwalking."

But everybody was too busy chatting and eating and trying to get their hot dogs toasted; nobody seemed to care that the sleepwalking girl was heading straight for the bonfire.

"Take me out to the ball game!" sang a boy.

"Take me out with the crowd!" About ten other kids joined in. With so many dreams to choose from, why were they all picking the same baseball dream? Maren didn't have time to think about it.

"Hal—Zoe!" she yelled. "Zoe Finch, where are you?"

There was no answer, so she went into rugby mode,

plowing through the singing crowd, not caring who she hit or whose foot she stepped on.

"Wait! Please wait!" The mob almost swallowed up the girl's words, but Maren heard her and swung sideways, knocking a cup of eggy beans out of somebody's hand.

"Sorry, but I did you a favor," she muttered, charging through the crowd. Finally, she spotted the girl again. Her invisible suitcase seemed to be stuck on something—she tugged and frantically waved her free arm at the dream train conductor.

"Wait!" she called.

Maren finally reached the girl and gently took her elbow. "It's okay, there's another train right after this one and it's going to…uh, where you're going."

Hallie popped out of the crowd, her worried eyes locked on them, and just seeing her sister dropped Maren's anxiety about fifty points.

"To Spain," said the girl. "I want to see the flamenco dancers."

"Yes, to Spain," said Hallie, taking the girl's other arm. "Here, let me get your suitcase. Don't worry, there are loads more trains, so you can let that one go."

"Are you sure?" The girl's voice trembled.

"Positive," said Maren. "Here, let's go find a bench on the platform. Excuse us. Sorry. Thank you."

Finally they reached the edge of the crowd, and Maren spotted a fallen log. She and Hallie helped the girl to sit.

"What's your name?" asked Hallie.

"Lucy," said the girl.

"I'm Zoe," said Hallie. "And this is my sister, uh…" Her eyes went wide with panic.

"Vesper," finished Maren, and Hallie mouthed *sorry* and made a mortified face.

Maren tried not to take it personally that Hallie had forgotten her alias. So what if her sister had barely been thinking or caring about her for two days? As long as she was focusing on the mission. And not on Evan the lifeguard.

"That sounds super dreamy!" came a goofy man's voice from the crowd. Hallie jumped up, disappeared briefly, and returned with an irritated camp co-director with a tiny "C" embroidered on the chest of his pajamas.

"Something's wrong with your dreams," said Hallie, pointing at poor Lucy, who was now sleep-crouching on the ground, rummaging through her invisible suitcase. "She's sleepwalking and we can't wake her up."

Calvin edged toward Lucy and poked her arm. "Hey there, camper! Time to wake up!"

"Genius," muttered Hallie. "Why didn't anybody think of trying that?"

Maren pressed her lips together to keep from laughing. This was serious.

"I'm sure she'll be fine!" said Calvin. "Some people are just, uh, prone to sleepwalking."

"Yeah, but this shouldn't be happening when they're taking the camp's dreams," said Hallie. "If the dosage of your sleep—" She caught herself and snapped her mouth shut. No regular camper would know about the proper dosage of sleeping agents.

Luckily, Calvin wasn't listening. He bent down and shook Lucy's shoulder. "Hey there, camper!"

"Her name is Lucy," said Maren.

"Hey, Lucy," said Calvin. "It's time to rise and shine!"

But Lucy's eyes stayed tightly shut. "Is there a vending machine in this station? I want a candy bar."

"I'll, uh…go and get you one!" Calvin leapt up, and before Maren or Hallie could stop him, he dashed away.

"Are you kidding me?" Hallie's eyes flashed fire as she helped Lucy back onto the log. Maren patted her arm reassuringly.

"Hey, I cooked your—What's going on?" Ivy emerged from the crowd, holding Maren's hot dog on its stick. Maren realized she'd dropped the rest of her dinner somewhere in the jumble of kids.

"This girl Lucy is dreaming," said Maren. "Kind of like what happened to Emma, but this time we really can't wake her."

"Oh wow." Ivy's feet shuffled nervously.

"Do you think your grandmother has a waking anti—" Hallie corrected herself quickly "I mean, like, some kind of thing to make people wake up or whatever?"

"I doubt it." Ivy glanced over her shoulder. "She just got this job last month. She pretends to be some big expert, but all she did was read the training packet they sent her and a couple of books about dreams."

"Help me get her up." Hallie draped one of Lucy's arms over her shoulder, and Maren was about to do the same when Calvin returned with a woman in a pink unicorn onesie.

"This is our head counselor, Judy," said Calvin.

"We know," said Maren, and Hallie gave Judy an awkward wave.

"Judy's going to bring Lucy..." Calvin snorted. "That almost rhymed!" When nobody laughed at his little joke, he continued: "To the health center, where they'll make her right as rain!"

"What will they do, exactly?" asked Hallie.

"Don't worry about your little friend!" Judy beamed her gummy smile. "She just needs to sleep it off in a safe spot."

She needs a waking antidote, thought Maren. Made with coffee and mint and powdered firefly and cayenne. If only she could go to the dream-crafting workshop and whip something up, she could fix this a lot faster. "Can we come visit her?" she asked.

"We'll see," said Judy in a tone that sounded like probably not. She wrapped her arm around Lucy's waist. "Now come on, camper. Right this way!"

"Are you the conductor?" murmured Lucy, reaching for her suitcase handle.

"That's me, Conductor Judy!" Casting a saccharine smile at Maren and Hallie, the head counselor led Lucy away, followed by Calvin.

"That was weird," said Ivy.

"Super weird," said Maren.

"Hi," Hallie extended her hand to Ivy. "I'm Zoe, Vesper's sister."

Ivy's eyes widened. "Nice to meet you. Vesper didn't mention she had a sister at camp."

"Did…did I not?" Maren stammered. "I'm sure I told you that."

Ivy shrugged. "Nope."

Maren's cheeks went hot. She'd been so worried about keeping her identity secret that she'd forgotten the parts that didn't need to be kept secret. She was utterly failing at this undercover thing.

"Love your hair," said Hallie with a big smile. "Do you mind if I borrow my sister for a second?"

"No problem."

Maren managed to grab her hot dog from Ivy before Hallie dragged her away. As they passed the food table, she snatched a bag of chips too. Once they were far enough from everyone, the sisters ducked behind a pine with dense boughs like a Christmas tree.

"We need to tell Gran-Gran about Lucy," said Maren. "One kid who can't wake up and another kid sleepwalking in one day can't be good."

Hallie stole a chip from Maren's bag. "Especially on top of that turkey sandwich fiasco. But I can't figure out how the two things are connected."

"If they even are," said Maren.

Back at the bonfire, a microphone squealed, and the crowd shushed. "Hellooo, dreamers and dreamettes!" yelled a goofy voice.

"I can't deal with those guys," said Hallie.

"Me neither." Maren crumpled up her empty chip bag and wondered if Malvin and Calvin might also not be as clueless as they seemed.

"Who's ready for some karaoke?" yelled one of the co-directors, and the campers cheered. "Hosted by our very own mistress of dreams, Carmella! Only songs about dreams, of course!"

"Mistress of dreams," muttered Hallie. "More like mistress of questionable fashion choices."

Maren rubbed her temples. "You know what we should do? Make our own waking antidotes and keep them on us in case this happens again. Maybe we could even sneak into the health center and give one to Lucy."

"Yes." Hallie's eyes gleamed. "Are you thinking what I'm thinking?"

Maren did a quick *shuffle hop step* and grinned. "The dream-crafting workshop."

Seventeen

ALL OF THE LIGHTS IN the dream workshop were on, casting an otherworldly glow through the trailing willow branches. The two sisters crept up to a window and peered inside.

"Wow," breathed Hallie as she took in the shelves full of dream ingredients.

"Looks pretty legitimate, doesn't it?" whispered Maren.

"Completely," said Hallie. "She's even got a sterilizer."

"How does she know this much about dreams, but not about dreamsalt or any other kind of sleeping agent?" said Maren. "Why would she think the dreams were going to work for everybody?"

Before her sister could answer, a door at the back of the room swung open, and a shadowy figure entered. It was Thalia, draped in a lacy black shawl and carrying an amber-colored antique jar. She set the jar down, dragged a step stool out, and climbed up to gather ingredients. Even though she was too far away for Maren to read all of the labels, she moved quickly and decisively. Like someone who'd spent a lot of time in a dream shop and knew exactly what she was doing.

The sisters watched silently as Thalia tweezed out purple flower petals and glittery crystal beads and dropped them into the blender, adding seeds and bits of foil, a finely powdered something that looked like sand, and a spritz from a green spray bottle. Maren had no idea what this dream was, but it looked enchanting.

A swarm of gnats wafted into her face, and as she ducked under the window to swat them away, one flew up her nose. "Gark!" she whisper-yelled as the overwhelming urge to sneeze hit her.

"Shh," hissed Hallie.

Please, nose, don't betray me like this. Maren dug her finger into her nostril, not caring that her sister saw, and fished out the bug, then pinched her nose shut to hold in the sneeze. Her eyes began to water.

Finally, Thalia turned on the blender, and under cover of the crunching roar, Maren let out a plugged-up sneeze that made her eyeballs feel like they were popping out. Hallie tensed beside her, but Thalia just switched off the blender and began spooning the powdered mixture into sachets. Then she unscrewed the lid of the antique jar she'd brought with her and used tweezers to remove its contents, adding a tiny pinch to each sachet.

"Is that what I think it is?" whispered Hallie, and Maren nodded, spellbound.

Thalia paused, then blew gently over all the sachets.

—

Thirty minutes later, Maren and Hallie crept out of the shadowy willows. Thalia had left shortly after finishing up her dreams, but she'd locked the door behind her. The sisters had checked every single window, but they were all firmly locked too. Maren wanted to break one and sneak in, but Hallie reminded her that they were still undercover and it'd compromise their plans if anyone found out there was an investigation.

"Gran-Gran can make waking antidotes," said Hallie. "I'll go find her now."

"I want to come too," said Maren. "Plus I know where her cottage is. Well, I'm not sure exactly which one it is, but we'll figure it out."

"Can you believe Thalia Mandrake actually has dream magic?" said Hallie as they hurried down the path that led to the staff housing.

"Yeah, I can, actually," said Maren. "I mean, look at her."

Hallie made a *hmph* sound. "She's trying a little too hard if you ask me."

"Do you think she's the one pulling all the strings behind the scenes?" An image of Obscura Gray's sinister shadow puppet show flashed through Maren's mind, and she shuddered.

"She has to be," said Hallie. "Everyone else is totally incompetent."

"She must have put too much dreamsalt in Emma and Lucy's dreams," said Maren. "But did she do it on purpose or was it an accident?"

"That," said Hallie, "is what we need to find out."

⌒

The sisters reached the little cluster of blue cottages and hovered at the edge of the clearing. The woods on this side of camp were quieter, full of chirping insects and whispering branches.

"Which one do you think is Gran-Gran's?" said Hallie.

"I don't know," said Maren. "Can you see inside any of them?"

Keeping to the shadows in the dimming evening light, the two girls crept closer, straining for a glimpse inside the cottages, most of which had their lights on and televisions flashing a multicolored glow. Maren missed her own house and television, but at least Hallie was here now. She fought the urge to reach out and hold her sister's hand—they were way too old for that now.

In the first cottage, two women played cards at their kitchen table. In the second, three older ladies shouted at a game show on their TV. In the third, a woman sat alone on her couch, reading a magazine. The light in a room at the back of the cottage was also on, but the curtains were drawn.

"I bet that's it," said Maren, who felt a spidey-sense of Lishta lingering in the air. She tiptoed closer and tried to peek around the edges of the curtains, but it was useless. "Should I knock on the window?"

"No," said Hallie, pulling her back into the shadows. "If it's not her, everybody will think we're Peeping Toms."

Maren wrinkled her nose. "Peeping who?"

Hallie waved her hand. "Never mind. Let's try to lure her outside."

"Cah-*caw*, cah-*caw*!" called Maren, not exactly loudly, but louder than her usual speaking voice.

"Shh, oh my God!" hissed Hallie. "Not like that!"

The curtains twitched, and Lishta's face appeared. Maren's heart leapt at the sight of her grandmother, and she stepped out of the shadows and waved. Lishta's eyes went big as grapefruits. Quickly recovering, she waved back, then pointed toward the side of her cottage.

"See, it worked." Maren nudged her sister, who groaned.

Seconds later, Lishta emerged, wearing a bathrobe and slippers and a slightly crooked wig. "What are you girls doing here?" she whispered.

Maren threw her arms around her grandmother and took a big whiff of her lemony scent. "There's been a big development."

Lishta tensed. "What kind of development?"

"Earlier this afternoon, we had a hard time waking up a girl in my group," said Maren.

"Then at the bonfire tonight, a girl named Lucy started sleepwalking and nobody could wake her," said Hallie.

"And everybody keeps singing this baseball song," added Maren.

"My goodness!" said Lishta. "Where is this poor Lucy? Is she still asleep?"

"Maybe," said Maren. "They took her to the health center."

"Did nobody think to give her a waking antidote?" Lishta patted the pockets of her robe like she might have one on hand.

"I don't think anybody knows what those are," said Hallie. "We would have suggested one, but then we would've blown our covers."

"Hmmm," said Lishta. "Quite right, but what a dilemma. I'll go over there now and give her one if she's still asleep."

"Do you want us to create a distraction?" said Maren. "I could faint, or Hallie could pretend to choke or..."

"I don't think that will be necessary." Lishta smiled and smoothed Maren's hair off her forehead. "You girls had better get back to your bunks. It's getting late, and we still need to maintain our secrecy. Thank you for coming and telling me this, though."

"We think it's Thalia Mandrake," said Hallie.

"You think who's what, dear?" Lishta lowered her glasses and squinted at her granddaughter.

"The brains behind the operation," said Maren. "Thalia Mandrake is the dream-crafting instructor. At first we thought she was a sham just like everybody else, but tonight we saw her using dreamsalt, or something just like it."

"And actually blowing on it," said Hallie.

Lishta's eyes went grapefruit-wide again. "Tanya Mangrove, you say?"

"Thalia," said Maren.

"Mandrake," said Hallie.

"Fascinating," said Lishta. "What does she look like?"

"She has gray hair." Hallie wrinkled her nose. "And she wears these wafty long dresses."

"But it's cool gray hair," said Maren. "She's young and she dyes it that color."

"As if old people's gray hair isn't cool?" Lishta sniffed.

"I didn't mean it that way—" Maren started, but her grandmother gave her a teasing smile.

"I know you didn't, dearie. At any rate, I've been meaning to visit this dream-crafting workshop, and I think I'll go over and pay Ms. Mangrove—"

"Mandrake," said Hallie and Maren.

"Mandrake," said Lishta, waggling her eyebrows, "a visit. I'll pretend I need some dreams to help with anxiety or gout or something, and then I'll gently question her, maybe get a look at that dreamsalt of hers. But before I do any of that, I need to pay a visit to poor, sleepwalking Lucy. And then I'll drive into town to call your mother and give her an update."

"Is there really not a phone you can use here?" asked Hallie.

Lishta shook her head. "Absurd, isn't it? They must have one somewhere, but *we're* not allowed to use it."

Unease trickled through Maren's gut.

"At any rate," said Lishta, "You girls need to get back to your bunks. I'll send your love to your mother."

Both girls nodded, and Maren's eyes stung again. She rubbed them hard with her fists and told herself to stop being a baby.

"Gran-Gran?" she said. "Are you worried? About the sleepwalking and stuff?"

"Not yet," said Lishta. "Unfortunately, this is what happens when inexperienced people dabble in dreams. It's precisely why we're here, keeping an eye on everybody. Are you worried, dear?"

"A little," she admitted, because Thalia Mandrake clearly knew more than she was letting on. But before Maren's anxiety had time to spiral, Lishta folded her into another warm, lemon-scented hug.

"Do you think we should sleep with nylons over our heads, just to be safe?" Maren asked.

Lishta laughed. "No, darling. Obscura Gray is one of a kind, and I doubt we'll see the likes of her trained moths ever again."

"And she's still in jail," said Hallie, patting Maren's shoulder. "She can't hurt you anymore."

The knot of worry in Maren's chest eased a little, but she couldn't shake the nerves completely.

"I almost forgot," she said, reaching into her pocket. "I found a stack of boxes in the laundry building with dreams inside. The logo on the boxes said Moonbeam Illusions. Have you ever heard of that?"

Lishta inspected the dreams. "No, I haven't. I'll take these apart tonight and analyze them. And I'll also whip up a batch of waking antidotes and give them to you at breakfast tomorrow, in case you need them again. Thank you for these dreams, darling. Good sleuthing, both of you. Now run along—I've got lots to do!"

"Bye, Gran-Gran," said Maren. "Love you."

"I love you too." Lishta kissed the palm of her hand and pretended to throw the kiss at her granddaughters.

As they stole back down the dark path with just the glow of Hallie's phone to light their way, Maren crept close to her sister and slid her arm through the crook of her elbow.

"It's going to be fine," whispered Hallie, and Maren badly wanted to believe her.

Eighteen

THE NEXT MORNING, MAREN STOOD in the cabin's shared bathroom, brushing her hair after a long shower, when Anika came thundering in.

"Have you seen what Peyton and Maddie are doing?"

Maren tugged on a tangle. "No, why?"

"They're acting super weird, and Kendall isn't here."

Dropping her brush, Maren dashed into the main room, where all the girls had gathered in a circle. In the center, Maddie lay curled up in a ball, and Peyton was wriggling around on her stomach, stretching out her neck and opening her mouth wide.

"Lollipop," she muttered as she chewed. "Swiss cheese. Pickle." She wriggled in the other direction, hunching her back up and down as she moved. "Chocolate cake."

"She told us she's a caterpillar," said Emma.

"A hungry one," said Ivy with a not-quite-repressed giggle. "And it looks like Maddie is already in her cocoon."

It's not funny, it's not funny, Maren told herself as she crouched beside Peyton, who kept worming—or caterpillaring—away.

"Peyton," she said, gently shaking the girl's shoulder. "Hey. Wake up. You're having a dream, but it's time to wake up now."

"Cherry pie," said Peyton, chomping at the invisible pie and licking her lips.

Maren wished with all her heart that she'd been able to make a waking antidote at the dream workshop last night, or that she'd gotten some from Lishta. She crawled over to Maddie in her cocoon and tried shaking her.

"I can feel my wings growing," whispered the girl with a blissful smile.

Maren couldn't decide if that sounded lovely or horrible. But she didn't have time to sit around thinking about it. She needed a waking antidote.

"I'll be right back," she said to Ivy. "If Kendall comes back, tell her I, uh…"

"Went to look for her?" offered Ivy.

"Yes, perfect!" Maren shoved her feet into her slippers and ran for the door.

"Watermelon," said Peyton, chomp-chomp-chomping.

The mess hall wasn't open yet, so Maren skirted around the back and peered through one of the foggy windows. She spotted Lishta by the grill, struggling with a tray of something lumpy that might have been eggs...or maybe potatoes...or possibly ham. Racing to the other window, Maren tapped on the glass. Lishta did a double take, the tray swung wildly, and Maren held her breath, but her grandmother managed to set it down safely on a counter.

Seconds later, Lishta whooshed out the door. "Dearie, you really shouldn't be here."

"It's an emergency," said Maren. "Two girls in my bunk are sleepwalking—er, sleepcrawling."

Lishta's gray eyebrows shot upward. "My goodness, it's spreading."

Maren nodded grimly. "Is Lucy okay now?"

"Yes, yes, she's perfectly fine," said Lishta. "I snuck into her room when nobody was looking, and she woke as soon as I gave her the antidote. She was back in her bunk by ten o'clock."

"That's a relief," said Maren. "And did you make another batch of waking antidotes?"

"I certainly did." Lishta rummaged in her apron pocket and pulled out a bag full of tiny sachets. "There's one batch for you, one for Amos, and one for Hallie. You take Amos's, and I'll give Hallie hers when she comes for breakfast."

"Thanks, Gran-Gran!" Maren spun on her heel and dashed away.

"Be careful!" called Lishta.

⟨‿⟩

By the time Maren returned to her cabin, Maddie had become a butterfly. She was leaping from bed to bed, flapping her arms and yelling "I am sooo beautiful!" A frantic Kendall chased her, yelling that it was dangerous to jump around like that with her eyes closed. The rest of the girls stood in small clusters, some laughing and some whispering. Everyone had forgotten about Peyton, who now lay curled up in her own cocoon.

While nobody was watching, Maren ran over and bent low over the sleeping girl. She opened her bag of waking antidotes and eased Peyton's mouth open.

"Not hungry anymore," groaned Peyton.

"Shh, it's not food," whispered Maren. "It's, uh, flower nectar."

"Okay," mumbled Peyton, and she let Maren poke the sachet under her tongue. Ten seconds later, her eyes flashed open. Maren sprang backward and bumped into someone's bed.

"What are you doing?" said Peyton, looking around groggily. "Why am I on the floor?"

"Look at how beeyooootiful I am!" sang Maddie, leaping over her friend and crashing into a fuchsia canopy, which detached from the ceiling and fell. Maddie's legs caught in the fabric, and as she twisted and flapped, getting more tangled by the second, she tumbled into the gap between the bed and the wall with a very un-butterfly-like shriek.

"Holy mackerel!" yelled Kendall from the other side of the room. "Is she all right?"

"I got her." Maren jumped onto the bed and pretended she was trying to pull Maddie out, but instead, she jammed a sachet into the girl's open, wailing mouth. "We need to move the bed," she called as Maddie's eyes fluttered.

Emma and Anika ran over to help Maren shove the bed aside, and Maren pulled a blinking and sore Maddie up from the floor.

"What did I just do?" moaned Maddie, rubbing her knee and hobbling.

"It wasn't your fault," said Maren. "Something was wrong with your dream, and you couldn't wake up."

"Are you okay?" said Kendall. "Hang on, I'll get the first aid kit!"

"I don't need the first aid kit." Maddie groaned as she

sat on the bed beside Peyton, whose face was just as red as hers.

"What do you mean, something was wrong with her dream?" said Anika.

Maren's face went hot. "I, uh, well, it seems like that shouldn't happen when you're taking dreams, doesn't it?"

A few girls murmured their agreement.

"Do either of you have a history of sleepwalking?" asked Maren.

"I used to do it a lot when I was little," said Peyton. "One time my mom found me in the cabinet under the kitchen sink."

"I hope you weren't being a hungry caterpillar under there," said Ivy with a dry laugh.

Maren glared at her friend. This wasn't funny. Okay, the caterpillar part *had* been a little funny, but what was starting to happen all over the camp was not.

"I'm sure it's nothing," said Kendall, bustling over with the first aid kit that nobody needed. "People sleepwalk all the time, and the dreams here are totally safe." She ripped the paper off a Band-Aid and held it out to Maddie, who shrugged and took it.

"Maybe nobody should take that caterpillar dream for now," said Maren. "Just to be safe."

Kendall paused. "Yeah, that's probably a good idea until I talk to Calvin and Malvin."

The dread in Maren's chest eased a tiny bit. Kendall might be way too overexcited about everything, but she did seem to have the campers' best interests at heart. That was something at least.

"Come on, girls!" said Kendall, all bright smiles and rainbows again. "We're going to be late for breakfast, and if we don't hurry, they'll run out of all the good stuff!"

"What good stuff?" muttered Ivy as everybody rushed around finding their slippers and getting ready.

"They make my school cafeteria look like a five-star restaurant," said Maren.

As the girls filed outside, Ivy sidled closer and dropped her voice to a whisper. "What did you give Peyton and Maddie?"

Maren's slipper caught on a tree root. "What are you talking about?" she said, hating how squeaky her voice sounded.

"I saw you put something in Peyton's mouth right before she woke up," said Ivy.

"No, I didn't." Maren stuck her hands in her pockets to hide their trembling. "I was just playing along with her dream, and I, uh, told her that if she ate some magical flower nectar, it'd wake her up. It was like a psychological trick, you know?"

Ivy's face fell. "Actually, I don't know."

"You need to tell your grandmother to get rid of that caterpillar dream too. This is getting really dangerous." Maren hadn't meant for her tone to sound quite so accusatory, and Ivy looked like she'd been slapped. "Not that I think it's her fault!" Maren added quickly.

"Yeah, I'll get right on it." Ivy sped up, dodging around girls until she was walking with Anika and Emma instead of Maren.

Maren sighed. Going undercover wasn't nearly as fun as she'd expected it to be. In fact, it was downright horrible.

Nineteen

"Did the antidotes work?" whispered Lishta as she served Maren five slices of floppy bacon.

Maren nodded. The mess hall this morning was calm and surprisingly quiet. The campers all looked bleary, and nobody was demanding turkey sandwiches or anything else.

"Your mother sends her love." Lishta leaned over the counter and shielded her mouth with her tongs. "She wants to know if you'd like her to come get you, given everything that's happening."

Maren gulped. The thought of going back to her cozy, safe house, where she could be herself and sleep in her own bed and not have to worry about people taking bad dreams or sleepwalking, was so tempting. But she couldn't leave now. Hallie wasn't leaving, and neither was Lishta. The campers needed them.

"No, I'm okay," she said. "I want to stay."

Lishta gave her a thoughtful look, then nodded. "Let's see how it goes. I'm off to visit Tanya after this."

"Thalia," whispered Maren.

"Keep it moving!" called a kid from the back of the line, and Maren's shoulders hunched up. "I'll see you at lunch," she said.

"Looking forward to it." Lishta gave her a wrinkly smile, then turned to the boy behind her. "Bacon, dear?"

The boy looked at the tray of shriveled, glistening meat and shook his head. Maren slid her tray along the rails, grabbed a double serving of toast, and folded everything inside a napkin. After chugging a glass of soapy orange juice, she slipped out the side exit and slunk into the woods.

⌒

The boathouse looked empty, but as Maren approached, a croak rang out from the trees overhead.

"MAREN IS A STAR-FART SKEETER."

"Thank you, Heinie," she said, and the bird gave an outraged squawk.

Amos's grinning face poked out one of the boathouse's broken windows. "Morning!"

"Morning," said Maren. "Have you seen Hallie yet?"

"Nope."

Hopefully she was just running late. Maren found a spot on the tiny strip of beach and unfolded her napkin. "Did you have breakfast?"

"Yeah." Amos eyed her food like a hungry wolf. "But I could always eat again if you brought extra."

"Help yourself to all of the bacon," said Maren.

"Awesome." Amos sat beside her and made a sandwich with toast and wet bacon. "How was your night?"

"Absolutely bonkers," said Maren. "This girl was sleep-walking and almost ran into the bonfire. We couldn't wake her up, and Calvin ended up taking her to the health center. Gran-Gran had to sneak in and give her a waking antidote. Then this morning, two girls from my bunk started crawling around on the floor like hungry caterpillars. They were asleep too."

Amos choked on his sandwich. "I would've paid money to see that."

"It was a tiny bit funny," admitted Maren. "Especially when Maddie turned into a butterfly." She pictured the flapping girl leaping from bed to bed and giggled. "But it's not actually funny at all. Something very shady is going on."

"Duh," said Amos. "We've got sleepwalkers, directors who don't know how dreams work, and random ladies delivering boxes of dreams. And the place is literally called Shady Sands."

"Right?" said Maren. "Why did all these kids' parents let them come here?"

Amos shrugged. "I guess dreams seem kind of silly and fun, and they don't realize how dangerous they can be. I only just found that out last year."

Remembering the derelict Starlight Theater and how glad she'd been to have Amos helping her escape, Maren shifted closer to her friend and took a bite of toast. She was glad he was here now too. Peering down the shoreline for some sign of Hallie, Maren wondered if she was busy doing something important or just busy hanging out with her new friends.

"DU HAST KOMISCHE ELLBOGEN!" said Henri, landing on the beach. Three of his duck friends waddled out of the bushes and quacked their hellos.

Maren tore off a few strips of crust and threw them to the birds, who gobbled them up. "Did you overhear anything else, Henri?"

Henri hopped closer and cocked his head. Maren threw him another chunk of toast. "I asked you a question."

"STAR FART SKEETER!"

"Henri," said Maren, holding up the last piece of toast. "Tell me what you heard, and this is all yours."

The parrot squawked and hopped in a circle, and the three ducks quacked, then imitated him.

"Oh great, he's like some kind of bird influencer now," said Amos.

"Of course he is," muttered Maren.

Henri waited for his friends to stop hopping, then puffed out his chest feathers. "Phase two is rolling out ahead of schedule," he said in a woman's voice Maren didn't recognize.

"I thought that wasn't until Tuesday," Henri said in an exact mimic of Calvin or Malvin. "After we got a chance to—"

"Don't worry about the timing," said the woman's voice. "Just stick to your assigned role, and don't question us."

Henri sneezed and flapped his wings again. "DONNE MOI LE TOAST!"

"Don't question who?" said Amos.

Henri launched himself at Maren, and before she could react, he grabbed the crust and flapped away into the trees. "AU REVOIR!" he called, his voice muffled by toast. The ducks waddled over to the water and glided away.

Maren sighed. "None of that makes any sense. Do you think the sleepwalking is phase two?"

"Phase two of what?" said Amos. "Making everybody look stupid?"

"I don't know," said Maren. "But one of those voices was definitely Calvin or Malvin, so do you think you could spy on them today?"

"Sure," said Amos.

"I guess Hallie isn't going to meet us," said Maren with a sigh. She pulled Amos's bag of waking antidotes out of her pocket and handed them over. "Just in case you find somebody sleepwalking, put this in their mouth. But don't let anybody see you doing it."

"Okay." Amos pocketed the sachets. "Got any more of that bacon?"

"Ugh, no," said Maren. "I have to get back to my group now. Good luck with your secret mission. I'll report back here at lunchtime so we can debrief."

Amos gave a little salute. "Yes, ma'am."

"TOAST!" yelled Henri, crunching in the trees.

Twenty

MAREN CAUGHT UP WITH HER group just as they were leaving the mess hall. But instead of heading for the beach, Kendall led them up a third path, one Maren hadn't noticed before.

"Where are we going?" she asked Anika, who was busy filling her mouth with as many pieces of watermelon bubble-gum as she could fit.

"Arfs an fwafs." Anika offered the nearly empty package to Maren, who shook her head.

"What?"

"She said arts and crafts," said Emma, who had braces and no gum.

"What are we making?" asked Maren.

"Mo hibea," said Anika.

"No idea," said Emma. "Maybe we're painting our dreams or something?"

Maren hoped she meant they'd paint scenes from their dreams, not paint the actual sachets, but nothing would surprise her. Humming the baseball song, Kendall opened the door of a low, white building and held it so the girls could file inside. In the brightly lit space, they found three rows of tables scattered with wrenches and hammers and screwdrivers and drills. On the front wall was a blank, old-fashioned chalkboard, and in front of it stood a tall woman with a messy bun and a purple polka-dot smock.

"Hello, children!" The woman gave a sweeping, theatrical flourish, her lime-green earrings swinging. "I'm Ms. Muffelatta, and today we're going to learn about deconstructing art."

The campers murmured confusedly as they took their seats. As Kendall waved goodbye, promising to return in an hour, Ivy dashed in and grabbed the chair beside Maren. She still made no eye contact, but Maren hoped this was a good sign that she wasn't upset anymore.

"Why do we need to learn this?" called out Avery, a sporty blond girl in the last row.

"Didn't you read the camp handbook?" said Peyton with a superior look. "It's all in there. Art, martial arts, coding, all that stuff."

"There was a handbook?" Maren whispered to Ivy, who shrugged.

"Quiet now, children." Ms. Muffelatta whirled around, purple smock flying, and grabbed a piece of chalk. With broad strokes, she began drawing a pedestal with triangles and squares stacked haphazardly on top. "Who can tell me what this is?"

More confused murmuring.

"A sculpture?" offered Emma.

"Well, yes." Ms. Muffelatta drew a big umbrella on top of her collection of shapes, then two long squiggles coming out of the sides. "But *whose* sculpture?"

Maren leaned forward, picturing the posters on Hallie's side of their bedroom. "It looks like Cleo Montclair's stuff."

"Exactamundo!" Ms. Muffelatta began drawing more odd, abstract sculptures, some with animal bodies and wheels for legs, others with machines for bodies and animal parts for limbs.

Maren picked up a wrench from her table, wondering if the "deconstructing" part was literal. This class was the most bizarre thing to happen in an already very bizarre few days, and her mind turned somersaults trying to make sense of it. Was this somehow linked to phase two? But what could sleep-walking and Cleo Montclair possibly have to do with each other? She wondered if Hallie had taken this class yet today.

Up at the chalkboard, Ms. Muffelatta began drawing arrows all over the sculpture illustrations. Ivy twisted a strand of pink hair around her finger, letting out a bored sigh every so often and still refusing to look at Maren.

"All right, then!" The teacher waltzed dramatically over to a closet at the side of the room and stepped inside. "Now for the deconstructing part!"

"This is so random," said Ivy under her breath.

Maren hoped it would start making some kind of sense soon. Ms. Muffelatta reemerged from the closet, pulling a cart that was filled with small replicas of Cleo Montclair's sculptures, each about a foot tall or wide, depending on their shape. Maren lifted off her seat a little, straining to see. Each little sculpture moved, whether it swayed or twirled on its base or gently drifted back and forth in a small area.

"These are battery powered, not magicked, so they don't feel emotions," said Ms. Muffelatta. "But that's perfectly fine for our purposes. Everyone, find a partner and come grab a sculpture and a box!"

Maren's head spun. They couldn't be crafting dreams from these sculptures, could they? Nothing was sanitized, and they didn't even have any sachets. *Why, why, why, why?* tapped her toes under the table. She startled as Ivy set an empty box and a faintly buzzing metal sculpture in front of her.

"Partners?" Ivy gave her a cautious smile.

Maren grinned back. "Sure."

Their sculpture was a lumpy orange ball with something like a face that had just one eye and a gently smiling mouth made of red cloth. All over the body, metal spirals stuck out in various directions, waving gently to and fro like the tentacles of some undersea plant.

"His name is George," said Maren.

"He totally looks like a George," said Ivy, and Maren's heart warmed. Most people would have thought that was weird.

"Now let's get deconstructing!" Ms. Muffelatta flashed jazz hands, and Maren cringed, both for this mortifying teacher and for the poor little pieces of art, even if they were battery-powered and couldn't feel anything.

Ivy picked up a screwdriver. "This is so ridiculous."

"Why are we even here?" whispered Maren. "Did you read this part in the handbook?"

Ivy poked a copper coil with her screwdriver, making a *sproing* noise. "Sorry, George! You're forgetting that I was dragged here against my will, so I didn't get a handbook."

Ms. Muffelatta jabbed her chalk at the largest arrow on the board. "First you need to locate the joint at the midsection of your piece. That's going to vary depending on the construction of each sculpture, but think of it like the waist of a person."

Maren squinted at poor George. There was nothing resembling a waist, and there was no joint at the center because the center was a ball.

"Now find your pliers and clip that center joint," said Ms. Muffelatta. "If this were the real sculpture, we'd use something bigger, like bolt cutters or a saw."

"Why the heck would we be taking apart the real sculptures?" said Ivy.

Ms. Muffelatta shot her an irritated glare. "Less talking and more clipping!"

Ivy jammed her screwdriver into the connection between the sculpture's body and one of its waggling appendages and snapped it off.

"George, no," whispered Maren, half expecting the sculpture's smile to turn to a frown, but the rest of George's spirals kept wafting back and forth, unfazed.

"Be careful, children!" called Ms. Muffelatta. "Our purpose is not to *destroy* these pieces of art! We are simply *dismantling*! Our goal is to *remantle* them at a later date!"

"That is so not a word," muttered Ivy.

Maren was relieved to hear this wasn't the end for little George. She leaned in close to Ivy. "I'm sorry I made it sound like your grandma was hurting kids with her dreams. That wasn't what I meant, but it's how it came out of my mouth."

Ivy jammed her screwdriver into another of George's arms. "It's fine."

"I'm just worried about those sleepwalkers," said Maren. "And I guess I was hoping that she could help keep people safe."

"The dreams are fine," said Ivy. "What's the worst thing that happened? Maddie looked like a dingbat?"

"A dingbutterfly," said Maren, trying not to smile.

"Ahem-hem." Ms. Muffelatta drifted past their table and cast a dubious glance at their work. "Try not to bend any of the appendages when you're removing them. We'll need them for *remantling*."

Maren stifled a groan and waited for their teacher to move on. "Maybe we can give your grandma a list of all the dreams that've made people sleepwalk so far, and she could put them aside?"

"I already told her, and she pulled them from the bins," said Ivy. "What kind of monsters do you think we are?"

Maren let out a shaky laugh. "Giant purple ones? With hairy toes?"

Ivy rolled her eyes but laughed, and the two girls settled down to work on George's surgery, Maren holding him steady while Ivy used the tools. It was hard work because the arms kept moving, and sometimes they broke in half when Ivy pulled them off, which made Maren flinch in sympathy. Finally, Ms. Muffelatta clapped her hands.

"Time's up! Everyone, grab your boxes and put your *dismantlements* inside."

"Also not a word," muttered Ivy.

"And please welcome my guest judge!" said Ms. Muffelatta.

The door swung open, and in walked Carmella, wearing a tiger-print jumpsuit and stiletto-heeled sandals.

"That outfit," moaned Ivy. "What is she even doing here?"

"Howdy, campers!" sang Carmella, clacking over to stand beside Ms. Muffelatta. "I bet you all didn't know this, but I'm a huge art fan!"

"Is she really?" This was so random, and Maren wondered if it was the reason why there were so many art-related dreams at camp.

Ivy just sat there, staring at her grandmother as if she were trying to figure out a complicated math problem. Maren nudged her gently with her elbow. "Earth to Ivy?"

Ivy stared blankly at Maren for a second. "Sorry, what did you say?"

"It doesn't matter," said Maren.

"Come on, don't be shy little mice!" boomed Carmella.

"Bring up those dismantlements! The winner gets a whole pound of dreams!"

That was a shocking amount of dreams, considering how little each sachet weighed. Ivy just sat there looking perplexed, so Maren set poor George and his dismantled arms in the box and carried them to the front of the room. Next to everyone else's work, theirs looked like a kindergartner had hacked it apart with safety scissors. The two judges barely gave George a second glance, instead selecting a box full of what looked like bendy straws.

"Absolutely fantastic!" raved Carmella. "Whose is this?"

"Ours!" Anika waved her hand, and Emma wiggled excitedly.

"Have you done this before?" asked Ms. Muffelatta.

"When would they ever have done this before?" said Ivy.

And when would they ever do it again? Who was this strange art teacher who took apart sculptures instead of making them? Thalia Mandrake didn't make sense as a teacher either, but at least her class was related to dreams. And why was Carmella judging a sculpture-dismantling contest? Maren felt like she was trying to put together a jigsaw puzzle where half the pieces were missing and the others were made of marshmallow.

As the girls filed out of the arts and crafts building, they found Kendall sitting under a tree with her knees tucked up tight.

"Kendall?" One of the girls nudged her shoulder. "We're all done now."

Their counselor's head snapped up. "Huh?"

"I think you fell asleep," said Emma. "We're done now. What's next?"

The girls gathered around their counselor and Maren couldn't see her anymore, but dread made her limbs heavy. She knew—just *knew*—that Kendall's eyes were not open.

"Watch out for the fairies!" cried Kendall. "We're trying to bowl and you're stepping in our lanes."

Twenty-One

MAREN PULLED A WAKING ANTIDOTE from her pocket and hid it in her fist. She had no idea how to get it into Kendall's mouth unnoticed with all these people clustered around.

Flap heel heel brush heel toe heel, went her feet as she pondered what to do. The only thing she could think of was pretending to do CPR, but the counselor was clearly breathing. In fact, she was on her feet now, shooing people out of the imaginary fairy bowling lane.

"Does anybody want to try?" she said picking up something invisible but heavy. "The acorn balls take some getting used to because they're not perfect spheres."

"That is *so* embarrassing," said Peyton, apparently forgetting that she'd been a cake-eating caterpillar earlier.

"I'm hungry," whined Maddie. "Come on, Kendall, wake up!"

"Back up and give her some air," said Anika, waving her arms to open up the circle around their counselor.

Emma started flapping her hands in front of Kendall's face. "Does anybody have some water we can splash her with?"

Someone handed her a water bottle, and she unscrewed the lid.

"Don't—" began Maren, but it was too late. Emma threw a big splash of water all over Kendall's face and shirt. With a shriek, the counselor lurched backward, clawing frantically at the air and gasping.

"You're going to turn this into a nightmare," said Maren, snatching the bottle away. Dreams were perfectly balanced, designed to work without interference. If you added other elements, like a sudden, gushing shock of cold water, the dreamer's brain could start incorporating them into the dream, altering its course. What started as a lovely day at the beach could end up as a disastrous tsunami. Maren had no idea what a splash of water to the face might do to a fairy-bowling dream.

"It's okay, it's okay," she said, taking Kendall's arm. "What's your score right now?" This wasn't the greatest question, considering most people in dreams couldn't read numbers or letters, but it at least gave Kendall something to focus on.

Kendall squinted at a far-off scoreboard. "Everything's wet right now, but I think I'm up to nine hundred and…forty?"

"Wow, that's amazing," said Maren. "Don't worry about the water. It'll dry in a second. Why don't you sit down and think about maybe waking up?" She nudged the waking remedy closer, waiting for the right moment.

"Is she okay?" Ivy leaned over Maren's shoulder, and Maren snapped her fist shut around the antidote.

"I don't know," she said. "It looks like another one of the camp's dreams is faulty. We'd better add fairy bowling to the list of bad dreams."

Ivy nodded warily. "I wonder if something got spilled in the bins or the sun was too bright on them."

"Maybe," said Maren, though she knew that wasn't the case. It was obvious at this point that somebody was tampering with the dreams, either as a practical joke or for some other, more sinister reason. Like phase two.

"We should go on another spy mission this afternoon," she said, thinking of the letter in Malvin and Calvin's cottage.

Ivy chewed her lip. "I'm supposed to help my grandma this afternoon, and I want to keep an eye on the dreams at the shack in case somebody is messing with them."

The girls exchanged a worried look, and a shiver raced across Maren's skin. Ivy was getting close to the truth. She wondered if she should tell her more, but she couldn't betray her family's spy mission without getting permission first.

From the woods came crashing and rustling. Three middle-school-aged boys tore out, ferns and leaves caught in their hair and clothing.

"There's the Mars rover!" shouted the tallest one, pointing at nothing. "Come on, guys!"

The second Ivy turned to see what was happening, Maren jabbed the waking antidote into Kendall's mouth. Crouching low with their eyes shut, the boys ran along the path, and as they reached the clearing, one of them yelled "Sniper fire!" and dropped into a clumsy barrel roll before lurching to his feet and running after his friends.

"Looks like a video game dream," mused Ivy.

Maren chewed her lip. Shooter games were dangerously close to nightmares if they weren't crafted carefully, and she was certain nothing was being crafted carefully here. Kendall groaned, and Maren nudged her shoulder, waiting for her eyes to open.

"Those mean pixies tied my shoelaces together," she said, thrashing her legs.

"Kendall, it's time to wake up now." Maren wished she could look inside her counselor's mouth to check if the sachet had dissolved properly.

"I *am* awake," insisted Kendall, her eyes still firmly shut. "And now it's my turn to bowl, but I can't walk."

"Here, I'll untie them," said Ivy, touching Kendall's foot gently, then the other. "There, all done."

With a dreamy smile, Kendall got to her feet. *Wake up,* thought Maren. *Wake up, wake up, wake up.* But Kendall bent to pick up another imaginary bowling bowl, and then she did a funny hop and skip and launched her ball down the invisible lane.

"Strike!" yelled Ivy.

"Woohoo!" yelled Kendall, swinging her hand in the direction of Ivy's face for a high five.

"You're so good at this!" said Ivy, who somehow managed to smack Kendall's hand instead of getting smacked.

"That's great, but it's time to wake up now." Maren took hold of Kendall's elbow so she wouldn't run off. The waking antidote should have worked by now. It should have worked minutes ago. Maybe she'd held it too long in her hand and gotten it damp.

"Oh my gosh, is that a baby fox?" said Maren, pointing into the bushes.

"Where?"

As Ivy turned, Maren shoved another waking antidote into Kendall's mouth.

"I don't see a fox," said Ivy.

"Hmm, maybe it was just a squirrel," said Maren. *Wake up, wake up, wake up,* tapped her foot.

Ivy gave her a long look, and Maren tried to keep her face neutral. Kendall's eyes still weren't opening, and Maren had to fight down the swelling waves of panic in her stomach.

"She's not waking up," said Ivy, lifting an eyebrow, and Maren wondered, just for a second, if Ivy had seen what she'd done, if she suspected what Maren was trying to do. With a jolt, Maren wondered if maybe Ivy thought *she* was the one behind all this.

"We need to take her to the health center," said Maren. "They'll be able to help."

That was a massive lie, but she didn't know what else to do. At least the nurses would keep Kendall safe until Maren could send Lishta in with another remedy, hopefully a new batch or another combination of ingredients that worked better.

"Why don't we just let her bowl for a while and keep an eye on her?" said Ivy. "I'm sure she'll wake up eventually."

"No," said Maren, guiding Kendall down the path toward the health center. "We also need to find those video game kids. What if they fall in the lake?" She stopped short, and Kendall bumped into a tree. "Oh God, the lake! Can you go down there and ask your grandmother to close the dream bar for now? And keep an eye on everybody on the beach?"

"That's Evan's entire job." Ivy scrunched up her nose. "Okay, he's terrible at his job. I'll go down there."

Maren took a slow breath and ground her heels into the dirt. Freaking out wasn't going to help anything. Lishta would know what to do. "I'll meet you there soon," she called, and Ivy waved over her shoulder.

By the time Maren got Kendall to the health center, the counselor had played two more frames of fairy bowling and seemed no closer to waking than ever.

"I'm sure she'll be fine, just like that other girl last night," said a nurse in an ill-fitting white dress that looked more like a costume than a uniform. "Come on, honey, let's get you into bed."

"Thank you!" yelled Maren, already sprinting off toward the mess hall.

Twenty-Two

Maren found Lishta and Hallie behind the mess hall, next to the dumpster that swarmed with flies and smelled like the worst nightmare Maren could think of.

"Oh, thank goodness you're here," said Lishta, pulling her in close. "Hallie tells me things are getting out of hand."

"My counselor's sleepwalking and the waking antidotes aren't working," said Maren. "I gave her two."

"The same thing happened to me," said Hallie. "Three girls from my bunk, and the antidote did absolutely nothing."

"I saw three boys sleeprunning through the camp on the way here, but I couldn't go after them." Maren's voice had taken on a screechy, embarrassing tone, but she no longer cared. "What are we supposed to do?"

"Hush, hush, it's going to be all right," said Lishta, pulling

Maren closer. "Now I'm not sure it matters anymore, but do you know which dreams they took?"

"Fairy bowling," said Maren. "And some kind of adventure video game."

"Two of the girls in my bunk were swimming with mermaids, and the other one was licking everything and saying it was made of candy." Hallie shuddered visibly. "I gave her a lollipop to lick instead, but I don't know how long it'll last."

"Do you think you could get your hands on any of those dreams that've been causing problems?" said Lishta. "I'd like to analyze them and figure out what's causing them to go wrong."

"I can try," said Maren.

"Excellent. In the meantime, I'm going to find Kelvin and Melvin."

"Calvin and Malvin," said Hallie.

"Yes, yes." Lishta waved her hand dismissively. "And I'm going to insist that they shut down the dream shack and immediately stop every camper from taking dreams. This has gotten entirely out of hand, and it may be even worse than we think."

"What do you mean?" asked Maren.

Lishta glanced all around her, then beckoned the girls closer. "This is starting to look like the handiwork of the Sandwoman."

"The who?" Hallie's forehead furrowed. "Is that, like, the Sandman's wife?"

"Far worse," said Lishta. "The Sandman is an imaginary character who sneaks around sprinkling sand in people's eyes to put them to sleep. The Sandwoman is a living, breathing person. Nobody's heard from her since the eighties, long before you two were born."

"Have you ever met her?" asked Maren.

"No, and for that I am extremely grateful," said Lishta. "She's a highly dangerous criminal. Back when your mother was a girl, there were multiple robberies involving businesses all over the world. Employees were stealing massive amounts of money or valuable goods and disappearing, only to return a few days later empty-handed and with no memory whatsoever of what happened."

"What do you mean?" asked Maren. "How do you forget something like that?"

"They had no idea they'd stolen anything," said Lishta. "Because they were sleepwalking the entire time."

"Whoa," said Maren.

"Cool," said Hallie, and Lishta gave her a sharp look. "I mean, it's not actually cool," she added. "But it's a pretty smart—and evil—idea."

Maren's skin went cold as she remembered the last evil

plan she'd gotten caught up in that involved dreams and mind manipulation.

"At first, nobody believed the employees, and a lot of people went to jail," said Lishta. "It took ages to figure out the pattern because it was happening so sporadically. First a bank in Santiago, then an armored truck in Hong Kong. Then nothing for a year, then a jeweler in Moscow. It took close to five years and miles of surveillance tape before the international authorities figured out that those employees weren't lying. But since they couldn't remember what they'd done with the stolen goods, and because this was before the internet existed"—Lishta waggled her gray eyebrows dramatically, and Hallie pretend-gasped—"it was impossible to figure out where it had all gone."

"So how did they know it was the Sandwoman?" asked Maren.

"Excellent question." Lishta tapped Maren's nose with her fingertip. "A forensic psychologist from Johannesburg had the brilliant idea to use hypnosis to help the convicted employees recall the events leading up to their crimes. You can imagine how difficult it was to get the police to agree to this."

Maren and Hallie nodded. The police weren't anti-magic, per se, but since magic was impossible to prove or show evidence of, it was very hard to get them to pursue any crimes that were suspected of being magic-related.

"As it turned out, there was a pattern," said Lishta. "Every single time, every single robbery."

Maren's foot tapped a nervous beat.

"Each employee had just come back from their lunch break," said Lishta. "And they all recalled seeing a woman smoking outside their building."

"Is it somebody with smoke magic like Cedric?" asked Maren.

"Who?" asked Hallie.

"The guy who was helping Obscura Gray," said Maren. "He could blow smoke into shapes like dragons and stuff." She thought of that foggy night when she'd found Cedric sitting alone at a bus stop and shivered.

Lishta pursed her lips. "Perhaps her magic is a distant cousin to Cedric's, though it's much more powerful and linked to sleep."

"But I don't get it," said Hallie. "The kids here are taking dreams, not inhaling smoke."

"I don't quite get it either," said her grandmother. "But I wonder if she's figured out a way to blend her magic with the magic of dream sachets. She seems to be testing it out right now."

"Yikes," said Maren.

"So how does anybody know the Sandwoman's name?" asked Hallie.

"That's the fascinating bit." Lishta's eyes twinkled, but Maren's skin felt like it was covered in spiders. "During their hypnosis sessions, the employees all spoke of a woman who visited them in their dreams, even after their crime was done. Always with the same message."

Maren's throat had gone dry. "What?"

"The Sandwoman is watching you," whispered Lishta.

"Guh," said Hallie, rubbing goose bumps off her arms.

Maren swallowed hard. This was just as bad as Obscura Gray and her nightmares. "Why didn't you ever tell us about her before?"

"Well, she hasn't been heard from in decades, and none of us work in a bank, so it seemed quite unnecessary," said Lishta. "And you know how strong the power of suggestion is, dear. When you were younger, if I'd told you about a strange woman whispering in people's dreams, pretty soon you'd have started dreaming about her all on your own."

Hallie laughed. "That's so true. Remember all those nightmares Maren used to have about the Easter Bunny?"

Maren's cheeks went hot. "It's totally creepy for a man-sized rabbit to go skulking around people's houses at night. Even if he does bring candy."

Lishta pinched her younger granddaughter's cheek. "I agree, sweetheart. Very creepy. Now back to the matter at hand, which is more than a little bit worrisome. Your waking antidotes don't seem to be working this morning, and things are getting out of hand."

"It's got to be Thalia," said Hallie, pounding her fist into her palm. "She's the Sandwoman."

Their grandmother shook her head. "It sounds like she's too young to be the Sandwoman. But every time I've stopped by the dream-crafting workshop, it's been empty. I'm starting to wonder if she's avoiding me."

"I bet she's working for the Sandwoman," said Hallie.

"She's the Sandwoman's henchwoman!" added Maren, with a tiny peep of a giggle.

"Now, now, let's not jump to conclusions," said Lishta.

"But she's the only person at this whole camp who knows about dreams," said Maren. "And she's hiding her knowledge."

"We'll find out soon enough, I suspect," said Lishta. "In the meantime, I've sent Henri to look for her and repeat all of her conversations back to me."

"Do you actually think he'll do it?" asked Maren.

Lishta pursed her lips. "There's at least a fifty percent chance. Now girls, I must go. I need to find Kevin and Devin and tell them to put a stop to all dream-taking at the camp."

"Good luck with that," said Hallie.

"I can be very persuasive when I mean to be." Lishta's

gray eyebrows straightened into a severe line as she tightened her apron strings. "In the meantime, I want you girls to try and wake any sleepwalkers you find with the waking antidotes we've got. If they're not working, try adding some crushed spearmint leaves—I saw some growing over beside the health center. And I'll make us a new, stronger batch by the end of the day. If you can't wake people, make sure they stay safe. Take them to the health center or keep them immobilized. Got it?"

"Got it," said Hallie and Maren.

"I'll call your mother this afternoon to give her an update," said Lishta. "In the meantime, make sure to keep your identities secret. It's more important than ever, now that we know something's afoot. There's no way of knowing who we can trust."

"Yeah, like Evan the *dreamy* lifeguard," said Maren. "Maybe we should cool it with boyfriends for now."

"Evan is not my boyfriend!" Hallie chewed her lip. "Okay, I'm not going to lie, he's cute—" Maren started to interrupt, but Hallie cut her off. "But he's not the sharpest guy, and I'm sure he could never pull off any kind of secret scheme."

"Well I don't like him," said Maren.

"Nobody said you had to," snapped her sister. "And I haven't told him anything."

"I'm sure your sister is doing her very best to protect the

mission," said Lishta. "Now, it's time to head back to your groups. Watch out for smoke, and don't eat any suspicious foods. Only what I give you at the mess hall."

Maren's stomach wobbled with hunger and nerves. Shivering in the warm sunlight, she said goodbye to her grandmother and headed back to camp with a slightly resentful Hallie.

Twenty-Three

MAREN FOUND ONE OF THE sleepwalking video gamers leaping and dodging around invisible obstacles at the edge of the bonfire clearing.

"Yeah! I made it to Jupiter, guys!" he yelled to nobody, pumping his fist and then launching into a weird dance that involved flapping his arms and squatting repeatedly. He looked like a chicken trying to lay a difficult egg.

"Take me out to the ball game!" he sang, even though he clearly wasn't taking a baseball dream. Maren crept closer as he adjusted his invisible headset and called out to the rest of his squad, then listened for their response. Even though she knew the whole thing was happening inside the boy's head, Maren found herself straining to listen too.

"Hold still," she whispered, pulling an extra-minty

waking antidote from her pocket. She'd cut a tiny hole in the edge of the sachet to add the spearmint. Although she didn't have any way to sew it back up, it was holding together fairly well.

"Copy," said the boy. "We're all clear for phase two!"

Maren froze. Could this dreamer be talking about the same secret plans as Calvin and Malvin and the mysterious letter writer? He started checking his pockets and loading invisible weapons, and she realized she didn't have time to stop and wonder. She had to wake him before he ran off again and hurt himself. Slowly, silently, she crept closer, then reached out and tapped his shoulder.

"AARGHH!" The boy swung around, brandishing his invisible gun, and as he yelled, Maren stuffed the waking antidote into his mouth. He yelped again and spit it out onto the ground.

"No!" Maren was not a gamer, and she racked her brain for the appropriate lingo, something she'd heard Amos and his friends say. "That was your...um...your power-up."

"My what?" The boy whipped his head around, evidently unable to see Maren in his dream.

"The, uh, thing that gives you extra energy and strength," said Maren. "You have to eat them on Jupiter."

"My energy boost?" said the boy, looking dubious.

"Exactly!" Maren picked the antidote out of the grass and wiped it on her shorts. She didn't have enough to waste this one. "Open up."

"Eh, I don't know," said the boy.

"Do you want to win or not?" asked Maren. "There are like ten guys heading this way. You'd better, um, energy-up."

The boy shook his head again, but Maren didn't wait. She stuffed the waking antidote back into his mouth and gave him a thump on the shoulder. "There, now you're at like four thousand...energies. And maybe you might want to think about opening your eyes?"

"My eyes *are* open," The boy did the flapping/squatting dance again with his eyes firmly shut. "Thanks for the boost!"

With no warning, he launched forward, slamming Maren's shoulder with his and sending her toppling backward.

"Stop!" she yelled, scrambling to her feet. But it was too late. The boy had disappeared into the woods.

"I *saw* you do it this time."

Maren spun around, and there stood Ivy, arms folded over her chest.

"It's not...what you think," stammered Maren.

"I don't get it." Ivy took a step backward, like she was worried Maren was going to stuff something in her mouth too. "Why do you act all worried about people when you're the one doing this to them? Is it all just part of your act? Do you think this is funny?"

"I think this is the farthest thing ever from funny," said Maren. "I'm trying to help them, not make them sleepwalk."

Ivy scoffed. "How?"

Maren's hand went to her pocket. Lishta's words echoed in her mind.

There's no way of knowing who we can trust.

Ivy was her closest friend here, her snooping companion who'd helped her spy on Calvin and Malvin. If there was anybody she could trust with the truth, it was Ivy, but she couldn't be sure that Ivy wouldn't tell her grandmother. And if her grandmother told Calvin and Malvin, it'd all be over.

"I tried to give him some spearmint," said Maren. That wasn't a lie. "I remembered reading that it could wake people up."

Ivy's eyes narrowed. "Where did you read that? The same place you learned how to make dreams?"

Maren's breath hitched. Ivy couldn't possibly know that. It was just a bluff. "Um, it was in the handbook."

"I thought you didn't get a handbook."

"I...just found one. I wanted to read it because of that whole art dismantling thing." Maren's words were tumbling out way too fast to be believable. "In the section where they talk about safety rules, you know, like using those harnesses down by the lake and stuff? If somebody's dreaming and in trouble, you should give them spearmint."

"Just stop talking." Ivy's hands balled into fists. "I thought you were my friend, but you're a liar. I'm done with you. I'm done with this whole stupid camp." She stalked away across the grass.

"Ivy, wait!" Maren started after her. "It's not what you think. I just…can't say more than that."

Ivy's shoulders hitched up, but she didn't turn around. "I'm moving into my grandma's cottage until this nightmare camp is over."

Maren fought to think of some way she could explain everything without coming totally clean, but there was just no way to tell Ivy that she knew all about dreams but had pretended not to because she'd infiltrated the camp on a secret mission. It had been so nice to have a new friend, even for such a short amount of time, but now she'd lost her. A big, empty hole opened up in Maren's chest as Ivy stormed off.

⌒

"…extremely dangerous, and a great liability for every single young person here!"

Lishta's sharp words cut through the trees as Maren reached the path that led toward the staff housing.

"Now, now, let's take a gentle, calming breath together," said Calvin or Malvin. Maren crept to the edge of the path. "No? I promise it'll make you feel bett—"

"You're not taking this seriously, young man!"

"My dear lady, I assure you my brother and I are taking this very seriously. We just want everyone to stay calm and dreamy while we're discussing such important matters."

"Dreamy shmeamy," spat Lishta. Maren ducked under a bush and crawled as close as she dared. Her grandmother stood with the co-directors in front of their cottage. Squinting through the leaves, Maren could just make out a C-shaped pin on the twin closest to Lishta.

"I want to know exactly what you plan to do to keep these kids safe," continued her grandmother.

"They're perfectly safe," said Calvin, taking Lishta by the elbow like she was some frail old biddy he was helping across the street. "They've all woken up on their own, aside from that one unfortunate young woman last night, and the nurses revived her quickly."

Lishta yanked her arm away. "That's because I—" She froze, then shook her head. "Because I care about their safety, and it's just not safe to be running around with their eyes closed. What if someone fell into the lake or down a flight of stairs?"

Calvin and Malvin exchanged an uneasy glance.

"Or wandered off into the woods?" continued Lishta. "Have you considered that possibility? They could get lost and you'd never find them."

"I assure you, Ms.,.." Malvin trailed off, clearly having forgotten Lishta's name, if he'd ever known it in the first place, "Madam, that we know exactly what we're doing here, and the campers' safety is of the utmost importance."

"Pah!" Lishta shouted. "You have no idea what you're doing. The two of you couldn't dream your way out of a box!"

Both twins' mouths popped open, and even Maren gasped quietly. She'd never seen Lishta this angry before. The tiny old woman was almost levitating with fury, and it was both spectacular and slightly frightening.

"I beg your pardon—" began Calvin.

"You'll be begging the pardon of those kids' parents if you start losing them," interrupted Lishta. "Not to mention the police."

The twins' expressions darkened in perfect unison.

"Is that a threat?" asked Calvin.

"Perhaps it is." Lishta took a menacing step forward, but the twins didn't budge.

"And what do you think the police will do if you call them?" Malvin's voice was low and even, the goofy tone suddenly gone. "They'll see a camp full of kids dreaming, which is exactly what their parents paid for. And two very reasonable directors who know exactly what they're doing and how to keep everyone safe."

"And who do you think they'll believe?" Calvin gave a snooty little chuckle. "Us or a ridiculous old lunch lady?"

"I am *not* a lunch lady." Lishta's nostrils flared like an angry bull's.

"Oh, excuse me." Calvin rolled his eyes. "A food services professional. At any rate, it doesn't matter, because you're fired."

Lishta balled up her fists and shoved them into her apron pockets. "Fine."

Fine? Maren almost tumbled out of the bush.

"I refuse to be a part of these shenanigans any longer," said Lishta.

Now is the part where she reveals her true identity. Maren braced herself, ready to spring out from the bushes and back up her grandmother.

"I'll go get my things," said Lishta. "But I expect to be paid for this morning's work."

"What?" whispered Maren.

"We'll mail your check," said Malvin, rolling his eyes.

Before Maren could fully process what was happening, Lishta stormed off, muttering something that sounded like "not on my watch." The brothers watched her go.

"You don't think she'll actually call the police, do you?" said Calvin.

"No," said Malvin. "I think she's hiding something too."

Maren threw her hands over her mouth. Could the brothers know about her and Hallie too?

"We'd better get our stuff ready," said Calvin. "Do you have the tickets?"

Malvin patted his pocket.

"Good," said Calvin. "Keep them on you just in case."

The two brothers went inside their cottage, and Maren counted to fifty before creeping out of the bush and dashing to Lishta's house. She peered inside her grandmother's window, but the room was empty. All of the other rooms were empty too. Maren scurried down the path back into camp, but Lishta wasn't in the mess hall or the health center or down by the lake, although Hallie was there, giggling with her friends and—big surprise—Evan the lifeguard.

Plywood boards covered the front of the dream shack, and Carmella was nowhere to be found. At least nobody was getting any new dreams for now. Maren jogged over to Hallie, dragged her away from her friends, and cupped her hands around her sister's ear.

"Meet me at the boathouse in five minutes."

Twenty-Four

As Maren waded through the cool, shin-deep water, she wondered if she'd ever get a chance to swim in the beautiful lake. It seemed less and less likely as time went on. At this rate, she'd be lucky to make it out of here with all of the campers unscathed. There had to be a way to get everybody to stop taking the remaining dreams. Maybe she'd pretend to sleepwalk and do something so utterly embarrassing that nobody would ever want to take one again. But that was risky, not to mention humiliating.

The water lapped gently at the shore and the birds chirped in the trees. Maren wished she were a bird singing on a branch, not a person with all these worries and dangers. All she'd think about was flying around, building a cozy nest, and finding nice, juicy worms to eat. On second thought, Maren didn't wish she was a bird.

Amos sat on the beach, eating a granola bar and quacking at the ducks, who scattered as Maren approached.

"Wait up!" called a voice from behind her, and Hallie came dashing through the water. "What's going on?"

Maren trudged out of the lake and sprawled on the beach. "Gran-Gran just got fired."

"She *what?*"

"Malvin and Calvin fired her, and I don't know where she is now," said Maren.

"Wait," said Amos, waving his granola bar. "Start from the beginning. What did she do to get fired?"

Maren caught him up on the events of the day, as well as Lishta's story about the Sandwoman. "We can't be sure it's her, but Gran-Gran tried to get the co-directors to ban dreams, just to be safe, and they fired her."

"I hate those guys," said Amos. "Why did the antidotes stop working? Do you think somebody changed the dream recipe or whatever?"

"Probably," said Maren.

"Definitely," said Hallie. "By the way, I found the rest of those gamer kids and woke them up."

"How come your antidotes worked and mine didn't?" asked Maren.

"I put a *ton* of spearmint in them," said Hallie. "So much

that I could barely shut them. But even then, they took a really long time to work."

"That's good to know," said Maren. "Amos, did you discover anything on your stealth mission this morning?"

"Kind of," said Amos. "I followed Calvin and Malvin to that office building that nobody ever goes in. I tried listening outside the window, but I couldn't hear anything."

"Rats," said Maren.

"Turns out I'm not the greatest secret agent." Amos dragged his hand through his curls, making them spring in all directions. "But after they left, I snuck inside and found this office with a big filing cabinet. I looked through all the drawers, but it was mostly just camper files and handbooks and stuff, and the computer wouldn't turn on. There was another room down the hall, but it was locked. I wonder if—"

"Hang on," said Maren. "Were there camper registration forms, like the ones their parents filled out?"

"Yeah, I think so."

"Did you see a phone in there too? Like a landline?"

"Yeah," said Amos. "It was one of those old-fashioned ones with the dial thing, but I know how to work it."

"This is great!" Maren leapt up, scattering sand every-where. "Those forms will have their phone numbers on them.

We can go back there tonight and call everybody's parents and tell them there's been an emergency and they need to come pick their kids up right away."

"Awesome," said Amos. "What kind of emergency? Are you going to tell them about the sleepwalking?"

Maren tapped her foot. "I don't know if that's urgent enough. Some of them might not realize the seriousness of the situation. I think we'd better lie, and then when they get here, we'll deal with it."

"How, exactly, are we going to deal with it?" asked Hallie.

Maren shrugged. "We'll figure something out."

"No offense, but the last time we went into a situation with a vague, hand-wavey plan, we got kidnapped." Amos threw a piece of his granola bar to a wayward duck that had paddled over.

"Don't feed it that!" Maren snatched away the rest of his bar. "It'll get sick." She stopped and pondered. "Actually, speaking of sick, maybe we could put something in the cafeteria food tomorrow morning that makes people throw up."

"That sounds super gross," said Hallie.

"Yeah, and pretty mean, actually," said Maren, who hated throwing up. "What do you think we should do?"

"Hmm," said Hallie, staring out at the lake, but Amos leapt up, startling the ducks.

"We'll tell them there's an escaped convict in the woods around the camp! No, an escaped *axe murderer.*" Amos's eyes gleamed. "We'll say it hasn't hit the news yet, but it's about to, and the police need everybody to go home right away. Nobody's going to let their kid stay at a camp with a murderer roaming around. That's like Horror Movie 101."

"Yesss." Maren's scalp tingled at the perfection of it. "We'll sneak in tonight after everybody goes to bed and make the calls. How about midnight?"

"BONJOUR, CROTTE DE NEZ!" came a screeching voice from right behind Maren, and she leapt about three feet into the air.

"Henri…have you seen…Gran-Gran?" asked Maren, gasping for breath after the sudden startle.

Henri inspected Amos's empty granola bar wrapper, then hopped over to his duck friend. "GUTEN TAG!" he yelled, and the duck quacked hello.

"*Gran-Gran*, Henri," repeated Maren. "You know, the gray-haired human you love? The one who gives you crackers? Have you seen her?"

The bird cocked his head. "GRAN-GRAN-GRAN?

ALLONS-Y!" With a hoppy, flappy, running start, he launched himself into the trees and disappeared.

"Ugh," said Maren. "I don't know why I ever expect him to listen."

"No." Hallie jumped up. "He said 'Let's go.' He wants us to follow him."

Twenty-Five

IT FELT LIKE THEY HAD been shoving through bushes and brambles and swampy mud for at least half an hour, and Maren was certain they'd just passed the same boulder for the third time.

"Henri, are you taking us in circles?" she called.

"ALLEZ LES VACHES," yelled Henri from somewhere ahead.

"We're not cows," muttered Amos.

"Did either of you have arts and crafts today?" she asked, smacking a mosquito off her forehead. "This teacher made us take apart replicas of Cleo Montclair's sculptures and then Carmella judged how well we did."

"How dare they." Hallie untangled a prickly green branch from her shirt. "I had coding workshop, but instead of learning how to actually code, we learned how to hack into those security PIN pads with the numbers."

"Okay, that is just flat-out weird," said Maren.

"You think that's weird?" said Amos, panting as he jogged to catch up. "I had virtual crane operating."

"Virtual *what* operating?" said Hallie.

"Crane," said Amos. "You know, those big machines at construction sites that lift heavy stuff? But we didn't have actual cranes, so we did it all in virtual reality."

Maren peered over her shoulder to make sure Amos wasn't joking, but his face was serious. "What do any of those things have to do with each—oof!"

She had walked straight into Hallie, who had stopped at the edge of a clearing. A faded red tent stood in its center. Maren didn't recognize the tent—it might belong to Lishta, but it might also belong to some random camper or a homeless person who lived in the woods. Or an escaped axe murderer.

Henri zoomed into the clearing and landed in front of the tent.

"Henri, are you sure this is—" whispered Maren, her heart thundering.

"BONJOUR, BONJOUR!" he yelled. "MAREN PARTRIDGE IS A BAR-FIGHT CHEATER!"

The zipper on the tent slid upward, and Maren and

Hallie clung to each other. Seconds later, Lishta's wrinkly face poked out. "Hello, Henri," she said. "What's that you said about Maren?"

"He said she's a bar-fight cheater," said Hallie, stepping into the clearing. Lishta gave a little jolt, then beamed at her granddaughters and their friend as she clambered out of the tent.

"Did my lovely little bird bring you here?" she asked.

"I don't know about lovely," said Maren. "But yes, he did, and it was pretty helpful, so…" She groaned inwardly. "Thank you, Henri."

"BUCHERON A BARBE SALE," yelled Henri, who had found a saltine cracker somewhere and was busy crunching it into crumbs.

"Henri, dear, let's not call anyone a dirty lumberjack's beard," said Lishta, hurrying over to hug Maren, Hallie, and Amos for good measure. "You're probably wondering why I'm here. Something terrible has happened."

"I know," said Maren. "I overheard your whole conversation with Malvin and Calvin."

"Those nincompoops." Lishta's eyes flashed angrily.

"Why didn't you tell them the truth?" asked Hallie.

"Because I gave them an alias when I applied for the job, dearie," said Lishta. "And I want them to forget about me immediately, not start digging up dirt. I fear that dreadful Kevin is right. If the police came, they'd just see a camp full of dreaming children doing things they didn't understand, and they'd believe those foolish co-directors that nothing was amiss. Except for the lunch lady who lied about her name and background. I fear they might arrest me for that."

"We just came up with a plan to get the place shut down," said Maren. "If it works, everybody's parents will come pick them up tomorrow."

Lishta's gray eyebrows lifted.

"You know that little office building in the camp center?" said Amos, and Lishta nodded. "There's a phone in there, and also all of the campers' files. We're going to sneak in there tonight, call all the parents, and tell them there's an escaped convict hiding out in the woods and they need to come get their kids right away."

"Let's hope nobody goes searching for the convict and finds this." Lishta jabbed her knobby thumb at the tent.

"Oh," said Maren. "That's a good point."

Her grandmother broke into a wrinkly grin. "It's fine, dear. I'll stash my tent in the car. And it's a perfect plan." She gave Maren's cheek an appreciative squeeze. Hallie ducked out of the way before she could grab her face, and Amos looked nervous.

"I called your mother," continued Lishta, "and she's going to drive up tomorrow. She'll be here by lunchtime. If for some reason you can't manage to convince all the parents to come and get their children, we'll call the police then and hope for the best."

Maren's heart sang with relief. Everything would feel safer with her mother there, even if the parents didn't come and they had to take on Calvin and Malvin and somehow convince the police there was a problem. She couldn't wait to give her mom the biggest hug in existence.

"My plan for the night is to churn out superstrong waking antidotes of all different kinds so we can figure out what works best," said Lishta. "I've got a miniature factory set up inside the tent. Do you need help with the phone calls?"

"We should be fine," said Hallie. "There's only one phone, so it's not like we need more people to do it."

"More importantly, do you feel safe doing this by yourselves?" said Lishta.

"Totally," said Hallie, and Maren leaned a little closer, hoping to absorb some of her sister's confidence.

"All right, then," said Lishta. "I'm going to send Henri to keep an eye on you from the trees, and he's under strict instructions to fly straight to me if anything happens."

"DEGUEULASSE COMME UN PET DE RHINOCEROS," yelled the parrot.

"No one smells like a rhinoceros toot." Lishta cast a disapproving look at her bird, who fluffed his feathers and did not look remotely sorry. "We'll also use a code word if you need Henri to come and find me. The word is 'baloney.'"

"SALAMI!" yelled Henri. "MORTADELLA!"

"Baloney," repeated Lishta firmly. "In the meantime, I need you three to destroy as many dreams as you can at the camp. Stop the sleepwalking before it starts."

"I know where they're storing a bunch of them," said Maren. "In boxes in the laundry building."

"Perfect," said Lishta. "Those will be simple—just open up the boxes and pour water inside. And if you're feeling brave, you can try something similar with the dream shack, perhaps with hoses or sprinklers."

"It's closed right now," said Hallie.

"Interesting," said Lishta. "Let's keep an eye on that. Now, the trickiest part will be getting the dreams that the campers already have in their possession."

"We can sneak back to our bunks and soak all the dreams we find," said Amos.

"Excellent," said Lishta. "Just be careful, my dears. And just to be safe, you'd better sleep with nylons over your faces tonight."

The thought of anybody slipping dreams into her mouth

while she slept turned Maren's skin cold. "Do you think we really need to?"

"Better safe than sorry." Lishta clambered inside the tent and reemerged with three limp stockings in a strange shade of pale blue.

Amos held his up between two fingers, looking dubious. "What am I supposed to do with this?"

"I'll explain on the way back," said Maren, thinking she'd die if any of her bunkmates saw her sleeping with this thing on her face, and it'd be a hundred times worse for Amos. Thank goodness for the canopies.

"We should get back," said Hallie.

Maren wished she could stay longer with her grandmother, sitting under the quiet trees far away from sleepwalkers and chaos, but Hallie was right. They had a lot to do, and she wanted to check on Kendall.

"All right, sweethearts," said Lishta. "Be careful. Remember the code word."

"LIVERWURST!" yelled Henri.

Twenty-Six

After saying goodbye to Hallie and Amos and stealing away through the lengthening afternoon shadows, Maren crept up the steps to her cabin and eased through the creaky screen door.

"Hey," called a voice from the back of the room, causing her to nearly jump out of her slippers. Kendall sat on the edge of her bed, her long hair loose around her face. "Everybody's at the dream-crafting workshop right now."

"You're awake," said Maren.

"Yeah, I woke up a half hour ago and came back here. Judy's looking after the group." Kendall's face was pale, and her mouth turned down in the opposite of her usual cheerful smile. "Was I acting super embarrassing?"

"No!" Maren sat on the bed beside her. "You were fine. It was mostly just cute. Do you remember any of it?"

"Literally all I remember is bowling with some fairies." Kendall sniffed. "I can't believe everybody knows I still like fairies now."

Maren handed her a tissue from the box on someone's bedside table. "I'm sure loads of people your age still like fairies."

Kendall groaned. "Did any of the other counselors see me?"

"Just Judy and the girls from our bunk," said Maren. "Maddie and Peyton were a hundred times more embarrassing when they were acting like caterpillars, so don't worry about it."

Kendall nodded and wiped her nose. "Thanks. That was pretty freaky though, doing all that stuff without even knowing I was doing it."

Goose bumps whispered up Maren's arms as she thought of Lishta's story about the Sandwoman. "Yeah, that is kind of freaky." At least nobody at the camp had stolen anything or broken any laws. They'd just made fools of themselves, which wasn't the end of the world. And it'd all be over tomorrow when everybody's parents came.

"Didn't you want to go to the dream-crafting workshop?" said Kendall.

"Nah," said Maren. "I've got a headache."

"Me too," said Kendall. "I have to go get everybody in a few minutes, but you can stay here and rest if you want. Maybe take one of those mint relaxation dreams and see if it helps?"

"Do you think taking any of these dreams is a good idea, considering what happened to people today?" asked Maren.

"I...don't know," Kendall said. "I mean, that's why you're all here, right? But it does seem like something's wrong with some of them."

"And we don't know if there are more bad ones," added Maren.

"Yeah." Kendall's voice drooped with exhaustion. "To be honest, I don't know what to tell you, Vesper. If you don't feel safe taking them, I one hundred percent support your decision. We'll have a talk later with the whole bunk, okay?"

"That sounds good." Maren rubbed her temples and winced. "I'm going to lie down."

"Feel better." Kendall flashed a strained attempt at a smile as Maren crawled under her canopy and lay there, waiting for her to leave. To pass the time, she rummaged through her personalized sachets of dreams.

Flying
Snorkeling with mermaids
Tango on Mars

Singing alphabet soup
Everything is made of candy
Step inside a painting

She dug down to the bottom, to the dreams she'd only briefly glanced at on the first day.

Ice cream sundaes with Pablo Picasso
Your best friend is a statue
Skiing through the Louvre Museum
Magic crayons
A world of watercolor

"What is it about art?" she muttered. And what could today's sculpture dismantling class possibly have to do with code breaking and crane operating? Were they related, or were they completely random activities designed to distract and occupy the campers for some other purpose? The Sandwoman—if that's who was really in charge—had an extremely weird and confusing plan. Thankfully it would all come to an end tomorrow.

The floorboards creaked as Kendall passed Maren's bed, humming the baseball song. The screen door swung shut.

Maren counted to ten before climbing out from under

her canopy. There wasn't much time. She needed to steal one of those fairy bowling dreams from Kendall's stash and get Henri to bring it to Lishta. Then she needed to find and destroy everybody else's dreams. It was such a sad waste.

Maren dashed to Kendall's bed. The counselor had set up her trunk as a bedside table and covered it with a bright pink scarf. Careful not to disturb Kendall's arrangement of personal items, Maren eased open her dream packet and sifted through until she found the ones labeled *Fairy bowling: A capricious escapade*. She took one, closed the bag, and set it back in place. Then, on a whim, she swiped Kendall's phone's screen to see if it had any signal, but it didn't. Quickly, Maren crept to the door, poked her head outside, and whisper-yelled, "Baloney!"

No response.

"Baloney!" Maren tried a little louder.

Still nothing.

"Henri, are you even there?"

"ROUGE A LEVRES POUR LES COCHONS!"

"Shh!" hissed Maren. "Be quiet and come here. I need to give you something for Gran-Gran."

A whirring sound came from the branches above, and moments later Henri landed on the staircase railing.

"Thank you for listening," said Maren. In response, Henri

pooped on the stairs. With a heavy sigh, Maren held out the tiny sachet. "Bring this straight to Gran-Gran, okay?"

"Voleuse," whispered Henri.

Maren remembered this word from the last time she'd stolen dreams. "I know, but this time I'm stealing for the right reasons."

Henri squawked doubtfully.

"Shh," she whispered. "Give this to Lishta. Gran-Gran."

"GRAN-GRAN-GRAN!"

Maren groaned. "Just go, okay? Before somebody sees you." She held out the sachet, and miraculously, Henri took it.

"Hurry, and then come back," she said as Henri let out another dropping and then launched into the air.

"AU REVOIR, GROS PAMPLEMOUSSE!"

Twenty-Seven

MAREN FILLED A BUCKET IN the bathroom sink and headed back into the main room to start drenching dreams. But then she stopped. If everybody came back and found their dreams soaking wet, they'd know someone had sabotaged them. And since Maren was the only one who'd been alone in the cabin besides Kendall, she'd be the prime suspect. Not to mention she'd already been telling people not to take their dreams. This was no good at all.

There had to be some other way to deactivate the dreams so nobody would notice until they woke up having not dreamed. Setting down the bucket and kicking off her slippers, Maren stretched her calves and rolled out her ankles. As she pondered what to do with the dreams, she barefoot-tapped her way through the spring recital routine.

"What are you doing?"

With a gasp, Maren spun around and found Ivy standing in the doorway. "Tap-dancing?" she squeaked.

Ivy folded her arms. "In the dark? By yourself? With a bucket?"

Maren nudged the bucket with her foot. "I spilled something and was just cleaning it up."

"What'd you spill?"

"Oh, um, just some sunblock," said Maren. "I tried to squirt it on my legs, but it went all over the floor. I didn't want somebody to slip in it."

"That was nice of you," said Ivy. "It's weird, though. I don't see a puddle or even a wet spot."

"Oh, I did it a while ago." Maren cursed her ridiculous voice, which insisted on leaping up an extra octave whenever she lied. "It's probably dry by now. I just forgot to put the bucket away."

"Mm-hmm." Ivy fixed an even gaze on Maren, who fought the urge to squirm.

"I thought you were moving in with your grandma until camp ended," Maren said, desperate to change the subject to anything that wasn't her bucket of guilty plans.

"She said I can't sleep there." A lonely, lost expression flickered across Ivy's face.

"That stinks." Maren's heart ached for this poor girl who was getting shuffled around all summer because everyone was too busy. She felt awful for making it worse by lying to her and hiding secrets when they were supposed to be friends.

"Do you ever feel so incredibly frustrated with all the stuff that grown-ups think you're too young to understand?" said Ivy. "Especially when you're trying to help?"

Maren nodded, though she felt that Lishta and her parents did a pretty good job of being open with her. But Ivy had a point. It wasn't just about family: it was other grown-ups, teachers, counselors, and awful camp co-directors. Loads of people thought kids were too stupid to understand or handle the truth. It was exhausting.

"I'm sorry," said Maren.

Ivy shrugged. "It's not your fault."

"I know," said Maren. "But I'm sorry about that other stuff. And you were right—I'm not being totally honest with you. But it's not because I don't think you can understand or handle it. It's because I literally can't tell anybody."

Ivy grimaced. "Guess I'll just add you to my list of people who are shutting me out."

"Okay, listen." Maren took a deep breath and ran through all the things she could tell Ivy without blowing her cover. "The sleepwalking thing that's happening all over camp? I don't think it's an accident. I think somebody's tampering with those dreams before your grandmother is selling them. Or maybe even after."

Ivy looked unsurprised. "Who do you think is doing it?"

Maren wondered if she could tell her about the Sandwoman. Those crimes must be public information, but Lishta hadn't mentioned whether the public knew the actual truth. That might be too much dream-insider information to know or share.

"I don't know exactly," she said, which was technically the truth. "But I think it's getting really serious."

"How are you waking them up?" Ivy leaned forward into Maren's space. "I know you've got something."

Maren stepped backward and her heel hit the bucket, sloshing water onto the floor. "It's like a…remedy thing to wake people up. I asked…um…Thalia to help me make it in the dream-crafting workshop."

This was risky, bringing Thalia into it when Maren had no idea what Thalia's true intentions were. But it was also the most plausible reason for having waking antidotes.

"The remedies don't work perfectly, though, which is why I've been adding spearmint," said Maren. "I wasn't lying about the spearmint, for the record."

"Can I have some?" asked Ivy.

Maybe it wasn't the worst idea to let somebody else help with the antidotes, even if they didn't know exactly why they were doing it or where the antidotes came from. There were so many kids to keep track of, and Maren, Hallie, and Amos already had their hands full.

"Okay," said Maren. "But you have to promise to keep it a secret. And I can only give you a couple."

"I solemnly swear," said Ivy, eyes shining, and Maren felt a twinge of pity for this poor girl who'd been left out of everything else. She wished she could include her even more, but it just wasn't possible. Maren pulled two sachets out of her pocket and set them in Ivy's outstretched palm, cringing at what Hallie would say if she found out. But antidotes couldn't hurt anything, and Maren wasn't giving away any more of their secrets.

"You'll have to add your own spearmint," she said. "There are patches of it growing near the health center. Do you know what it looks like?"

"I think so."

"Just make sure you don't pick poison ivy," said Maren. "That's everywhere too."

"I'm the only poison ivy around here." Ivy broke into a maniacal grin that made Maren laugh.

"Can I start calling you that?" she said.

Ivy waggled one eyebrow, an impressive feat.

"Vesper? Are you still in there?" Kendall's face poked in through the door, causing both girls to jump. "Oh, hey, Ivy! I'm *super* glad you're back! Are you girls ready for dinner?"

"Is it bonfire hot dogs again?" asked Maren, her stomach simultaneously gurgling and sinking at the prospect.

"No, we're at the mess hall tonight," said Kendall. "It's taaaco night!"

"I can't wait to see how they mangle those poor tacos," said Ivy.

"Promise me that you'll keep this secret," whispered Maren as they filed out of the cabin.

"Pinkie swear," said Ivy, hooking her finger around Maren's.

Guilt crawled around like a big, fuzzy caterpillar in Maren's stomach. She wondered if giving the waking antidotes to Ivy was smart. It felt like she had just opened a brand-new can of worms next to an already open bucket of worms. On top of that, she hadn't managed to destroy any of her bunkmates' dreams, and this had been her last chance before tonight, when everybody would be taking them. Hopefully they'd all stay fast asleep in their beds this time, but that seemed less and less likely.

Twenty-Eight

MAREN LAY IN HER BED with sketchy tacos doing the cha-cha in her stomach. She'd approached every single girl in her bunk that evening, begging them not to take their dreams anymore, but nobody believed her, and Ivy had left the mess hall right after finishing dinner. So much for helping. Maddie and Peyton had flat-out laughed in Maren's face, and even Emma and Anika had only promised not to take the dreams that had made other people sleepwalk.

A mosquito whined around the canopy of Maren's bed, zooming away every time she swatted it, and she wanted to scream at the futility of absolutely everything. The minutes on her cell phone's screen seemed to move at one-hundredth their normal speed.

11:03.

Footsteps tromped past as the last girl went to bed.

11:04.

Giggling broke out from under either Maddie's or Peyton's canopy.

Go to sleep, thought Maren as hard as she could. *But don't take your dreams.* Hopefully if anybody sleepwalked, they'd stay in their cabin. She wished she could lock them all inside, but that would be a fire hazard.

Please be safe, please be safe, thought Maren. *Just hang in there until your parents come.*

11:07.

The rhythmic sound of sleep-breathing slowly filled the cabin. Someone snored. Someone else mutter-sang the baseball song.

11:11.

Maren eased her legs over the edge of the bed. She'd sneak out the back exit so she could pretend she was heading to the bathroom if anyone saw her. But nobody emerged from their canopies, not even Ivy, whose flashlight cast a yellow glow on the blue fabric. As she crept past her friend's bed, the floorboard creaked, and she froze, holding her breath.

Silence. The papery flick of a page being turned. Maren let out her breath and continued creeping.

The air outside was thick and muggy, like walking into

a bathroom after someone had just taken a hot shower. In the distance, thunder rumbled, but it wasn't raining yet. Once she was far enough away from the cabin, Maren switched on her phone's flashlight, cupped her hand around it to dim the brightness, and ran down the path toward the office. In the faint glow, the tree branches looked like reaching arms with long, spindly fingers, and Maren shuddered every time their damp leaves brushed her skin. It was hard to see the twists and turns and the roots sticking out, but she didn't dare shine any more light. If only there'd been a moon instead of a dark, stormy sky.

As she neared the main clearing, raindrops began to fall, first tiny little pinpricks and then larger, fatter globs. All of the buildings were dark except for the health center. At night, it looked more like an abandoned ghost camp than a real one. Thunder rumbled again, louder this time. Dropping to a crouch, Maren ran across the clearing, and just as she ducked under the eaves on the side of the office building, the sky opened up. Rain clattered onto the roof and gurgled down the drainpipe, which emptied straight onto Maren's foot. With a squeak, she leapt sideways.

"Watch out!" hissed a voice, and Maren had to clap both hands over her mouth to keep silent. It was Hallie, her clothes considerably dryer than Maren's, which meant she'd gotten there earlier.

"You almost gave me a heart attack," said Maren. "Why didn't you say—"

Hallie made a cutting motion with her hand and jabbed her thumb at the window on her other side, which was faintly illuminated. "Because I was trying to hear," she whispered. "Now shhh."

Maren pressed her ear against the splintery wood at the edge of the window. She heard a man's low voice and then a woman's—a silvery, singsong voice that rose in agitation.

"Thalia," whispered Maren, and Hallie nodded.

Footsteps squelched in the dark, and then a body hurtled into Maren, stomping on her already soaked foot.

"Watch it," she hissed, then pressed her hand over Amos's mouth. "And shhh."

"Fforry," he mumbled. Maren let go of his face, then pointed at the window. With a nod, Amos crouched underneath.

"You have no idea who you're dealing with," said Thalia.

Two male voices broke into goofy, snorting laughter.

"Do you honestly think we're afraid of you?" said one of the brothers.

"I don't care whether you are or not," said Thalia. "You'll find out soon enough that it doesn't matter. You're both in way over your heads."

"Yikes," whispered Amos.

"Shh," hissed Hallie.

"Our job is to keep everything running smoothly," said Calvin or Malvin.

"And that's exactly what we're doing," said Malvin or Calvin.

"Are you joking?" From inside the office came a loud thump, and Maren, Hallie, and Amos all jumped. "This is a complete disaster! You should be ashamed of yourselves."

Maren couldn't figure out if Thalia thought it was a complete disaster because kids were sleepwalking or because *not enough* kids were sleepwalking.

"Do you think we don't know who you really are?" said Calvin or Malvin.

"Whoa," whispered Maren.

"Do you think I care?" said Thalia with another thump. "You'd better watch yourselves or you'll have far bigger problems than just me."

At this, both brothers broke into their sneering chortle again.

"Get out of here," said one of them.

"With pleasure," said Thalia. A door banged, and Maren, Hallie, and Amos flattened themselves against the building as the dream-crafting teacher burst outside. She stormed away through the rain, her black nightdress billowing behind her.

"What was *that?*" whispered Amos.

"I have no idea," whispered Maren.

"Shh," said Hallie, but the brothers were silent. Moments later they came out and one of them opened a polka-dot umbrella, which they both huddled underneath as they scuttled away.

"She was being pretty aggressive," said Amos.

"Maybe she's just trying to help, like we are," said Hallie.

"But she's not undercover," said Maren. "And they know about her dream-crafting abilities. I just don't get how this all fits together."

"Tell me about it," groaned Amos.

"I'm going to follow her," said Hallie. "Can you two manage the phone calls?"

"Sure," said Maren. "There's only one phone, so it's not like we need all of us."

"Okay," said Hallie. "I'll be back in twenty minutes."

Maren's gut twisted as her sister jogged off into the dark. It wasn't like she was going anywhere dangerous, but this whole night felt way more dangerous than anything so far. It was probably just the thunder, but Maren's knees started wobbling.

"She'll be fine." Amos nudged Maren's arm with his elbow, like he could read her thoughts.

"Baloney," she said.

"No really," said Amos. "I think she's—"

"I know, and thank you," said Maren. "Baloney! Henri, are you even out there?"

"BON SOIR, NOUILLES MOLLES!" Henri's screechy voice echoed through the eaves, and Maren almost leapt out of her skin.

"Hey, who are you calling a floppy noodle?" said Amos.

Maren groaned. "Why can't you just listen for the code word, Henri? We need you to follow Hallie and make sure she stays safe."

"VACHE TYRANNIQUE."

"Maybe she has to be a bossy cow because you don't listen," retorted Amos.

"Enough!" Maren glared up into the darkness. "If you care about our family, you need to go right now. If something bad happens to Hallie, you fly straight back here. Got it?"

Henri let out an offended squawk, but he took off into the night without another rude word.

Maren groaned. "Why couldn't Gran-Gran get a dog?"

"I kind of like him," said Amos. "As long as he's not pooping on me."

"You have no idea," said Maren. "Come on, let's start making calls."

Amos tugged on the front door, but it was locked. Maren

tried the window, but it didn't budge. Neither did any of the other windows, and there wasn't a back entrance.

"Should we break in?" asked Amos.

Maren shrugged. "I guess so. By the time Calvin and Malvin find out what happened, the parents will already be on their way here."

With a devious grin, Amos pulled a rusty hammer from his backpack.

"What are you doing with that?" asked Maren.

"Breaking in." Amos swung the hammer at the nearest window, shattering the glass.

Twenty-Nine

"Okay, maybe I should rephrase my question," said Maren, stepping carefully through the shards of grass littering the ground. "*Where* did you get that hammer? And why?"

"Found it in the boathouse," said Amos. "It probably used to be a boat-fixing tool, but I figured it might come in handy."

"You mean in case we needed to maim any dangerous criminals?" said Maren.

"Or break into any random offices." Despite his usual crooked grin, Amos looked different to Maren now that he'd just smashed a window. Older, somehow, and a little bit dangerous, which was sort of scary and sort of thrilling.

Pulling an extra T-shirt from his bag and wrapping it around his hand, Amos swept the broken glass from the windowsill. "You want to go first?"

Maren didn't really want to go first, but she also didn't want to look like a wimp, so she nodded and Amos boosted her up onto the sill. "Watch out for glass on the other side," he said, and Maren carefully squinched herself through and landed on the other side without injury. With her slipper, she nudged the biggest shards of glass out of the way before Amos came awkwardly slithering through.

The office was musty and carried a faint old typewriter smell that gave Maren pangs of homesickness. On the desk sat an ancient computer with a box-shaped monitor. To its left was an even more ancient phone with a rotary dial. Maren picked up the black receiver, but it was hard to tell which way it went.

"The end with the wire is the part you talk into," said Amos, tugging open the bottom drawer of a filing cabinet. Maren sheepishly turned the phone around and listened into the earpiece, which was silent.

"This thing is cool," she said, twirling the dial, which made a satisfying tickity sound as she let go and it spun back into position.

Amos dumped an armload of folders onto the desk and opened the top one. "Okay, let's start with Elizabeth Aaronson. Do you want me to dial?"

"No, I want to do it." Maren gave the wheel another spin. "Just show me how."

"Okay, so if you want a five, you stick your finger in the five hole and then pull it back to this silver thingy." Amos demonstrated. "Then let go." The phone made the lovely, tickity sound again, and Maren tried a six, a seven, and a zero for practice.

"Got it," she said. "What's her parents' phone number?"

Amos read out the string of numbers and Maren dialed them one by one, then listened carefully into the receiver.

"It's supposed to sound like a regular phone when it rings, right?" she said.

"Yeah, that part is the same." Amos shuffled Elizabeth's folder aside and opened the next one.

"How long is it supposed to take?" asked Maren.

"I don't know, about the same as a regular phone?"

"Hmmm," said Maren, still waiting.

"Did you get a dial tone when you picked it up?" asked Amos.

"I don't think so?" said Maren.

Amos took the receiver. "Don't you guys have a landline at the dream shop?"

"Yeah." Maren felt her face getting hot. Of course she knew how landlines worked, but she'd just assumed everything about this phone was different. Who knew when dial tones had been invented?

Amos held the receiver to his ear, then tapped the little buttons where it hung up a few times. "Great," he muttered. "It's dead."

"Are you sure?" said Maren. "Maybe it's just not plugged in? Where's the cord?"

Following the cord sticking out of the back of the phone, Amos crawled under the desk. "It's plugged in," he said.

"Rats and double rats," said Maren. "What's even worse than double rats?"

"Rabid groundhogs?" suggested Amos.

Maren grimaced. "Definitely worse. Let's check if there's another phone."

She and Amos dashed down the hall and found a dingy waiting room, a green-tiled bathroom, and a kitchen that smelled of stale coffee and mothballs, none of which had a phone.

"There's got to be one somewhere at this camp," said Maren, slumping against the kitchen counter. "Considering there's no cell signal here, they'd need at least one landline in case there was an emergency."

"Maybe the health center?" Amos opened cabinets at random until he found a dust-coated box of Girl Scout cookies.

"But the nurses are there," said Maren. "We can't just show up with an armload of folders and ask to borrow the phone for a couple of hours. Don't eat those cookies. That's not even what the boxes look like anymore."

"I bet those weasel-faced co-directors have a phone in their cottage," said Amos, pulling out a half-empty sleeve of cookies and sniffing it.

"Those rabid-groundhog-faced co-directors," added Maren. "And I'm serious. Don't eat those."

"Hey!" came a hissing whisper from the office. "Maren!"

Maren ran into the office and found Hallie at the window, water dripping into her eyes, which gleamed in a maniacal way. "You'll never believe what I just saw."

Grabbing hold of her sister's slippery, wet arms, Maren hauled her into the room, and the two girls nearly toppled into the desk.

"What was it?" said Amos through a mouthful of cookie. He stopped chewing as Maren gave him a horrified look. "What? They taste fine! A little chewy, but totally edible. Want one?"

"No!" said both sisters.

Hallie pulled out the desk chair and flopped onto it. "I followed Thalia to her cottage, which is right behind the dream-crafting workshop. And then she grabbed some keys, went out to her car, and drove off."

"Do you think she's gone for good?" asked Maren.

"She didn't pack any of her stuff," said Hallie. "But get this. Before she left, I saw her sticking pins into this map on her wall. I couldn't really see what it was, so I took some pictures with my phone. Look at this."

Everyone huddled around Hallie's screen as she pulled up the photos and zoomed in. On the wall of Thalia's cabin was a hand-drawn map of the camp, each cabin labeled with its number. Maren checked her bunk, number seven. Four pins were stuck into it.

"Four sleepwalkers," she murmured. "She's tracking them."

"Or she's targeting them," said Hallie.

A full-body shudder washed over Maren. "Do you think she's working for the Sandwoman?"

"Maybe she *is* the Sandwoman with plastic surgery," said Amos. "Or a really good disguise."

"There's no way somebody Gran-Gran's age could manage to look that young, no matter what they did," said Maren.

"Okay, so she's working for her," said Amos. "Maybe she's in training to become the next Sandwoman once the original one kicks the bucket."

"I doubt that's how it works," said Maren, but who even knew?

"How many calls have you made?" asked Hallie.

"None," said Maren. "The phone's broken, and we can't find another one."

"Let's check the other buildings," said Hallie. "They've got to have one for emergencies somewhere."

"That's what I said," said Maren.

"I'll bring the files," said Amos, trying to stuff the folders into his already stuffed backpack.

"Give me some of those," said Maren, and Hallie took an armload too. Leaving the front door locked, they climbed back out the window and into the rain, which had slowed to a halfhearted sprinkle.

"How about that one?" said Hallie, pointing to the laundry building.

"I didn't see a phone when I was in there, but I wasn't really looking," said Maren.

"We can sabotage those extra boxes of dreams while we're in there," said Amos.

They jogged over to the laundry building, which was unlocked, and ducked inside. While Amos checked the supply closet at the back, Maren and Hallie turned on their phones' flashlights and swung the beams all around the washing machines and dryers, the corners and the laundry piles and the tables, but there was no phone—and no boxes of dreams.

"We're too late," said Hallie. "They must be at the dream shack already."

"No phone back here," said Amos from the supply closet.

"Rabid groundhogs," muttered Maren.

Hallie's hand clamped around Maren's forearm. "Where?"

"Ouch, it's just an expression," said Maren, extricating herself from her sister's grip.

"Shh, someone's outside!" Amos hissed, dropping to the ground and gesturing for Maren and Hallie to do the same. Quickly, they covered their phone lights. "What is it?"

"Absolutely absurd," said Calvin or Malvin's smug voice. "Who does she think she is?"

"Who cares?" said his brother. "Once phase three starts, it won't matter if she's the queen of England."

A chill washed over Maren's skin. Phase three was certain to be even worse than sleepwalking.

The other brother's chuckle broke off. "What happened to the office window?"

Maren gulped so loudly she wondered if the co-directors could hear it. Even through the dark, she could feel Hallie giving her a death glare.

"It looks like somebody broke in," said the other brother.

There was the sound of running feet through wet grass, and Amos inched closer.

"We have to get out of here," he whispered.

"No kidding, Sherlock," said Hallie. "They're going to search everywhere. We need to get back to our bunks. Amos, can you take all of the files and hide them somewhere safe?"

"Sure," Amos stuffed a few more inside his bag, and they piled the rest in his arms.

"We'll try again tomorrow," said Hallie. "I'll meet you both at the boathouse at six a.m. sharp. Forget about sticking with your groups. Just make up an excuse."

Maren nodded, relieved that her sister was taking charge because she had no idea what to do. Amos kept watch out the window until the co-directors had unlocked the office and gone inside, and then the three kids raced around the edge of the clearing, keeping to the shadows until they reached the path to the cabins. Amos branched off first, and Maren grabbed her sister's hand for the last few moments before she had to do the same.

"ATTENTION!" called a screechy bird voice. Seconds later, two cloth pouches dropped from the sky, one landing on Maren's head and the other bouncing off Hallie's shoulder. Maren scooped hers up and looked inside.

"It's Gran-Gran's new waking antidotes," she said, pulling out a sachet. It gave off a strong scent of peppermint, as well as something a little…meaty.

"Bacon," laughed Hallie. "That always gets me out of bed in the morning."

"Me too." Maren had to admire their grandmother's creativity. "Thanks, Henri!"

"DE RIEN, PETIT CHEVRE."

"I think he just called you a little goat," said Hallie with a snort.

Maren shrugged. "He's called me worse."

"True," said Hallie. "Okay, I'll see you first thing in the morning. Don't forget the nylon over your head tonight."

"I won't." Maren's stomach churned at the possibility of someone sneaking dreams into her mouth as she slept, but after all of today's disasters and stress, she was sure she'd never fall asleep anyway.

But as soon as her exhausted, nylon-covered head hit the pillow, Maren fell into a deep and dreamless sleep. And she woke five hours later to utter chaos.

Thirty

WHAM.

Maren sat bolt upright, gasping and unable to figure out what the sound was or why her nose felt so crushed. Then she remembered the nylon stocking and ripped it off.

Wham-wham.

Wham. Her bed jerked sideways.

"What's going on out there?" Maren pulled her canopy open and immediately wished she hadn't. All of the girls in her bunk were running around the enclosed space like a swarm of ants. But because they all had their eyes shut, they kept crashing into beds and tables and walls. Somehow they'd all managed to put on their Camp Shady Sands T-shirts and *Dreamer!* hats.

"Kendall?" Maren called, hoping against all odds that

her counselor had somehow been spared and could help. But Kendall hopped past, trying to put on her slippers without stopping.

Wham. Kendall caught her shin on the corner of someone's trunk. "Everybody, come on!" she called, oblivious to the collision that would surely leave a nasty bruise. "It's time for the field trip."

"What field trip?" said Maren, but everybody was too busy dashing around. Maddie ran by with a toothbrush hanging out of her mouth and toothpaste all down the front of her T-shirt. Maren tried to stuff a waking antidote in her mouth as she passed, but Maddie turned her head and the sachet landed in the toothpaste on her shirt.

"Where are we going?" Maren tried again.

"On…a…field…trip," enunciated Kendall like she was talking to someone with a very basic grasp of English. "The bus is leaving in ten minutes and we need to get to the parking lot!"

"I've been waiting all week for this trip!" said Emma, who was trying to pull a sock on over her slipper.

"Oh no, not you again." Maren pulled out another antidote. "Hey, it sounds like we're not going to have time for breakfast before we leave. Do you want some of my granola bar?"

"What kind?" said Emma, still wrestling with her sock.

"What kind do you like?"

"Chocolate chip or s'mores," said Emma. "But I can't have the chewy ones because they get stuck in my braces."

"It's the crunchy kind, so you'll be fine," said Maren. "And it's chocolate chip. Open your mouth and I'll put it in."

Emma's nose wrinkled. "That's kind of weird. Can't you put it in my hand?"

"But you're so busy getting ready," said Maren, low and steady like she was speaking to a frightened animal. "I'm just trying to help."

Emma sighed and tried the sock on her other slippered foot. "Okay, fine." She held her mouth open, and Maren dropped the sachet inside. Immediately Emma started chewing. The other girls were now filing out of the cabin, and Maren fought down a wave of panic. She hoped they'd all gather somewhere to get on their imaginary bus, and she'd be able to give them all sachets then.

"This thing is terrible!" Emma chewed a few more times, then gagged. "It's like minty...bacon?"

"Just keep it in your mouth and don't chew so hard. It'll taste like chocolate chips in a second." Maren felt terrible because it wasn't ever going to taste like chocolate chips, but it had to be done. Emma kept on chewing, then swallowed. Her eyes fluttered, and Maren's heart soared. Lishta's new antidote was working.

Emma's eyes snapped shut again. She threw her sock on the floor and jumped up. "Thanks for sharing, but please don't ever give me one of those again!" she yelled, running out of the cabin after all the other girls.

Ivy was nowhere to be found in the chaos of sleeprunning girls, and her bed was empty. Throwing on her own slippers and pulling her camp T-shirt over her pajama top, Maren grabbed her hat, her bag of antidotes, her backpack, and her phone and raced for the door.

As soon as she stepped outside, all the breath went out of her. The path was jammed full of campers, all with their eyes shut, all wearing the same T-shirt and hat.

"Take me out to the ball game!" they all sang at once, and Maren's entire body went cold. This had to be phase three. It was already blowing the first two phases out of the water.

"Hallie!" she yelled at a group of girls who looked Hallie's age. "Are you there?"

From the jumble, a hand shot up and waved. As they got closer, Hallie made eye contact with Maren, then pointed forward, indicating that she should follow.

You okay? she mouthed.

Maren was decidedly un-okay, but she gulped and nodded.

"Baloney!" she yelled. "Bah, forget it. Henri! Henri!" It wasn't like anybody was going to notice the parrot with their eyes closed and the field trip dream—whatever that was—playing through their minds.

Henri landed on the stairs. "BALL GAME!" he squawked, holding his wings out stiffly and hobble-hopping like he was sleepwalking too.

"Don't make fun of them," said Maren. "Go find Gran-Gran and tell her to meet us at the parking lot. Right now!"

Henri cocked his head and peered at Maren with one beady eye like he was waiting for something.

"Please," added Maren.

With an urgent screech, the bird launched skyward.

~

The parking lot was filled with sleepwalking campers milling around, singing, and chattering about the field trip. At least there wasn't an actual bus, so they couldn't get into any major trouble. Maren searched for her sister in the crowd, wondering how they'd manage to corral this many people and give them all waking antidotes. Hopefully Lishta would have a plan when she got here. And, with any luck, her waking antidotes would work better than the one Maren had just given Emma. It probably hadn't worked because she'd chewed it, Maren reasoned, praying that this wasn't another ineffective batch. It was possible that whoever was making the dreams was staying one step ahead of them, but she didn't like to think about that possibility.

Maren edged through the crowd, catching snippets of conversations as she stuck as many waking antidotes as she could into people's mouths. They didn't seem to be working, but she kept trying anyway, both because it gave her something to do and because a stubborn part of her brain refused to accept that they might fail.

"When's the bus going to get here?" asked a short-haired girl.

"I'm so excited!"

"Did you bring money for the gift shop?"

"Buy me some peanuts and Cracker Jack!"

It was virtually unheard of in the dream-making world for this many people to be sharing the same dream at the same time. The campers would all have had to put the sachet in their mouths at the exact same moment, and it would have to be interacting in the exact same way with their subconscious minds, which were as unique as snowflakes. Maren couldn't figure out how the mastermind—whether it was Thalia (likely) or Malvin and Calvin (fairly unlikely)—had pulled it off.

"Hey." Hallie touched Maren's back, and Maren whirled around with a gasp of relief.

"I can't tell you how happy I am to see you awake," Hallie said.

"Me too," said Maren.

"Are your antidotes working?"

Maren peered through the crowd at the people she'd managed to give them to. "Not yet."

"Mine either." Hallie sighed. "I don't think they're ever going to." She turned to a boy about Maren's age who was standing by himself, gently swaying and smiling. "Open up!"

The boy obeyed, and Hallie popped a sachet into his mouth. Both sisters watched as the boy swayed and swayed, but his eyes never even fluttered.

"Can't wait for the bus to get here," he mumbled. "It's gonna be so much fun."

Maren kicked the curb, then immediately wished she hadn't, because slippers weren't as protective as shoes. "Have you seen Ivy anywhere?"

"The girl with the pink hair?" said Hallie. "No."

"She wasn't in our cabin this morning," said Maren. "I wonder if she's sleepwalking, because she said the dreams don't work on her."

Hallie shrugged. "No sign of Mom yet, right?"

"She won't be here for hours." Maren's heart sank even lower.

"There's Amos!" Hallie stood on tiptoe and waved. As soon as Amos spotted her, his cheeks went pink, and Maren groaned. Even in the middle of a total catastrophe, someone was crushing on Hallie.

"This is really, really bad, isn't it?" Amos said.

"So incredibly bad," said Maren. "Have you seen Gran-Gran?"

"Nope." He mopped his forehead. "I was trying to get the guys in my bunk to calm down when Henri showed up and started screaming in this wacky French-German hybrid. I don't know what you'd call it. Frerman? Grench?"

Maren made a whirling gesture with her finger, signaling for Amos to get on with his story.

"I threw on my camp T-shirt so I'd blend in, and Henri led me into the woods," said Amos. "I thought the plan had changed and we were all meeting up at your grandmother's tent, but nobody was there."

"Gran-Gran wasn't there?" said Hallie, eyes bulging.

"The tent was empty," said Amos. "There was a sleeping bag and a bunch of dream ingredients in there, but no grandmothers."

"Did you check the woods around the tent?" asked Maren. "Maybe nature called right before you got there?"

"Yeah, I checked," said Amos. "I'm glad I didn't see your

grandmother peeing in a bush, but I'm also worried that I couldn't find her. I thought maybe she'd gone into camp, so I left Henri at the tent and came here."

Maren's stomach had dropped to somewhere down around her knees. "I haven't seen her."

"But that doesn't mean she's not around." Hallie's words were a little too high-pitched. "Maybe she's talking to Calvin and Malvin again."

"That would be a good idea," said Maren. "Even they must be freaking out about this." She gestured at the horde of closed-eyed, babbling campers.

An engine rumbled in the distance.

"Here comes the bus!" somebody yelled.

Maren's stomach dropped from her knees to her ankles as a yellow school bus rounded the corner and stopped at the edge of the parking lot.

"Oh God, there really is a bus," whispered Hallie.

"Phase three is not messing around," said Maren.

"I don't even want to think about phase four," said Amos.

The campers surged forward in a single, noisy mass. There was no one to control the crowd—all the counselors were sleepwalking too, and there wasn't a grown-up in sight. No Calvin or Malvin or Judy or Carmella or Ms. Muffelatta or...

"Whoa." Hallie grabbed Maren's arm so hard she hissed in pain.

In the midst of the surging kids, a silver-haired head stuck out. Thalia Mandrake's eyes were firmly closed, and she held her long skirt up as she rushed forward with the others.

"The bus, the bus," she murmured. "We have to get on the bus."

"Guess she's not the mastermind after all," said Amos.

Maren should have been relieved that Thalia Mandrake wasn't the culprit. But seeing the teacher caught up in this scary scheme made her queasy.

"We need to find Gran-Gran right away," she said.

"Maybe she drove into town to call the cops?" said Amos.

"She didn't want to call them," said Maren. "But maybe she saw this and figured it was best."

"It *is* best," said Hallie, pulling out her own phone and glaring at the screen.

The school bus doors swung open.

"All aboard!" called the lady behind the wheel. "Who's ready for the field trip?"

A giddy cheer rose up from the crowd, but Maren's stomach felt like a bag of microwave popcorn. They were about to find out who the mastermind was. Blindly, she reached for Hallie's hand, which was cold and clammy.

"Maybe we should get on the bus," she said.

"What?" said Hallie and Amos at the same time.

"For starters we can't just let her kidnap all these kids," said Maren. "And second, once we get out of the woods, we'll have phone signal so we can call the police. And Mom's cell phone."

"What about Gran-Gran?" said Hallie. "We can't just go off and leave her. What if she's in trouble?"

"I'll go on the bus, and you stay here," said Maren.

"I want to go on the bus too," said Amos.

Hallie opened her mouth to argue, then stopped. "How will you let us know where you are?"

Maren grinned. "Messenger parrot."

"Henri!" all three kids yelled.

"FILS D'UNE SIRENE POILUE!"

Henri buzzed over the crowd and landed on Amos's shoulder.

"I told you he's starting to like me," said Amos. "Even though he just called me the son of a hairy mermaid."

"NOUVEAUX REMEDES," Henri said, dropping a little drawstring bag into Maren's hand. Lishta should have made more of these waking antidotes, and Maren wondered where the rest of the bags were. Still, it was better than nothing, and hopefully they were an even stronger new formula.

"Henri, where's Gran-Gran?" asked Maren.

"IN THE STARLIGHT THEATER!"

The bus driver honked. "Hurry up, campers!"

Gritting her teeth, Maren beckoned to Henri. "We don't have time for this. Get in my backpack."

"NON!" yelled Henri.

"I know it sounds terrible, but this is really serious," said Maren, casting a nervous glance at the bus.

"JE SUIS UN OISEAU INDEPENDENT," said Henri in a pouty tone.

"We know you're an independent bird," said Amos. "But we're asking you to help us."

"I'm pretty sure there are some safety pins in my bag," said Maren.

Henri's bird eyes went starry.

"You can have all of them if you just hop in and stay there for a little while," said Maren. "Then when we get…wherever we're going," she gulped, "you'll fly back to Hallie and Gran-Gran and tell them where we are."

"DONNE-MOI LES EPINGLES." Henri was already on her backpack, trying to unzip it with his beak.

"Great," said Maren, unzipping the pack so Henri could dive inside. "Go get 'em."

The bus horn honked again. Almost all of the campers, including Thalia, had now boarded.

"We need to go," said Amos.

Maren's throat filled with cement. "Take a few of these just in case," she said, pulling out three of the new waking antidotes and handing them to her sister. "I'll see you really soon."

Hallie pulled her into a hug so tight she couldn't breathe. "Be so, so careful."

"I will," said Maren. "You too."

"Come on," said Amos. "Shut your eyes and let's go."

Hallie ducked behind a tree, and Maren and Amos shuffled across the parking lot with their eyes mostly closed. By the time they reached the bus, the lot was empty.

"Howdy, you two!" called the driver, whose drawling voice Maren was beginning to recognize.

"Can't wait to go on the field trip," mumbled Amos, stumbling up the steps.

"There's an empty seat way in the back for you two," said the driver, and it took every ounce of Maren's strength to not peek as she passed the woman, but she caught a flash of cheetah print and froze.

"Go on, don't be a shy little mouse," said the driver, and Maren tripped on the back of Amos's shoe.

It was Carmella.

Thirty-One

Ivy's GRANDMOTHER WAS THE SANDWOMAN. Maren's thoughts swirled like a kaleidoscope. She, Hallie, and Amos had suspected almost everyone else at the camp, but somehow they'd missed one of the few people who were old enough to actually be the criminal mastermind. But Carmella had seemed so clueless, so loud, so…animal-printy. It was the perfect con, and everyone had fallen for it.

Maren shuffled past all the campers, peeking out from under her lashes so she didn't walk into anything. She wondered how all the other kids had found their seats with their eyes shut. It must have something to do with the fact that they were all simultaneously experiencing the same dreamscape. It was mind-boggling—and slightly impressive, if she was being honest—that Carmella had pulled it off. But then, this was a woman who'd pulled off multiple international robberies and never gotten caught.

As she passed row after row of chattering, sleeping campers, Maren searched for Ivy, but she wasn't on the bus, which gave her a squirmy feeling somewhere between anger and worry. Ivy had complained several times about her grandmother shutting her out of plans, and Maren wondered how much she knew. She couldn't believe she'd felt guilty for lying to her "friend" when all the while Ivy was lying too, and her reasons were far worse.

On top of that, Maren had told the granddaughter of the *Sandwoman* about waking antidotes and then given her a few. Those antidotes were their key weapon, and Maren had handed them over to the enemy like it was candy.

"Field trip, woo!" yelled Amos, pumping his fist, and all the campers cheered along with him.

"Can you not?" muttered Maren as they dropped into their seat and the bus pulled out of the parking lot. "The less attention we call to ourselves, the better."

Despite the fact that the campers were packed three to a seat, the one behind Maren and Amos held only a single person: Thalia Mandrake, who leaned against the window with mirrored sunglasses over her eyes and a blissful smile on her lips. She didn't budge as they sat down, not a flicker of recognition.

Maren's full-of-Henri backpack was wriggling and squirming. She tried to set it on the floor, but there was already a big yellow bag down there.

"ATTENTION!" came a muffled yell from her backpack.

"Sorry," she whispered. "Now shh!"

"Can you believe *Carmella* is the Sandwoman?" whispered Amos.

"No," said Maren. "But yes. How did we miss that?"

She felt a little tug on her braid, and a voice from behind her seat whispered, "Hello, Maren."

With a gasp, Maren dropped her head forward and forced her face to look flat and asleep, even though her heart was rattling like a snare drum in her chest.

"It's okay," whispered Thalia. "I'm undercover too. And I'm not sleeping, obviously."

The entire bus broke into a rowdy, shouting rendition of the baseball song, and Maren leaned her head back over the seat.

"How do you know my name?" she whispered.

"I knew who you were the minute you stepped into my workshop," said Thalia. "You might not realize this, but your family is quite famous in the dream-crafting world."

"Do you think Carmella knows who I am too?" asked Maren.

"It's possible, but I doubt it," said Thalia. "The Sandwoman's never been very big on networking. She doesn't really see herself as part of our community."

"Are you sure that's really her?" asked Maren, though she couldn't imagine who else it could possibly be.

"Nobody's seen the Sandwoman in almost forty years, and there aren't any photos of her anywhere, but I'd bet money on it," said Thalia. "No one else has the skills to pull off an operation like this. It's quite impressive, if I'm being completely honest."

"I know, right?" said Maren.

"I work at a dream shop in Sedona," said Thalia. "We were suspicious of this camp when we heard of it too, so I applied for a job to keep an eye on things. Calvin and Malvin weren't planning to offer dream-crafting, but I managed to convince them it'd be a great addition to their program. Of course I didn't teach anybody how to make real dreams—can you imagine what untrained children might make with activated dreamsalt and random ingredients?" She gave a little shudder. "But the power of subconscious suggestion meant that the dreams did actually work for a few people, even though they did all that work on their own."

Maren nodded along, keeping her eyes half-shut and a dreamy expression on her face. Some of the tension in her jaw and shoulders was easing now that she knew Thalia was on her side and that there was an actual, responsible grown-up on this bus who might know what to do.

"Once the sleepwalking started, I tried to track which campers it was happening to and which dreams they had taken," continued Thalia. "I even made a map. But there was no clear pattern. Some campers would take a certain dream and sleepwalk, and others who took the same one wouldn't."

"I guess phase two was a test run to make sure whatever she did to the dreams worked?" said Maren.

"Shh, she's looking in the mirror." Thalia slumped back in her seat and Maren swayed a little, then leaned her head against the window and let out a snore. Amos started yammering about the field trip, mimicking the campers around them.

"…such an awesome day…can't wait to start dismantling!"

"What?" said Maren under her breath.

"No idea," said Amos. "That's what the kid across the aisle just said."

"All clear," said Thalia, and Maren wished she'd thought to wear mirrored sunglasses like Thalia's so she could open her eyes unnoticed. She wished she owned mirrored sunglasses, period. They looked very cool on Thalia, although pretty much everything did.

"Why do you think kids are talking about dismantling?"

asked Maren. "Do you think it has something to do with that arts and crafts workshop? Or code breaking or crane operating?"

"I've honestly got no idea," said Thalia. "There are several pieces of the puzzle that I haven't found spots for yet. But I imagine we'll find out soon enough."

Maren nudged the yellow bag at her feet, and it clanked. Henri squawked and she hissed at him to be quiet, but none of the campers paid him any attention. She wondered what they were all seeing inside their dream landscape.

"Does your cell phone have any service yet?" asked Amos, who was sneakily looking at his in his lap.

Maren slid her phone out too and shook her head. "It feels like we're going even farther from civilization."

"That's what I'm afraid of," said Thalia. "Apparently Greenleaf Valley is a dead zone for cell signal. It's time to put a stop to this field trip before things get any more dangerous."

"What are you going to do?" asked Amos.

"I'm going to sleepwalk down the aisle, give Carmella a taste of her own medicine, and take control of the bus," said Thalia. Maren fluttered her eyes and saw a little white sachet pinched between her fingers. "Now that I've got proof that she's trying to kidnap a bus full of campers, I'm going to drive straight to the police and turn her in."

"Do you need help?" asked Amos, squirming with pent-up energy.

"If you're up for it," said Thalia. "You can help me tie her up. I've got rope in my purse." She patted a large black bag on the seat beside her.

"Of course we're up for it," said Amos, and Maren agreed. It was time to put a stop to this whole operation before phase four started.

"All right," said Thalia. "I'll go first, and you two wait until I'm all the way up there before coming. I don't want to tip her off."

"Got it," said Maren.

"We'll bring your bag," said Amos.

"Excellent." Thalia eased out of her seat, swaying and humming quietly. "Let's do this."

As she passed, she dropped her purse into Amos's lap. Maren's snare-drum heart beat a wild rhythm as she peeked at Thalia dreamily making her way up the aisle. The campers were singing again, and none of them paid her any mind, but Carmella watched in the mirror. Surely someone as young as Thalia could overpower an old woman, but that old woman also happened to be driving a bus. And she was an unpredictable criminal. And the bus was picking up speed.

Maren strapped her backpack onto her front and wrapped

both arms around it. No matter what happened, she wasn't going to leave Henri.

"CHAUSETTES SALES!" yelled a muffled bird voice as Maren and Amos slid out of their seat.

"It's going to be okay; we're going to be fine," she whispered, more to herself than to Henri. After what felt like an eternity, Thalia reached the front and bent low to speak to Carmella.

"Now!" said Maren.

They crept down the aisle, trying to look nonchalant and sleeping. Maren couldn't hear what Thalia was saying, but Carmella stared straight ahead. The bus sped faster, tires humming along the road and trees whooshing past.

"I hope Thalia's not going to make us crash," muttered Amos over his shoulder.

"I'm sure she knows what she's doing," said Maren, but she wasn't sure at all. She barely knew Thalia and had no idea if she was the sort of person who made solid plans or just winged things.

In the rearview mirror, Carmella's expression darkened and everyone tipped backward as she stomped on the gas. Maren let out a tiny shriek as Carmella jerked the wheel and everyone swung sideways.

"Come on," said Amos, launching into a run. But a

pajama-clad leg stuck out in front of him, and he sprawled flat on his face. Maren tried to leap over him, but someone grabbed her arm. She whirled around and found Evan the lifeguard, his eyes wide open and his mouth twisted into a sneer.

"I *knew* I didn't like you," said Maren as someone grabbed her other wrist. Then Evan was behind her, his hand closing over her mouth, and something papery hit her tongue. She tried to spit it out, but there was nowhere for it to go. Tears flooded Maren's eyes as a piney bitterness filled her mouth. She thrashed her legs, trying to scream for Amos, but two girls had pinned him on the floor and were forcing a sachet into his mouth.

Maren wanted to vomit. She, Hallie, and Amos weren't the only ones pretending to be campers. This plot was so much bigger than she'd imagined.

The bus swerved again, and several dreaming campers fell out of their seats. Maren hoped it'd knock Evan off her, but he held tight. The colors of everything were bleeding together, like water poured over a chalk drawing. With one last ragged gasp, she slammed her elbow into Evan's chest. He grunted and they toppled backward, but it was too late.

Everything went black.

Thirty-Two

MAREN SAT UP WITH A gasp. She'd been fighting, then falling, but now she and Amos were back in their seat. The bus was different. Or had it always been like this? Her seat was so… bouncy. She looked down and discovered she was sitting on a pink, sparkly, inflatable couch. All of the seats in the bus were sparkly inflatable couches. The floor was painted in rainbow stripes, and streamers hung from the ceiling, studded with all kinds of candy.

This doesn't seem right, thought Maren, but as hard as she tried to remember why it wasn't right, her brain just wouldn't connect. Outside, trees with giant puffball tops floated by, and the sky was orange with green clouds. A baby elephant with butterfly wings flew past, waving its trunk. Hesitantly, Maren waved back.

"This field trip is awesome," said Amos, pulling a streamer down and biting a jelly bean off the paper.

"So awesome," said Maren, but something in the pit of her stomach told her it wasn't. Her backpack was strapped to her chest for some reason, and even though she couldn't remember what was inside, she knew it was important.

The bus turned down a long driveway and a huge blue-brick building came into view. The bushes in front had been pruned into fantastical topiaries, and the sign over the door read PINE RIDGE MUSEUM OF ART.

Something pinged in the back of Maren's mind when she looked at the sign. Some kind of connection, some subtle warning, but she couldn't make her brain focus. She just wanted to eat candy and bounce on her lovely inflatable couch. Beside her, Amos was busy stuffing his face with red licorice.

Her backpack squirmed, and she jolted.

"GENOU D'ELEPHANT," it said.

"Did you hear that?" she asked Amos. "My backpack is talking."

"Cool," said Amos, waving to a camel with bat wings that zoomed past their window.

The backpack wiggled again, and Maren unzipped the top a tiny bit to peer inside.

"LACHE-MOI!" yelled a horrible, croaking voice.

"Your backpack wants you to let it go," said Amos. "Probably because you're wearing it wrong."

"No, there's something inside." Maren was almost too afraid to touch the zipper again, but the wiggling had turned to thrashing, and she didn't want to keep whatever was in there inside any longer.

Zip.

A green rabbit's head poked out.

"MAREN PARTRIDGE IS A STAR-FART SKEETER!" it yelled.

Maren and Amos sat there blinking at the rabbit.

"A what?" Again, there was that tickly something bumping around in Maren's brain, but she couldn't quite grasp it.

The bunny cocked its head. "FIELD TRIP?"

"Yes, we're on a field trip," said Maren. "It's pretty cool, right?" It sounded like a rhetorical question, but she honestly hoped for some kind of confirmation that this was, in fact, cool.

"ZUT ALORS," said the rabbit, and then it dove back inside the bag.

"Guess it doesn't want to come out after all," said Amos.

The backpack started thrashing around again, and Maren almost dropped it, but then the bunny stuck its furry green head out. Clutched in its mouth was a tiny something that looked like a tea bag.

"MANGE ÇA," it croaked, dropping the item into Maren's hand.

Maren vaguely recognized the little sachet—it was important in some way, but every time she felt close to remembering why, her brain drifted to the candy, or the bouncy couch, or the orange sky outside. Or to that weird sensation that whatever was about to happen inside that museum was going to be *amazing*.

"It wants you to eat that," said Amos, wrinkling his nose in disgust.

Maren held the little packet up to her nose and got a whiff of spearmint and coffee and bacon. "It smells like minty breakfast."

"I don't think it's a good idea to eat stuff that rabbits give you," said Amos as a couch-sized crab wearing a top hat scuttled sideways past the bus, clapping its claws like castanets.

"You're probably right," said Maren, but she still wasn't sure.

"All right, campers, it's time to go inside!" The bus driver rose from her seat and turned to face the group, and Maren caught her breath, because something about the woman was surprising. She wore a long, midnight-colored robe dotted with silver stars, and her moon-white hair hung down to her waist. Though her face was creased with deep wrinkles, her eyes were a shocking shade of turquoise, so bright it felt like they gave off their own light.

"Whoa," whispered Amos, clearly awestruck too.

"There's a yellow bag on the floor for each of you," said the woman. "Make sure to take it before you exit the bus."

Maren's chest grew warm at the woman's words. All she wanted in the world was to make this dazzling person happy. She felt certain that whatever they were about to do was the exact, perfect, right thing to be doing. But as she started to reach for her bag, something sharp poked her cheek.

"Ouch," she said to the rabbit, which had climbed onto her shoulder and was trying to stick one of those funny little sachets into her mouth with its own mouth. "Ugh!"

"*Réveille-toi*," it whispered, jabbing more urgently.

"Cut it out," she hissed back. "Amos, can you help me here?"

"Sorry, I have to go," said Amos, who was already filing down the aisle with the other kids. "This is really important."

"I know!"

There was sudden, chaotic flurry of flying fur and aggressive bunny paws, and Maren fell backward. The rabbit wedged one of its feet on her nose and the other on her chin, and with a sharp shove, it popped her jaw open. Then Maren's mouth filled with a minty, coffee, bacony, slightly rubbery flavor, and everything around her began to melt and smear.

Blink.

She lay on a musty seat in an emptying school bus. The couches and streamers were gone, and everything smelled vaguely of feet. Henri—not a rabbit after all—stood on her chest, head cocked, watching intently with one beady black eye.

"Thanks for that," she muttered, rubbing her chin where his claw had made a scratch and feeling queasy. She remembered everything from the dream—Lishta's remedy must have counteracted whatever made Carmella's victims forget—but waking felt like coming up from a deep underwater dive very suddenly. A whine sounded in her left ear, and everything seemed slightly slanted.

"LE GARÇON," said Henri urgently.

Maren rubbed her eyes. "You know I don't understand French. Is the bus driver gone? I need to find Amos, but I want to let you go first."

"AMOS, GARÇON, OUI!" Henri hopped back and forth, then dove back into the bag and emerged triumphantly with a shiny silver safety pin.

"Good bird," said Maren. "I promise I'll buy you a whole package of those if we make it out of here in one piece."

Henri made a burbling, happy trill.

"Now can you please check if the bus driver is gone?" asked Maren.

Henri peeped over the top of the seat in front of them, then bobbed his head.

"Yes, she's gone, or yes, she's still here?" said Maren.

"AARRAAWWWKGONE!" yelled Henri. "ELLE EST PARTIE."

"Good," said Maren. "Now quickly, I'm going to open the window, and I want you to fly straight back to Gran-Gran."

"GRAN-GRAN-GRAN," yelled Henri.

"Tell her you know where we are, and tell her the new waking antidotes work," said Maren.

"MAREN IS IN THE STARLIGHT THEATER."

"No, don't tell her that. Tell her I'm at the"—she checked the sign on the building—"Pine Ridge Museum of Art. Pine Ridge must be the name of the town."

"TWINE BRIDGE," said Henri. "MAREN PAR-TRIDGE IS IN THE SWINE FRIDGE."

"Ugh." Maren rummaged in her bag, looking for another safety pin. "You know what? Just tell her to follow you and fly here. Do you think you can do that? Wait, do you know how to get back to camp?"

"ABSOLUMENT!" screeched Henri.

"I sure hope that means yes," said Maren, sliding the window open.

"AU REVOIR, STAR FART SKEETER," yelled Henri as he launched into the sky.

A wave of loneliness hit Maren as he disappeared. But there was no time to sit around feeling sorry for herself. She needed to find Amos and wake as many kids as she could with the few antidotes Henri had given her. She peeked at the seat behind her, but Thalia was gone. Maren hoped the dream-crafting instructor was here, sleepwalking like everybody else, and that Carmella hadn't thrown her off the bus.

After checking her phone for cell signal—there wasn't any—Maren zipped up her backpack and stuffed it into the big yellow bag, between a wrench and a pair of worryingly large bolt cutters. What was she supposed to do with these? More importantly, what would she have done with these if she hadn't woken up? A cold, jittery sensation filled her gut, and Maren felt certain that phase four was going to be very intense.

Thirty-Three

"Everyone, get in line!" Evan and a dark-haired girl from Hallie's bunk rounded up the sleepwalking campers, who were still as excited as ever. Peeking through her eyelashes, Maren was surprised that the museum was completely unchanged from how it had looked in her dream, and she wondered why. It must have been important for the campers to see it exactly as it was.

Thalia was nowhere to be found, but Amos stood admiring a giant bush in the shape of a boat. As quickly as she dared, Maren drifted across the parking lot, but a pair of leopard-print, high-heeled shoes stepped into her path. Now that Maren wasn't dreaming anymore, the midnight-robed, long-haired Sandwoman was gone, and Carmella was back to her usual animal-print self. Maren shut her eyes all the way and pasted a dreamy smile on her face.

"This place is amazing," she said, making her voice sparkle with enthusiasm.

"It certainly is." Carmella's voice carried a dangerous edge. "What color is the sky, Vesper?"

"It's, like, the most beautiful shade of orange." Maren tipped her chin upward but kept her eyes shut and her breathing deep and slow. At least Carmella still thought her name was Vesper. "Like the inside of a cantaloupe. And there are all these wispy green clouds. Green is my *favorite* color." She felt a finger under her chin and fought the urge to flinch. "Did you see that flying camel? So cool."

"Of course I did," crooned Carmella. "Now get in line with the others. And remember, the Sandwoman is watching you."

A shiver crawled over Maren's skin as she joined the line behind Amos. She wondered what kind of crime all these kids could possibly be expected to pull off inside a museum, of all places. How much money could there be to steal? And why the tools clunking around in these bags?

Squinting and wishing again for mirrored sunglasses, Maren peered at the posters in the museum's front windows.

JUNE 8–AUGUST 31
CLEO MONTCLAIR
ART IN MOTION

"Oh no, no, no," she whispered.

Dismantlement.

Those miniature replicas in the arts and crafts workshop had been a practice run. They were going to dismantle Cleo Montclair's actual sculptures. Hallie was going to have a heart attack when she found out. Maren already felt like she was having one herself.

"Psst," she whispered to Amos as the line lurched forward. "Amos!"

Amos turned, his mouth half open, and Maren shoved a waking antidote inside. "Gark!" he said, but Maren put her hand over his mouth before he could spit it out.

"Just keep walking," she whispered before letting go. "And don't open your eyes. It's me, Maren. Just do what I say."

His eyelids fluttered, but he kept them closed and kept his feet moving, and three seconds later, his shoulders hunched up and he snorted.

"Whoa, that was wild," he whispered. "Are you awake too?"

"Yes," said Maren. "But we need to pretend not to be. We can't get caught again."

"Hey, you two!" Evan the lifeguard sauntered down the line, whistle swinging around his neck. "What color is the sky?"

"Orange," said Maren and Amos at the same time.

Maren couldn't see Evan's face, but she felt the weight of his assessing gaze. "I don't want these two near each other," he said to someone else. "Judy, take this girl and go to the end of the line."

A rough hand grabbed Maren's elbow and she staggered sideways, her heavy bag sliding off her shoulder. "Sir, yes, sir," Judy muttered sarcastically, sounding nothing like her old bubbly self as she pulled Maren to the end of the line. "Who died and made *you* the boss?"

"Your hair looks amazing," offered Maren, gazing admiringly with her closed eyes.

"Really?" Judy's tone brightened. "That stupid unicorn onesie made it so frizzy. Ugh, I'm so glad to be done with that dreamy nonsense."

"Whoa, did you see that?" Maren pointed at the sky. She wanted to figure out how much of the collective dream Judy knew about, since she clearly wasn't dreaming along with them. "What *is* that thing?"

"I...uh...wow, I don't know," said Judy.

"It looks like a turkey in a hairnet smoking a cigar," said Maren.

"Errr...yeah?" said Judy.

"No, wait, that's definitely a pipe." Despite her crushing nerves, Maren was sort of enjoying this. "Do you think he knows that smoking is bad for you?"

"Of course he…" Judy scoffed. "Whatever. Just stop talking and keep walking."

Following the feet of the kid in front of her, Maren shuffled along until they reached the building.

"Welcome to the Pine Ridge Art Museum!" boomed a voice over the loudspeaker as she stepped inside the brightly lit, air-conditioned space. It smelled like floor polish and rubber and metal, and Maren's fingers itched to take samples to make a dream of this place, even though she'd barely had a chance to look at it.

"Come on through, Camp Shady Sands," said a man near the turnstiles. "You're all paid for."

Maren snuck a peek at his polished shoes and navy blue pants as she pushed through the turnstile. He might be a security guard, someone she could turn to for help. Or he might work for Carmella. It was hard to get a feel for anything when you couldn't open your eyes. If he did work for the museum, Maren reasoned, surely he must find it strange that a whole group full of kids had just walked in with their eyes closed.

"Hey Judy! Give me a hand!" called Evan, his voice echoing in what seemed to be a very large space.

Judy muttered a stream of insults under her breath, and Maren found herself agreeing with each one, though she couldn't believe *this* Judy was the same person who'd checked them in at camp.

"Stay with the group," Judy growled, then went back to help her fellow henchperson.

Once Judy's footsteps were far behind her, Maren opened her eyes. She stood in a high-ceilinged atrium with sunlight streaming through its glass ceiling. Hanging from the ceiling were huge birds made of metal and stained glass that cast rainbow-colored shadows onto the white floor. A gentle air-conditioned breeze made the birds sway and their shadows dance.

This actually was a pretty cool field trip. Too bad it was being run by a mind-manipulating criminal for some nefarious purpose. Again, Maren wondered where Thalia was, and she hoped Henri would hurry up and bring Lishta and hopefully her mother.

"Psst," said a headless statue holding a basket of grapes in the corner.

Maren squinted into the shadows.

"It's me," said the statue in Amos's voice, and then a hand stuck out from behind its leg and waved.

Now murmuring at a quiet volume, the campers were heading toward the back of the atrium. Maren drifted along with them, then broke off and dodged behind the statue.

"It's creepy how they seem normal, and then all of a sudden they all do the same thing at the same time," said Amos.

"That's all part of the plan." Maren shuddered. "They're heading for the Cleo Montclair sculptures." She pointed to a doorway at the back of the atrium, where the group had clustered underneath a sign for the special exhibition. "I'm pretty sure they're going to take them apart."

"Why?" said Amos.

Maren pondered. "Maybe to steal them?"

"Aren't those things huge, even if you take them apart?" said Amos. "They're not going to fit on our bus."

"There's probably more to the plan," said Maren. "We need to look for Thalia. And also see if Malvin and Calvin are here."

"Maybe they're already at the exhibition," said Amos. "What's your plan for the waking antidotes?"

"I don't know," said Maren. "I don't have enough for the whole group, and I need to save one for Thalia—if we can find her."

"Maybe wake the older kids first?" suggested Amos. "They'd probably be the most helpful if we need to overpower Carmella."

Maren chewed on her lip. "At least two of them are

working for her, though, and I don't know who else is pretending to sleepwalk."

"Good point."

"Maybe I'll try talking to the museum staff," said Maren.
"But sleepwalk-kidnapping is kind of a ridiculous concept for
people who don't know about dreams, and apparently they've
been expecting us."

"She must have called ahead and booked this like a normal
field trip," said Amos. "But it wouldn't hurt to try them. They
must be wondering why everybody's eyes are shut."

"Let's hope they don't work for Carmella," said Maren.
"I'll go ask them a few questions without giving anything
away, and we'll see what happens."

"And I'll go with the campers and look for Thalia and the
directors," said Amos.

"Sounds like a plan," said Maren. "I'll come find you."

Amos shuffled across the floor to join the stragglers at the
back of the group and then headed through the doorway. Once
they were gone, Maren doubled back toward the turnstiles.
Evan and Judy were gone, and she hadn't seen Carmella since
they got inside, so she didn't bother to close her eyes.

The guard who had welcomed her to the museum turned
out to be a gray-haired, barrel-chested man. He was kneeling
by the entrance, tying the lace of his shiny shoe.

"Excuse me," said Maren.

"Yes?" he said, concentrating on his lace, which he was busy twisting into a double knot.

"I was just wondering…" Maren had no idea how to casually broach the subject of dreams or sleepwalking with a total stranger. Usually people came to her shop to ask about that stuff if they were interested. The man tugged and twisted and then tied another knot in his lace, which seemed like a lot of knots for one shoe.

"Yes?" He finally looked up, and Maren's hopes fell all the way down to her own shoes.

The security guard's eyes were firmly shut.

She let her breath out in a long whoosh. "Never mind," she said, heading for the ticket windows. But every single employee behind the glass panes looked the same: closed eyes, half-open mouth, gentle breathing. Carmella moved fast.

"Can I use your phone please?" Maren asked a lady with mousy hair and a pen tucked behind her ear.

"Phones are all broken," said the woman, her words as flat as her hair.

"It's an emergency," said Maren. "Can I just try?"

With a closed-eyed shrug, the woman stuck the receiver of her desk phone through the gap under the ticket window, and Maren leaned forward to listen for the dial tone. There was none. "Does your cell phone work?" she asked.

"No signal here," intoned the woman. "Greenleaf Valley is a cell service dead zone."

Maren fingered the waking antidotes in her pocket. She wasn't sure it was worth wasting them on people who might not believe her anyway. Better to save them for people she was sure would help, like Thalia. And possibly herself, if she got put under again.

Her heartbeat ratcheting up, Maren jogged through the rainbow shadows on the floor. "Hurry up, Henri," she whispered at the sky beyond the windows, hoping he'd made it back already and was telling Lishta everything. It would take a minor miracle for him to relay all that information correctly, but hope was the only thing keeping Maren going, and she clung to it.

The doorway led to a hall lined with paintings, and from somewhere at the end, Maren heard clanging and crunching and grating. Her stomach turned. The campers were using their tools already. THIS WAY TO CLEO MONTCLAIR, said a sign, and everything was coming together, but in a way that Maren still didn't quite understand, which made her feel even sicker. As she dashed down the corridor, the clanging and crunching grew louder. At the end, she paused, composed her face into a sleeping expression, and took a deep breath before rounding the corner.

"Whoa, whoa! Don't let that fall," called Evan. Maren snuck a peek and tripped over her own foot. The gleaming space was even bigger than the atrium. Scattered all through the space were Cleo Montclair's minivan-sized abstract sculptures. Maren even spotted the real George, his springy metal tentacles wafting back and forth, and she felt a pang of guilt for what she'd done to the tiny version of him.

About half of the sleepwalking campers, including Emma and Anika, were climbing all over the sculptures, using their tools to loosen and remove the smaller pieces and adding them to large bins. The rest of the kids were fanning out and moving to other areas of the museum, tapping away at security PIN pads on the walls, or—Maren gulped—operating machinery. In the center of the room, a tall crane lifted a wooden pyramid off the top of what looked like a dog's body with steamroller wheels instead of legs. Maren *really* hoped it wasn't Amos inside that crane.

"Everybody out of the way!" called a black-haired girl as a garage door at the back of the atrium rumbled open, allowing two more trucks to roll inside. For a long moment, Maren just stood there, speechless. Phase four was absolutely breathtaking in its sheer audacity. It was so far beyond Maren's imagination that it felt like a dream.

"Let the truck through!" yelled Judy, and the sleepwalkers shuffled out of the way. The driver wore a baseball cap slung low over her eyes and a pair of mirrored sunglasses. Pulling a heavy, oil-stained wrench from her yellow bag, Maren drifted over to the closest sculpture, an upside-down purple umbrella that gently opened and closed. The closer she got, the faster it opened and shut, responding to her fear, and she forced herself to breathe slowly and unclench her jaw. It didn't help.

Kids began loading various sculpture parts into the back of the truck, and Maren inched closer to the passenger side. The driver was busy tapping something into a phone.

"Thalia?" Maren whispered, rapping gently on the window.

The driver's head snapped up, and as her mirrored eyes made contact with Maren's, her mouth fell open.

It wasn't Thalia. It was Ivy.

Thirty-Four

IVY JAMMED THE TRUCK INTO gear, and as it jolted forward, Maren yanked the door open and threw herself inside. She rolled into the footwell as Ivy slammed on the brake.

"You can't drive like that in here," Maren hissed. "You'll hit somebody!"

"I know," Ivy hissed back. "What are you doing?"

"I could ask you the same question." Part of Maren wanted to hug Ivy, and part of her wanted to scream at this liar who'd pretended to be her friend and was now driving a sculpture-stealing truck.

"Hang on, we're not done loading!" yelled somebody from the back of the truck.

"That's enough for now," called Ivy. "Close it up!" She turned to Maren. "Are you awake?"

"Yes."

Ivy let out an incredulous laugh. "Stay down there, okay? I'm going to drive out of the building."

"Are you bringing me to your grandma?" asked Maren.

Ivy snorted. "No way. I have no idea what's going on right now, but this is bananas."

The tension in Maren's body eased by a fraction. "Do you know how to drive?"

"Sort of," said Ivy, fumbling with the gearshift. "I've played a bunch of driving games and it's not that much different." She let out the clutch while shifting, and the truck made a hideous grinding sound.

"But what…"

"Shh!" Ivy waved frantically for Maren to get down lower. "Do *not* make a sound or move," she hissed through smiling, clenched teeth as she waved to someone outside the truck.

"Ow!" whispered Maren as her yellow bag shifted and something cracked against her shin.

The truck's gears made another grinding screech, and Maren's teeth ached at the sound. Then she heard the whooshing, rolling sound of a garage door shutting behind them, and sunlight flooded the truck. The wheels bumped down over a curb.

"Hang on one more second," said Ivy. They turned right,

then left, and finally shadows and cool air filled the truck as Ivy cut the engine. "You can come out now."

Maren crawled onto the passenger seat and blinked at their surroundings. They were parked in the shade of a white eighteen-wheeler truck.

"Do you know where—" she started, but Ivy spoke at the same time.

"I have to get out of here in about three seconds, so we either need to talk very fast or you need to come with me."

"Where are you going?" asked Maren.

"I'm driving to the nearest town to find a police station," said Ivy. "I've tried calling 911 a million times, but there's no signal."

"I know," said Maren. "But wait, why are you here if you're not helping?"

Ivy gritted her teeth. "My grandma thinks I'm helping. But I'm not. Can you believe she didn't tell me about any of this until today?"

"I mean, I can't believe she's doing any of this," said Maren. "But that must have been quite a shock."

"I knew she was up to something," said Ivy. "I've heard stories about the stuff she used do to before I was born, but she swore to me and my mom that she was done with crime."

Maren laughed at the idea of anyone's grandma swearing off crime, but Ivy grimaced.

"Sorry," said Maren. "It's not funny."

"No, *I'm* sorry," said Ivy. "I've been running around trying to figure out her plan—trying to undo everything without her knowing—but she's been one step ahead of me the whole time. When I found out you were also trying to help, I should have told you the truth, but I didn't want my grandma to get in trouble. I just…" Ivy dropped her head into her hands. "I thought I could fix everything myself."

Maren nodded, remembering the blackmailing disaster with Obscura Gray, when she'd also been too scared to ask for help. "I understand your situation better than you think."

Ivy looked up, her eyes shining with tears. "Really?"

"Yeah," said Maren. "It's a long story that I'll tell you some other time."

"So will you come with me to the police?" said Ivy.

Maren shook her head. "I can't find Amos, and I'm afraid to leave him. And hopefully my grandmother and my sister are on their way. And maybe my mom."

"Wish mine was." Ivy's voice was full of such dejected longing that it made Maren's chest ache.

"Why don't you wait here with me?" said Maren. "It's got to be safer than taking this truck out on the road. I'll pretend to sleepwalk and you can pretend you're still going along with your grandma's plan, and when my family gets here, we'll fix everything." Her words sounded a lot more certain than she actually felt, but people always said confidence was half the battle, so she tried to believe herself. "How much of your grandma's plan do you know?"

"Not as much as I *should* know," scoffed Ivy. "All she told me is that we're borrowing these sculptures and we'll give them back when we're done."

"Borrowing?" Maren tapped her foot on the yellow bag: *clunk clunk clunk.* "What's the point if she's not selling them to make money? But how could she even sell something that big and not get caught?"

"She won't tell me," said Ivy bitterly.

"How does she make people sleepwalk?" asked Maren. "And how are all of the kids dreaming at the same time like this?"

"That's one of the things I've been trying to figure out," said Ivy. "I know she has sand magic."

"Hence the Sandwoman title," said Maren.

"The what?" Ivy blinked at her.

"The Sandwoman," said Maren. "Don't you know that's what everybody calls your grandmother?"

"But why would—" Ivy stopped. "Oh, with the sand and the sleeping, duh! Anyway, yeah, she can put people to sleep and make them do stuff, sort of like puppets. If I were giving her a name, it'd be the Puppeteer."

Maren laughed. "That doesn't sound quite as mystical and dangerous as the Sandwoman."

Ivy laughed too. "Fair point. Anyway, I'm pretty sure she's been experimenting with mixing her sand into dreams at the camp. At first when people couldn't wake up, I thought it was a random mistake with the dosage of whatever's in the dreams, like I said to you, but then I caught her actually cutting open those little packets."

"Sachets," said Maren.

Ivy's eyes narrowed. "How do you know so much about dreams, by the way? And where did you get those wake-up thingies?"

"My family owns a—"

Tap tap tap.

It came from the other side of Maren's window. Both girls hissed in their breath as a knobby-knuckled hand with gold fingernails did a creepy little wave.

"Oh no," whispered Maren, and Ivy whispered her own, ruder version as Carmella's makeup-coated, smirking face rose into view. The door swung open, and Maren wanted to run, but her escape route was blocked. Ivy sat frozen in the driver's seat as her grandmother's clawlike fingers closed around Maren's ankle.

"Hello, Maren Partridge," she said.

Thirty-Five

"Ivy, give me the keys." Carmella's voice was ice.

Ivy looked at Maren, who mouthed, "*Go along with her.*"
With an almost imperceptible nod, Ivy pulled the keys from
the ignition.

"I found this girl awake," she said, her voice steady. "I told
her to get in the truck so I could take her to you."

The old woman's eyes narrowed. "It's quite a coincidence
that Maren has somehow woken up twice now."

"How do you know my name?" asked Maren, clutching
the seat and resisting the urge to kick the woman.

Carmella's laugh was just as brash and hearty as ever.
"Your friend talks in his sleep."

Maren froze.

"Why don't you come out and we'll have a little chat,"

said Carmella, stepping back and gesturing for Maren to follow. "Not you, Ivy."

Ivy seemed about to respond, then clamped her lips together.

"Where is Amos?" asked Maren as she climbed slowly out of the truck.

"With the other children," said Carmella. "He's a good little helper when properly motivated."

"You mean when you've mind-controlled him," said Maren, hoping again that Amos wasn't operating that crane but suspecting he probably was.

Carmella shrugged, a smile playing across her frosty pink lips. "I'm sure you'll be a good little helper too."

Nerves fluttered like moths in Maren's chest. "What did he tell you about me?" she asked, easing away from the truck.

"That you're from Rockpool Bay and you work at a dream shop with your grandmother," said Carmella, and Maren's stomach plummeted. "I should've known something was up when you and your sister kept asking me those silly questions about my dreams. You were feeling me out, weren't you?"

"I've heard of that dream shop in Rockpool Bay," said Ivy.

"Well, I haven't," snapped Carmella, waving a hand dismissively. "So it can't be that good."

"They sell nightmares too," said Ivy.

Her grandmother's mocking sneer faded, and her eyes flickered with interest. "Is that so?"

Maren clenched her jaw. "We used to, but not anymore."

"You're shadier than I thought." Carmella drifted closer, and Maren shrank back against the side of the truck. *So are you*, she thought. *Way shadier.*

"I'm not making any nightmares for you," she said, and Carmella roared with laughter.

"Darling, I don't *need* nightmares. I catch more flies with honey."

Maren's relief vanished as she pictured a huge jar of honey swarming with flies. She thought of all those campers crawling over the sculptures like insects, and her stomach flip-flopped.

"Are you going to make everybody do your dirty work and then take the fall for you?" she asked. "Like you did with the bank robbers?"

"So you *do* know who I am." Carmella's bony chest puffed out a little. "Once I've got all the things I need, they'll get back on their little bus and go back to their little camp, and then they'll wake up in their little beds with no memory of ever coming here."

Maren swallowed, realizing she wasn't included in this plan. "Why are you borrowing the sculptures?"

Carmella's eyes shot daggers at Ivy, who flinched. "That's none of your business, little mouse."

Hurry up, Gran-Gran, Maren thought as forcefully and telepathically as she could.

"It's time for you to join your friend now," said Carmella, reaching into the pocket of her cheetah-print dress and pulling out a velvet drawstring pouch. Maren took another step backward and bumped into the truck. She was trapped.

"Look at your watch," whispered Ivy.

"What?" whispered Maren.

Carmella took a pinch of something from the velvet bag and held it to her lips, and as she blew, a silvery cloud came sparkling out.

"No!" Maren spun sideways and shoved off the truck, but the cloud swirled and swallowed her up. She covered her mouth with one hand and swatted the fog with the other, but she could feel the gritty grains of sand filling her nostrils and wafting down her throat.

Hurry up, Gran-Gran! was her last lucid thought before slipping under.

Thirty-Six

MAREN WAS BACK IN THE art museum, staring at the most beautiful, magnificent showcase of sculptures she'd ever seen. The ceiling was miles away, higher than the pink clouds floating overhead. The floor was paved in gold and silver mosaic, and a dazzling rainbow arced from the tips of Maren's shoes all the way to a huge, lumpy orange sphere with half a face and tendril-like coils that waved gently back and forth.

George, thought Maren, though she couldn't remember why it had that name. She tested the rainbow with her left toe. It was solid. With a giddy laugh, she stepped onto it with both feet. It bounced in the most soothing, rubbery way, and the colors swirled around her ankles, letting out a fruity scent. Hefting her yellow bag over one shoulder, Maren ran up the rainbow and then sat and slid down the other side, landing on top of George.

"That was amazing!" she called down to a girl using a wrench to remove the bolts that attached George to the floor.

The girl nodded, and then sang, "Take me out to the ball game."

"Take me out with the crowd," Maren sang back.

To her left, kids swarmed all over the umbrella sculpture, which was still slowly opening and closing. Another sculpture, a toaster with spider legs, lay on its back while campers detached its appendages. But Maren somehow knew that the umbrella and the toaster weren't her responsibility. George was the only thing in the world she wanted to work on.

Look at your watch, whispered a voice from the deepest depths of her mind.

My watch? Maren thought. How strange. She never wore a watch.

"Can you help me?" called the girl on the floor. "This bolt is stuck."

Maren jumped down and pulled a huge wrench from her bag. "Let's try mine." She fitted the wrench onto the bolt, and both girls grabbed hold of its long arm, straining and tugging. As she pulled, Maren's heart filled with longing. The only thing she wanted in the whole world was to free this beautiful sculpture from its prison.

Look at your watch. The voice was familiar somehow, but Maren couldn't place it. Was it a friend? Someone she'd recently met?

With a rusty crunch, the bolt let go, and Maren and the girl tumbled backward, landing in a laughing heap.

"Amazing!" shouted the girl, untangling her legs from Maren's. "Let's get the next one!"

"So amazing," said Maren, but she couldn't stop hearing that voice. *Look at your watch.* "I don't wear a watch," she muttered, but she looked at her wrist anyway.

To her utter shock, there was a watch. A gold contraption with a purple strap and an iridescent blue face.

"Whoa," she whispered, holding it closer. The second hand twirled in the opposite direction from the minute hand, which seemed wrong, but Maren couldn't remember why. She tried to read the numbers, but they started at 7 and skipped to 23, then 11, and the 8 kept changing into 18 and back again.

Then she remembered Ivy's tips for lucid dreaming. This was a reality check. And that wasn't a real-life watch.

"I'm dreaming," whispered Maren.

"What?" said the girl, straining to remove the next bolt.

Maren blinked, and the ceiling was back to its normal

height, the rainbow was gone, and the floor was plain white. The sculptures, the trucks, the machinery, and the campers were all still there. "I was dreaming," she said. "You're *still* dreaming."

The girl laughed. "What are you talking about?"

Maren checked her pocket—her last waking antidote was gone. "I'll be right back," she said.

"The Sandwoman is watching!" called the girl as Maren jogged away and veered down the hall.

The atrium was empty, the stained glass birds gently drifting overhead. There were no campers, no museum visitors, no staff at the turnstiles or the ticket windows. No Henri or Lishta or Hallie here to save them. No Amos. Maren froze. She'd forgotten to look for Amos back at the exhibition.

Outside, the sun beamed off the parked cars, and Maren edged closer to the doors. Maybe it was better to wait out there, away from Carmella and her treacherous sand clouds. Maren could hide in the woods beyond the parking lot, keep an eye on the museum, and make sure Amos got back on the bus with Anika, Emma, and the other campers. Then once everyone was gone, she'd walk to a main road and flag down a car. Someone was bound to help a girl all by herself.

Shivering, Maren looked at her wrist, but there was no watch. Not dreaming. She headed for the turnstiles at a speed-walk pace, and no one yelled for her to stop.

Maren's speed walk turned into a jog. Her jog became a run, then a sprint, the slap of her slippers echoing through the open space. Slowing just long enough to shove through the turnstile, she raced for the glass doors, which whooshed open to the parking lot. Maren shielded her eyes against the dazzling sun.

It seemed strange that Carmella would just let her escape like this, but she didn't have time to think why. She just needed to run. Heart pounding, she wove and darted through the parked cars. The forest loomed closer, filled with birdsong and the faint smell of pine.

The window of a car rolled down, and a puff of what looked like cigarette smoke wafted out. Maren veered left, but the cloud doubled in size, then tripled. She stumbled and banged her hip on an SUV's bumper, then whirled around and ran in the other direction. The forest was so incredibly close, she could almost reach out and touch the leaves with her fingertips.

But the cloud was faster than she was.

"Amos!" Maren yelled as cold sweat flooded every inch of her skin. "Gran-Gran! Henri!"

The world around her started to drip like an ice cream cone in July sunshine.

Thirty-Seven

SHE FELL ONTO HER HANDS and knees in a dark, echoing place. Behind her, there came a rolling rumble, a familiar sound she couldn't place. By the time she realized it was the back of a truck closing, the door had crashed shut. The engine roared to life, and she was thrown backward as the vehicle shifted into gear.

This was very, very bad. Maren swallowed a sour mouthful of panic and steadied herself against the wall as the truck picked up speed. She tried to step forward and banged her shin on something metal. Crouching low, she swept her hands around until she found the top of whatever it was, then climbed over. Slowly, she made her way through an invisible obstacle course of rolling and shifting sculpture parts until she reached the front of the compartment.

"Hello?" she called, tapping on the wall.

A little screened window slid open and a shard of light pierced the darkness.

"Hello, little mouse," said Carmella.

"Am I still dreaming?" asked Maren.

"What do you think?"

Maren pinched her check, then held her wrist up to the shard of light. No watch.

"Awake?" said Maren.

"Bingo."

Maren's relief at being firmly back in reality was quickly replaced by a bolt of fear. "Where are we going?"

"To my compound," said Carmella.

Maren gulped. A compound was more than just a house or even a mansion. It was right up there with evil lairs.

"Where are the other campers?" she asked, fighting to keep her voice calm.

"On their way back to camp," said Carmella. "They'll all sleep like babies tonight after their *amazing* trip to the museum. Unfortunately, you and your curly-haired friend know who I am, so I can't send you back with them."

"Where is Amos?" Maren's heart leapt into her throat.

"He's perfectly fine, don't worry," said Carmella. "You'll see him soon."

Maren prayed that Henri and her family had made it to

the museum by now. But even if they were there, how could they know that Maren was in a truck now, heading someplace else? Her foot tapped a nervous rhythm on the gritty floor.

Carmella spoke in a low voice to someone else in the truck. Maren pressed her eye to the tiny window, but all she could see was gray highway and trees out the truck's windshield. With a sudden *thwack*, something hit the screen and she tumbled backward.

"Sit down or I'll shut this," snapped Carmella.

"Okay." Maren eased herself down on something flat and relatively stable. "I'm sitting."

"Good girl. You'll catch more flies with honey too."

The last thing Maren wanted was flies. "Why are you doing all of this? Why borrow a bunch of sculptures?"

"I've got some fun experiments planned," said Carmella.

The truck rolled over a bump, and then its wheels ground and juddered. They were on a dirt road—a badly maintained one, judging by all the jolting and rocking.

"Like science experiments?" said Maren.

"You could say that," said Carmella.

"Since when are you into science? Or even art?" Ivy sounded crabby and tired, but Maren's heart leapt at the sound of her friend's voice. She wanted to peek through that opening again to see her face, but knew she'd get in trouble if she did.

"I've always been fascinated by some kinds of science," said Carmella. "Like the science of sleep."

"Why would you care about science when you've got magic?" grumbled Ivy.

"I've been doing all kinds of experiments this week," said her grandmother. "Mixing and matching my sleeping sand with those dreams. Testing things like food cravings and songs to see how long I could make them last after people woke up. The results have been absolutely fascinating. The dreams are a perfect amplifier. Normally my sand wears off faster and I have to blow more, but the dreams extend it for hours, and I have so much more control over what the sleepwalkers are seeing. Even better, I can coordinate large groups of them all at once!"

"Those kids aren't your guinea pigs!" snapped Ivy.

"That's right," whispered Maren.

"What they don't know won't hurt them," said Carmella.

"They just robbed a museum!" Maren couldn't hold back the words. "That's a serious crime!"

Carmella laughed. "They're children. Nobody's gonna blame them for being brainwashed at a dream camp run by a couple of criminals."

"Malvin and Calvin?" Maren sat up straighter. She wondered how anybody with a criminal record was possibly allowed to run a summer camp.

The truck slowed and turned another corner. Gravel and rocks clattered against the undercarriage as they picked up speed again.

"You mean Chad and Trevor snorted Carmella. "They've been in trouble with the law in some way or another since before you were born."

"Are they actually that goofy in real life?" Maren couldn't help asking.

"Even worse," said Carmella. "Thankfully, they're on a one-way plane ride to Paraguay as we speak. So while the police are busy tracking them down, I'll have plenty of time to finish up my final experiments, execute my plan, and disappear."

Goose bumps broke out on Maren's arms. "What's your plan?"

"I'm going to make those sculptures sleepwalk." Carmella's voice dripped with arrogant glee.

Maren almost fell off her perch. In the front seat, Ivy made an explosive spraying sound like she'd just spit out water.

"Wipe that up," snapped Carmella.

"How are you going to do that?" said Maren. "They don't have brains."

"Of course they don't have brains," said Carmella. "But they've got something in them that responds to feelings." The truck barreled around a corner that sent Maren tumbling.

"A consciousness, if you will. Very low level, nothing like a person, but if I can strengthen that consciousness with dreams, it should be just enough for my magic to work."

Maren rubbed her elbow where she'd banged it. This was the most far-fetched thing she'd ever heard. "But why are you doing this? Why not just get sleepwalkers to steal you more money? It's not like you can resell those sculptures without someone finding out."

"Because it's not money that I want," said Carmella. "Well, it's not *only* money that I want."

Ivy muttered something Maren couldn't make out, and Carmella slammed on the brakes, throwing Maren off her perch again.

"Excuse me, young lady?" said Carmella. "You're thirteen years old. You've got your entire life ahead of you. I've got twenty more years if I'm lucky, and nobody knows who I am. I want to leave a mark on this planet after I'm gone. I want people to tell stories about me."

"My grandmother told me a story about you," said Maren.

"Ah, but your grandmother is in the dream business," said Carmella. "I want normal people to know who I am too."

Maren bristled at the insinuation that her family was not normal, but it was technically accurate. "So, what's your plan? You get the sculptures to put on a big show so that everybody pays attention to you?" With a shudder, she thought of Obscura Gray's Shadow Show and hoped Carmella didn't have similar ideas.

The old woman roared with laughter and the truck fishtailed, skidding for a few sickening seconds before straightening out.

"A show, yes, that's a good way to put it—but not the kind of show you're thinking of. And that's all I'm going to say for now. You'll find out soon enough."

Maren's throat went paper dry. Suddenly the truck careened left, and she toppled in the other direction, hitting her forehead with a sickening clunk as the vehicle came to an abrupt stop.

"We're here," announced Carmella.

Thirty-Eight

THE TRUCK'S HEAVY DOOR RUMBLED open, and Maren blinked in the blinding light. Her forehead throbbed, and she felt carsick. From somewhere in the distance came the beeping sound of vehicles reversing and machinery clanging. In front of her stood a tall white fence that stretched far in both directions.

"What are you—" she began, before catching sight of the velvet pouch in Carmella's hand. "No, please don't!"

A silver cloud filled the truck. Maren tried to run out, but she kept tripping over the sculpture parts littering the floor. A papery taste hit her tongue, and then everything twisted and warped. A red door appeared in the center of the fence and swung open. Maren did not want to go through that door, but her feet were shuffling toward it all on their own.

Carmella's hearty laugh echoed around her, and Maren felt like she was tumbling through silvery fog as her brain let go of the threads of reality. Slowly, her feet took her closer to the red door.

"Have fun, little mouse!" Someone gave Maren a shove that sent her sprawling through the red door, which slammed shut behind her. She clambered to her feet, which immediately started shuffling forward again, and her jaw fell open.

Before her stood a rocket ship, gleaming blue in the fading afternoon light. But this wasn't any ordinary rocket ship. It had a column of rainbow-colored eyes running down its center, swiveling and blinking, and at its base were two chicken feet. As she stared up at the sculpture, Maren felt all her anger and fear start to ebb. This was the weirdest and coolest thing she had ever seen. She wanted to touch it. Her feet shuffled closer.

"Hey!" called a mustached man wearing paint-spattered coveralls and a headlamp. "Come give me a hand."

Maren glanced behind her, wondering who he was talking to, but there was nobody else there. The red door she'd tumbled through was gone, replaced by blank, white fence. She wondered what would happen if she ran back through that spot, but she didn't want to go anywhere. She really, really wanted to help the man in coveralls with whatever he needed.

That didn't seem right, though. She *should* be angry and

afraid, for some reason she could no longer remember. As she approached the man, he switched on his headlamp, picked up a pair of hedge trimmers, and began clipping the toenails of one of the rocket's chicken feet. Maren's lips turned up into a giant smile. It felt lovely, deep inside her heart, to help this man. She couldn't think of anything she'd rather be doing. And somehow, she knew exactly what to do.

Look at your watch.

Humming to herself, Maren picked up a rag from a bucket and began to wipe the side of the rocket, which was covered in black scuff marks.

Look at your watch.

"What watch?" she muttered. But when she looked at her wrist, there it was, bright orange with lime-green polka dots. As Maren peered at the spinning dials, they dissolved and the watch disappeared. Her mouth filled with sour nausea. But in seconds the nausea was gone, and she couldn't remember why she was just standing there, not helping, when that nice man in the coveralls needed help. She picked up the rag she'd dropped and resumed her polishing.

"I won't do it!" screamed a woman's voice from somewhere in the distance.

Maren paused again. There was someone she was supposed to be looking for, but it wasn't a woman.

"Don't worry about that." The man handed Maren a spray bottle, and her mouth stretched into that painfully wide smile again. Of course she wasn't worrying. She enjoyed the feeling of the sleek metal beneath her rag. The cleaning spray smelled like lemons, which reminded her of something lovely…

…of someone lovely…

…of feeling loved…

"Gran-Gran," whispered Maren. Her foot did a nervous shuffle-tap as she moved to the back of the rocket ship.

Look at your… What was it? Elbow? Shoe? Maren tried both and nothing happened.

"You can't do this!" yelled the woman again. "Let me go!"

"Who is that? And why are they so upset?" A vague inkling told Maren that she should also be upset, but she couldn't think why.

"It's nothing to trouble yourself with." As the man looked up, his headlamp beamed into Maren's eyes, making her wince but also shifting everything into a different focus. For a few seconds, he didn't have a mustache.

"Will she be okay?" stammered Maren, trying to catch that dazzling light again. But the man was busy clipping the other chicken foot now, his mustache firmly planted on his upper lip.

"You'd better keep cleaning," he said. "The Sandwoman is always watching."

Maren felt like a hundred spiders were crawling all over her. She tapped her toe once, twice, three times. It listened.

Shuffle ball change stamp, shuffle ball change stamp.

The painful, fake smile dropped off her face.

I'm dreaming.

Her eyes tried to snap all the way open, but she only allowed herself to peek through her lashes. "Where's the bathroom?" she asked, setting her rag in the bucket.

The space around her shimmered as lucidity took hold, and a building appeared on the other side of the rocket ship. It was a simple, two-story white building with a blue door. It looked like a back door, rather than a front door.

The man looked up from his clipping, and Maren forced the smile back on her face and shut her eyes all the way.

"Down the hall, third door on the right." He gestured with his chin at the blue door. "Come straight back. Remember—"

"The Sandwoman is always watching," droned Maren. She walked as slowly and dreamily as possible to the door and slipped inside.

"Get away from me!" yelled the woman, closer now. "You'll never pull this off. It's absolutely absurd."

Maren stood in a dimly lit hall. The yelling was coming from behind a half-open door near the end. She shrank against the wall and slid closer.

"Of course I'm going to pull it off." Carmella's voice, low and amused.

"They're sculptures!" said the other woman. "They don't have brains! Or even mouths to put the dreams in."

"I think there's another way to give them dreams," said Carmella, "and I think you're going to tell me what it is."

There are *other ways*, thought Maren, remembering the time the nightmares had soaked through Amos's backpack and saturated them both in horrible visions. She reached the door and paused. Inside the room, some sort of scuffle was happening. Very carefully, Maren peered around the edge of the door and saw a kitchen. A middle-aged woman with red glasses stood on a table, brandishing a rolling pin. Maren would have bet money that it was the same woman Amos had seen delivering the Moonbeam Illusions boxes to the camp.

"I won't tell you a thing!" spat the woman, lunging and jabbing with her baking tool. The table wobbled, and she nearly fell.

Carmella rolled her eyes. "Get down before you hurt yourself, darlin'."

"I can't believe I thought I was *helping* you out with your brand-new camp," said the woman.

"I paid you ten times your usual price," scoffed Carmella. "Who was helping who?"

"Whom!" yelled the woman.

Carmella paused. "Excuse me?"

"Who was helping whom!" The woman's cheeks were almost as red as her glasses now.

Carmella gave a trumpet blare of a laugh as she pulled out her velvet pouch, and Maren backed away, covering her mouth and nose. She held her breath until stars swam in her vision, then pulled her shirt up over her mouth and took a careful breath through the fabric. Reality stayed put.

"Now, let's try this again." Carmella's tone was as sweet as a lollipop. "Come on down from there."

A soft thump. Maren didn't dare look inside the kitchen, in case the silvery sand cloud was still present.

"That's right," said Carmella. "Now tell me, Pam, can you give someone a dream without putting it in their mouth?"

"Of course you can," said Pam in an empty monotone. "Just get the sachets wet and put them anywhere on their skin. They'll absorb right through."

Maren wondered if metal could absorb dreams in the same way as skin. Not all of the sculptures were completely metal, though. Some had paper or wood or fabric parts. That would definitely absorb things.

"Perfect," said Carmella. "Now was that so hard?"

"No, it was very easy," droned Pam. "I just want to help you."

"I know you do, sweetheart," said Carmella. "Now why don't you go help clean the sculptures for a while? We want them to look beautiful for their big day."

Maren shuddered, trying to imagine what could possibly be happening on their big day.

"That sounds great," intoned Pam. "Thank you so much."

Inside the kitchen, feet shuffled closer. Maren leapt backward into the hall and just managed to dive through one of the other doors before poor, sleepwalking Pam emerged. Pushing the door almost all the way shut, Maren peeked through the crack as the woman shambled down the hall, humming softly to herself.

"Psst!" Someone tapped Maren's shoulder, and she clamped both hands over her mouth to keep from screaming before whirling around. She was in a storeroom full of boxes, and in front of her stood a twitchy-looking Ivy.

"Are you awake?" asked Ivy, and when Maren nodded, she pulled her into a hug. "I am so, so sorry about what's happening right now."

"It's…okay," Part of Maren still wanted to blame Ivy for not telling anyone her grandmother was up to something terrible, but part of her understood why she hadn't. "But why is your grandmother planning to make the sculptures sleepwalk? What's the big plan?"

"She still won't tell me." Ivy kicked a box. "I'm pretending I don't care, but I'm so mad I want to burn this place down."

Maren contemplated setting a fire. It'd be a quick way to get rid of the dreams—the boxes would go up in a flash—but there was no telling how many sleepwalkers were in Carmella's compound. It might be impossible to get them all to evacuate. It also seemed cruel to burn Cleo Montclair's sculptures. What if they could feel pain?

"Have you seen Amos anywhere?" she asked.

"Yeah, he's around. Sleepwalking, but safe." Ivy said.

"Who are all these people?" Maren pressed her face to the crack again, but the hall was empty. She needed to get back before that mustached man wondered where she'd gone. "They're not all sleepwalking, are they? Some of them are helping her on purpose."

"I have no idea who they are, and I can't believe she's been hiding all of this from me and my mom." Ivy slumped against the wall. "Why, why, why didn't I tell anybody about this when I had the chance?"

"And why, why, why did your mom let you stay with her for the summer?" muttered Maren.

Ivy looked a little green. "Because she has nobody else to help."

"I'm sorry," said Maren. "That was really insensitive."

Ivy waved her off. "It completely stinks, but you're right. She definitely shouldn't be allowed to watch kids. Anyway, I'm going to fix this, so don't worry. I mean, you can worry a little bit." She let out a shaky laugh. "But at soon as it gets dark, I'm going to steal a truck and go for help."

"This time I'll come with you," said Maren. "And Amos too, if we can find him."

Ivy nodded. "I still have those waking thingies you gave me. I stuffed them full of spearmint."

"I'm so glad you kept them," said Maren as Ivy dug around in her pocket and pulled out two sachets and a small wad of lint.

"They seemed really important, even though you wouldn't tell me exactly who you were or why you had them." Ivy gave Maren a cringey smile. "Which was fair, considering. Here, take them."

"You keep one for yourself," said Maren, but Ivy shook her head. "Oh right, the dreams don't work on you. Does that mean your grandmother's sleeping sand doesn't work either?"

"Nope. Thank God."

Maren paused. "Do you have…sand magic like her?"

"I wish," said Ivy. "When I blow on that stuff, it just turns purple and does nothing."

"Hmm," said Maren. "Sounds like you haven't quite figured out your magic yet."

"Or maybe my magic is literally just changing the color of one very specific thing." Ivy sighed.

"Hey, little girl? Are you still in there?" Maren jolted. It was the sometimes-mustached man, knocking on a door across the hall.

"I have to go," she whispered. "Take one of these antidotes in case you run into Amos, okay?"

"Okay," said Ivy. "And tonight after everybody's in bed, I'll steal the keys to one of the trucks. When you hear somebody whistling…um…'Row, Row, Row Your Boat,' that's your cue to sneak out."

Maren snorted. "Of all the songs in the world, *that's* the one you're picking?"

"Who cares what the song is?" said Ivy. "At least it's not 'Take Me Out to the Ball Game.'"

Maren had to agree with that.

"When you hear it, meet me here," said Ivy. "Got it?"

"Got it." Giving Ivy a quick thumbs-up, Maren stepped out into the hall, her eyes mostly shut.

"What were you doing in there?" said the sometimes-mustached man.

"I was trying to find my way back from the bathroom." Maren made her words as sluggish as a sloth. "But these doors all look the same, and there's pink bunnies all over the floor."

The man glanced at the brown carpet and shrugged. "Come on, we have a lot of work to do before dinner."

"Awesome," said Maren, dreamily following him back outside.

Thirty-Nine

MAREN SPENT THE REST OF the afternoon with the sometimes-mustached man and Pam, the sleepwalking dream supplier, polishing various sculptures in various stages of dismantlement. It was hard to work while pretending to close her eyes, and Maren had smashed her forehead twice and her shoulder at least three times on overhanging sculpture appendages. As they worked, the sky grew dimmer until finally the mustached man mopped his forehead with his dirty rag.

"Time for dinner," he said, tossing his rag into the bucket. "Follow me."

Maren's stomach growled, even though she was nervous about putting anything made by Carmella into her mouth. Hopefully someone else did the cooking, and there was no need to tamper with it if everybody was already sleepwalking. Maren and Pam followed the man inside the white building and past the kitchen, where the hall turned a corner and led to a big room full of clacking utensils and chatter.

"Hey, Bob!" someone called out as they entered.

"You two can go sit with the other sleepers," said Bob, pointing to a table where a handful of people sat with plates full of sliced lunch meat. With a huge wave of relief, Maren spotted Amos, and she slid into the empty chair beside him before Pam could take it.

"Hey," she said under her breath.

"Hi." Amos was busy cutting a slice of bologna with his knife and fork and didn't look up. Maren wondered if Ivy had woken him already and he was just pretending to sleepwalk, or whether he was still asleep.

"How's, uh, the dinner?" she asked.

"*So* good." Amos grinned with his eyes firmly shut. "I can't remember the last time I had roast beef this good."

Maren eyed the slice of limp lunch meat dangling from his fork. Amos had very low standards for food, but this didn't seem right. She nudged his foot under the table, but not a single muscle in his face moved.

"Here you go, hon." An older woman—Maren recognized

her as one of the lunch ladies from camp—set a plate in front of her. Thank goodness Lishta had been careful about hiding her identity from her cafeteria colleagues.

"Thanks, I love roast beef," Maren said, and the woman left. She ventured a quick glance at the non-sleepwalker table, where Bob, the sometimes-mustached man, sat with Judy, the two younger girls who had pinned Amos down on the bus, a few people she didn't recognize, and Evan, that slimy rat. They were all busy stuffing their mouths with actual roast beef and telling loud jokes, paying no attention to the sleepwalkers and their sad plates of processed meat.

Maren cut herself a bit of sliced ham and turkey and gave it a cautious sniff. It smelled sandwichy and didn't seem to be dosed with anything. She took a small bite, and it tasted fine. Before she knew it, she'd eaten everything on her plate, and her stomach groaned happily. Amos was still busy cutting his food and savoring every bite. Carefully, Maren eased the waking antidote out of her pocket, and after checking one more time that no one was watching, she dropped it onto Amos's fork as he lifted it to his mouth.

Amos's eyebrows twitched as he tasted the new flavor with his lunchmeat, but he kept on chewing, and for the first time ever, Maren was grateful for her friend's ability to eat pretty much anything. His eyes popped open.

"Shut them," hissed Maren, and Amos gave her a bug-eyed gawk before quickly obeying.

"Rabid groundhogs," he whispered. "How long have I been out?"

"A few hours," whispered Maren. "We're at Carmella's compound."

"That can't be good," whispered Amos.

"Who wants dessert?" The lunch lady reappeared, holding a platter of green Jell-O with lumps inside that looked like cottage cheese and possibly olives.

"Me!" yelled Amos, and Maren gagged as they each received a wobbly green scoop on their plates.

"Is this seat taken?"

Maren almost looked up at the sound of Thalia's silvery voice, but caught herself. "No, it's all yours."

"Thanks." The dream-crafting instructor dropped into the seat and picked up a spoon. "Ooh, angel food cake is my favorite."

"It's not—" Maren started, but the lunch lady was still at their table, doling out more lumpy Jell-O. Amos finished eating his and asked for seconds. Thalia began eating her own dessert with relish, and Maren cursed herself for only giving Ivy two waking antidotes back at camp. She desperately needed another one right now.

"Look at your watch," she whispered, hoping Thalia somehow knew the lucid dreaming trick, but the dream-crafting teacher just shrugged.

"I don't wear a watch."

They'd have to sneak out tonight without her. Hopefully it wouldn't take long to find a nearby town and a police station, and then they'd come straight back and rescue her before morning even came.

"There's a plan for tonight," Maren whispered to Amos. "Ivy and I are going to steal a truck and go to the police."

"Ivy, as in the granddaughter of the evil megalomaniac who just kidnapped us?" whispered Amos, stealing a spoonful of Maren's Jell-O.

She slid her plate over to him. "Yes. But she didn't know about any of her grandmother's plans, and she wants to help us."

"Sounds suspicious," said Amos.

"I know it does, but I think we can trust her," said Maren. "She's been trying to help all this time."

"Well she did a pretty terrible job." Amos swallowed the last wobbly green blob and scraped his spoon all over the plate.

"She's our only option," said Maren, and Amos reluctantly nodded. "So tonight, when you hear somebody whistling 'Row, Row, Row Your Boat,' that's our signal to sneak out. We're meeting in the storage room near the back entrance. It's the third door on the left before the exit."

"Got it," said Amos. "I just hope you're right about her."

Maren's stomach churned at all the trust she was placing in one girl's hands, a girl who had already lied to her multiple times. But then, Maren had lied too. They'd both had to lie for different reasons, but now everything depended on them being honest.

"I hope I'm right too," she said.

Forty

MAREN LAY ON A NARROW cot in a dark room with all the sleepwalkers, wondering if they were dreaming that they were asleep. As terrifying as this entire experience had been, she still desperately wanted to know how Carmella was making it all happen. She hoped someday, when this was all a distant memory, she'd learn some of the old woman's secrets—assuming this would actually be a distant memory someday. Maren didn't like to think of the alternatives, ones where she might stay kidnapped forever, end up in jail for theft, or worse.

The cot squeaked as she propped herself up, trying to see if Amos's eyes were open, but it was too dark and he was too far away. Hopefully he hadn't drifted off, because once they heard Ivy's whistle, they'd have to move quickly. As she waited, Maren made a list of everything she knew about Carmella's plan.

1. Trick two petty criminals into starting a summer camp for dreamers.
2. Test out sleeping sand combined with dreams to see how they interacted.
3. Make a bunch of kids sleepwalk and do highly embarrassing things.
4. Get the sand/dream ratio just right and then make the kids steal sculptures from a museum.
5. Give dreams and sleeping sand to the sculptures.
6. ???????

There was just no logical jump from step 5 to anything. What could Carmella possibly be planning to do with a bunch of giant, abstract, sleeping sculptures? She said she wanted people to remember her, and Maren had joked about putting on a show, but everyone would know the sculptures were stolen and the police would immediately shut it down. In the past, Carmella had gotten people to commit crimes for her while sleepwalking, but what crimes could sculptures possibly commit? And why bother with them when people were so much easier to transport and control?

Out in the hall, a floorboard creaked, and Maren held her breath and shut her eyes in case it was one of Carmella's henchpeople coming to check on them. The floor creaked again, and then softly, almost inaudibly, came a whistle.

Row, row, row your boat...gently down the stream...

Maren whipped upright, and, across the room, so did Amos. Easing off their cots, they crept to the door, and Maren tested the handle. It was unlocked, thankfully.

"Sorry, Thalia," she whispered. "We'll come back for you soon, I promise."

As she and Amos slipped out into the dark, empty hall, Maren prayed she'd be able to keep her promise.

———

Ivy met them at the door to the storage room.

"I've got the keys already," she whispered. "Let's go."

Amos and Maren followed her to the exit, and they dashed out into the summer night. The sky was ablaze with stars, and the woods around the compound practically roared with the sound of crickets and other nighttime creatures.

"I feel like I'm still dreaming," said Amos, and Maren agreed.

"This way," said Ivy, darting around the side of the building.

"You're absolutely, one hundred percent sure you trust this girl?" whispered Amos as they crept through the shadows.

"Like ninety-nine point nine percent," said Maren. "And we're all out of other options, so we'll just have to get over that one-tenth of a percentage, okay?"

"I guess." Amos stepped in a hole and almost fell, but Maren grabbed his elbow.

"Come on!" whisper-yelled Ivy, who stood beside a gate, poking numbers into a PIN pad. "We have to all go through at once and then I have to enter another code on the other side. If we screw this up, the alarm will go off."

Maren started forward, but Amos tugged her back.

"How come she knows so much about alarm systems but not her grandmother's actual plan?"

"I think she's on a need-to-know basis," said Maren. "Her grandmother doesn't trust her with all of the information, just some of it."

"Hmm," said Amos. "I don't like it."

If she was being honest, Maren didn't love it either, but the only other option was to go back inside and clean sculptures with a bunch of sleepwalkers until Carmella moved on to the next phase. It was time to get one step ahead of her plan and stop it. Tugging Amos behind her, Maren darted through the gate and waited while Ivy tapped in another code.

The gate swung silently shut. No alarm. Parked along the driveway in front of the building was a fleet of white trucks. Ivy pulled a key ring from her pocket and checked the number.

"Look for truck forty-seven," she said, but as she stepped onto the pavement, a light in front of the building flicked on. The three kids dove back into the shadows of the fence, not daring to breathe. Nothing inside the building moved, and no one came running outside.

"I think it's just a sensor light," said Ivy. "Let's go around the other way."

"I really don't like this," muttered Amos, and Maren wished he'd stop voicing her own thoughts out loud.

Keeping close to the fence, they snuck toward the back of the line of trucks. Each had a number stenciled on the driver's side door, but none of them went in order.

"There!" said Maren. "Forty-seven."

"On the count of three, and then run," said Ivy. "Those lights are going to turn on again, and we need to get out of here fast. One…two…three!"

Crouching low, they scuttled across the driveway toward the white truck. Just as Ivy's hand touched the door handle, the building light blinked on, illuminating them like a spotlight. Maren and Amos froze.

"Keep going!" yelled Ivy, gesturing for them to run to the passenger side.

As Maren darted around the back of the truck, she heard the door slam. Ivy was inside. But the engine wasn't starting. Maybe she was having trouble with the keys. Hopefully between the three of them, they'd manage to get the truck started and drive it to safety.

As Maren reached for the passenger door handle, Amos grabbed her arm.

"I still have a terrible feeling about this," he said.

Maren snatched her arm back. "We don't have time for feelings." She threw the door open and screamed.

Sitting in the passenger seat of the truck was Carmella, wearing a tiger-print bathrobe.

"Hello, little mouse," said old woman with a vicious grin. "Or should I say, little mice? How nice that you brought a friend."

For a long moment, Maren just stood there, gaping. Had Amos been right all along? Ivy sat in the driver's seat with a face like thunder, shoulders heaving. Then Maren's brain jerked into gear again, and she shoved Amos away.

"Run!" she screamed.

Without a second's hesitation, Amos sprinted for the woods, but Maren didn't follow. He had a better chance of escaping if she stayed here to distract Carmella.

"Why did you do this?" she yelled at Ivy.

"I didn't," said Ivy. "I swear!"

"She didn't." Carmella's eyes gleamed in the starlight. "Well, not on purpose anyway. But I had a feeling you weren't really sleeping, Maren, so I decided to follow my granddaughter and see what you two *besties* were up to. And then I noticed that truck forty-seven's keys were missing." She turned to her granddaughter and tutted. "Stealing vehicles? I thought I raised you better than this."

"Sorry, guess I should have gotten some sleepwalker to steal it for me," spat Ivy.

Carmella threw her head back and cackled. "If only you could make the sleeping sand work, sweetheart."

Ivy's face went even more thunderous. Tornado-like was a better way to describe it.

Maren wondered how far Amos had made it in the dark, if he had any idea how to get out of this compound. Maybe if he followed the driveway to the dirt road they'd driven in on, he'd eventually get to a main road and manage to flag down a car. It was only a tiny spark of hope, smaller than a fleck of dust, but it was better than nothing. Maybe if Maren played her cards right, she could run after him. Her foot slid backward, bracing.

"Grammy, you have to let them go!" pleaded Ivy. "Keep

the sculptures, but you can't just take people. Especially kids."

"I'll let them go once everything is done," said Carmella. Sour nausea filled Maren's throat, but she leaned back and waited for her moment.

"I want to call Mom!" Ivy slammed her fist into the steering wheel, and as Carmella startled, Maren swung her leg up, hooked her foot around the edge of the truck door, and kicked it shut. Then she bolted for the woods.

Faster, faster, she thought as her feet pounded the ground.

Her nose started to tickle.

Faster...faster...

Her eyes began to itch. The trees loomed closer, and she stretched out her hands as if they could somehow save her.

Fast...er...fa...s...ter...f...

Clouds filled her vision, and Maren tumbled, arms wheeling, into endless silver clouds.

Forty-One

SHE DRIFTED FOR A LONG time, flitting in and out of consciousness, vaguely aware of a cot under her body and a thin pillow
under her cheek. Sometimes the world was a dark room, and
other times it was whirling clouds or sandy deserts or orchards
full of apple trees or blue foxes with swishing tails. Each time
she tried to reach out and ground herself, her brain lost the
threads and she went drifting again, the images fading to
blackness or shifting into something so abstract she couldn't
focus on a single point.

And then suddenly everything was sharp and clear. The
cot was gone, and she stood in a parking lot surrounded by
tall, fantastically designed buildings in a rainbow of colors.
Something papery clung to the underside of Maren's tongue,
but she couldn't quite remember what it was, and it didn't

matter anyway. The sky was sun-dazzled pink, and a gentle breeze tickled her face. She smiled. Everything felt wonderful. Cities were fun places to visit. Especially this city, which she'd never seen before.

"Be careful of the springs!" someone shouted. "They're going to expand as soon as it comes out!"

Someone nudged Maren aside, and she watched as three men in paint-spattered coveralls pushed a ramp up to the back of a white truck. From inside the truck came a terrible scraping sound. Actually, it wasn't terrible—Maren loved the sound of that heavy metallic scrape, because it meant something wonderful was about to happen. Something she cared deeply about, even though she wasn't quite sure what it was.

Then people were leaping out of the way as a lumpy orange ball came rolling down the ramp. As it rolled, armlike appendages sprang out from its body in all directions.

"Now!" someone yelled, and a teenage boy dashed over and placed a wedge in front of the rolling sphere. It came to a gentle stop. A sideways, one-eyed half-face in the ball's center grinned at Maren, and she grinned back.

"Hey, George," she said, though she had no idea how she knew its name. Judging from the empty sockets and newly welded spots, George's arms had been rearranged so that he could roll, his face rotating like the hands of a clock.

Or a watch.

There was something about a watch that Maren was supposed to remember.

"Heads up!" Another truck opened, and out rolled a dog with a wooden pyramid for a head and steamroller wheels instead of legs. Maren didn't know the name of this sculpture, but a delighted flush went through her. She loved it too, and she couldn't wait to help with…whatever was happening next.

Yet another truck rattled open and Maren rushed over to help the others pull out a rocket ship that lay on its side on a wheeled trolley. Its blue metal sides gleamed in the sunlight, and pride filled Maren's heart. She'd helped make this one shine. A crane swung a rope with a huge hook overhead, and Maren waved to the operator, a boy she recognized—Amos, yes, that was his name. She clipped the hook onto a metal loop at the tip of the rocket, and Amos lifted it slowly up. Once the ship was vertical and standing on its chicken feet, everyone cheered.

On the sidewalk, a man and a tiny girl with a purple balloon tied to her wrist stopped to stare. "Is there going to be a parade?" he asked.

"There's going to be something even better than a parade." A long-haired old woman dressed in a midnight-colored robe dotted with stars strode out from behind a truck. Maren's heart filled with love and devotion. *This* was the person she cared most about in the whole, wide world. The lovely, mesmerizing Sandwoman, who was always, always watching.

The little girl clapped her hands. "I love parades!"

"Those look like Cleo Montclair sculptures," said the man. "I read something about them recently. What was it again?"

As he scratched his head, the Sandwoman drifted closer. Flashing a smile at the girl, she pulled a velvet pouch from her pocket and took a pinch of something, then blew it at them. The man's eyes snapped shut, and a dreamy look drifted across his face.

"I'm going to tell everyone to watch," he droned.

His daughter sneezed, then blinked at the Sandwoman. "Daddy, I want to go home."

"We will, sweetie," he said, leading her away. "Just as soon as we tell everyone."

The girl peeked back over her shoulder and stuck her tongue out at the Sandwoman, which Maren found very rude. But that didn't matter. It was time for things to begin. What things, she wasn't sure, but she was ready.

The Sandwoman ran her hand along the steamroller-dog's side and then checked her fingers for dust. "Where's truck twelve?" she asked Evan, a boy who made Maren feel irrationally angry.

"I don't know," he said. "Judy, have you seen truck twelve?"

Judy pushed a button on the handle of a massive purple umbrella that lay on its side, then leapt out of the way as it opened and flipped upside down. "I thought they were right behind us on the highway."

The Sandwoman strode over, robe billowing. "Apparently they were *not* right behind you. Why weren't you paying attention, Judy?"

"I'm…so…so sorry," stammered Judy, backing away.

"Where is my granddaughter?" The Sandwoman's voice went quiet and glacially cold, and Judy let out a frightened peep.

"I don't know," she squeaked. "I thought she was riding with Evan?"

Evan's mouth pursed like he'd swallowed about seven lemons, and Maren felt a strange and sudden wave of smugness. "She asked if she could switch to truck twelve, and I…uh… said that was…fine?"

"And you didn't think to ask me?" roared the Sandwoman. "Who else was on that truck?"

Evan picked up a clipboard and shakily flipped through its sheets. "Looks like B—Bob and Dave."

"And the sleepwalkers?"

"Heidi Henderson and…uh, Thalia Mandrake."

The Sandwoman snatched the clipboard out of Evan's hand and flung it. It hit one of George's waving arms, which briefly stopped moving, then started up again at a faster, more nervous pace.

"You put my granddaughter on the same truck as the woman who tried to overpower me on the way to the museum?" roared the Sandwoman.

"Uh…" Evan glanced around at his fellow henchpeople, who were all suddenly very focused on wiping down sculptures and inspecting the trucks. "Bob said it would be okay." He gulped loudly. "I'm pretty sure he said he'd already talked to you about it?"

"He most certainly did not!" yelled the Sandwoman. "I never would have allowed that!"

Maren felt bad for Ivy, who must have gotten lost. Now she was going to miss whatever incredible thing was about to happen.

"I'm s-sorry on B-Ben's behalf," Evan sounded like a croaking frog.

The Sandwoman opened her mouth to respond, then froze. In the distance, police sirens wailed. She tipped her head to listen, and so did Maren. The sirens were getting closer.

"Forget about them." The Sandwoman waved her hand dismissively and strode away. With a malicious gleam in her eyes, she pulled out her velvet pouch. "We're moving forward. Get ready, everyone!"

Maren cheered along with the others, but something deep in her gut told her this wasn't the right emotion to be having.

"Get me the dream bandages," the Sandwoman snapped at Judy.

Bandages with dreams didn't sound right, but Maren couldn't remember why. Judy dashed away and returned with a bucket, then followed the Sandwoman over to the steamroller-dog. Tugging on a pair of rubber gloves, she pulled out what looked like a foot-long Band-Aid and stuck it onto the side of the dog's wooden pyramid head.

"Quickly now!" shouted the Sandwoman, putting on her own gloves and dashing over to the rocket ship, where they wrapped a bandage around each of the chicken ankles. They slapped one on the umbrella's side and one over George's cloth mouth. In seconds, his arms began waving at a frantic pace, clocking Judy in the back of the head. The umbrella began snapping wildly open and shut and the rocket hopped back and forth on its skinny chicken feet.

"Gas masks!" shouted the Sandwoman, and Evan, Judy, and about half of the other people pulled out scary-looking masks with round valves on the front. Maren looked around for hers.

"Does anybody have my mask?" she asked.

"I don't have one either." Amos climbed out of his crane. "But I feel like that's totally okay, don't you?"

Maren thought for a second. "Yeah, I guess you're right. Who needs one of those silly things?"

They both laughed as the Sandwoman pulled a fistful of sand from her velvet pouch and blew over it, whirling in a circle as she did. A gigantic silver cloud engulfed the parking lot. Maren's feet tapped with nerves and thrills as the vapor swirled and then slowly dissipated. This was it.

The sculptures shuddered and twitched. Then they all surged forward.

Forty-Two

THE STEAMROLLER-DOG LED THE WAY onto the street, swiveling its pyramid head from side to side, though Maren had no idea if it could actually see without eyes. Maybe it had something like whale sonar to navigate. Then came the rocket ship, hopping and prancing on its chicken feet. Next was George, rolling along like a lumpy bowling ball, anemone-tentacles waving excitedly. Finally came the umbrella, lying on its side and swiftly opening and shutting to propel itself forward.

Maren squealed with glee, and Amos clapped and cheered along with the others as they followed the sculptures onto a quiet side street. Ahead on the main road, traffic zoomed past, but within seconds of the sculptures rounding the corner, there came the sound of screeching tires and blaring horns.

"What's going on?" someone yelled.

"Get them out of the road!" called somebody else.

Maren ran to catch up, dragging Amos with her. "Come on, we're missing all the fun!"

"What's the fun part again?" he asked, tripping over a curb.

"No clue!" said Maren. "But we have to find out!"

A siren blared behind them, and they stepped aside to let a police cruiser zoom past, blue lights flashing. Then came a fire truck. Maren and Amos waved to the firefighters, but they didn't wave back.

They rounded the corner onto the main road, and Maren stumbled to a stop. It felt like her eyes couldn't widen enough to take it all in. The street was lined with buildings of different heights and colors and shapes. Some leaned over the street, while others stretched toward the sky. Some had pointy roofs, some had transparent domes, and some had beautiful gardens on top. Maren had never seen such a stunning city before. She wanted to move there.

The street, however, was total chaos. All traffic had stopped, and people were fleeing their cars as the steamroller-dog crushed everything in its path. The rocket ship was more nimble, hopping around and over obstacles, but it still knocked over traffic lights, lampposts, and kiosks along the sidewalk.

Then there was George. The street had become his bowling alley, and the more people screamed, the faster he rolled. As he bowled toward a sidewalk café, everyone leapt up, knocking chairs and tables over and abandoning their beverages. George slowed, tentacles waving like he was shooing them all away, and then when the coast was clear, he tumbled through the empty furniture, sending it flying in all directions.

Bringing up the rear was the umbrella, snap-snap-snapping like some hungry, gobbling creature. It had already caught three traffic cones, a rubber boot, a newspaper, and a skateboard, and they tumbled around in its gaping maw. A little, yapping dog dashed after it, trailing a jeweled leash.

"Fifi, come back here this instant!" yelled a woman in a long fur coat.

Unable to fit down the gridlocked street, the fire truck had stopped, red lights flashing, and the firefighters, along with the police officers, were racing after the sculptures, trying to figure out how to stop them. But everyone was wary of the dog's steamroller wheels, and the umbrella kept snapping aggressively at anyone who got too close.

At a jewelry store across the street, two impeccably dressed women stood in the doorway, gawking at the pandemonium. As the Sandwoman strode closer, a silvery cloud wafted over them, and their eyes snapped shut. They rushed inside the shop, then returned with armloads of bulging bags. With a gracious smile, the Sandwoman gestured to a gas-mask-wearing assistant, who took the merchandise and dashed off.

Next the Sandwoman visited a watch store, and then a bank. Maren loved seeing that extraordinary woman get all the things she deserved, but she stayed on her side of the street, trailing behind the sculptures and their mayhem. Still, something was dragging her forward, a deep purpose she couldn't ignore.

Then she spotted it. The luxury car dealership. Maren scanned the row of cars at the front of the showroom, and her eyes landed on a green convertible. That was her car. She was going to drive it right out of the showroom. She wasn't sure how, but it was going to happen.

"The Bugatti." Amos pointed at the dealership. "She needs it. I'm getting it for her."

Maren wasn't sure which one was the Bugatti, but she knew who Amos was getting it for. The Sandwoman deserved everything her heart desired. Sticking close together, Maren and Amos glided across the street and waited for the old woman to blow her magic sand. This was going to be so wonderful.

"Help!" cried a man. "Get me out!"

The yelling came from inside the umbrella, which had snapped shut and was rolling back and forth with someone thrashing around inside. Maren wondered if she should help, but then she remembered the Sandwoman had a plan and she shouldn't interfere.

A woman screamed. "The little girl! Somebody grab her!"

The girl from the parking lot stood tugging on the string of her purple balloon, which was wrapped around a lamppost. The sidewalk around her was empty—everyone had dashed inside shops as the steamroller dog came roaring through.

"Run, sweetie!" someone yelled. "Let the balloon go!"

But she couldn't let go, Maren realized, because the balloon was tied around her wrist.

Crunch. The steamroller-dog pulverized a planter full of pink flowers. *Crunch.* It flattened an empty bus stop bench.

"Somebody grab her!" yelled a woman, but no one was close enough, and all of the police officers and firefighters were gathered in the middle of the street, line dancing to music nobody but they could hear. Maren tried to run to the girl, but her feet just kept walking toward the car dealership. She grabbed Amos's arm.

"We have to—" she started, but he shook her off and dashed away to the dealership, which was now full of silver clouds. Maren's feet started to follow, but she dug in her heels. This wasn't right. It couldn't be right. But if the Sandwoman wanted it, it had to be right.

One of the gas-masked helpers ran past with an armload

of stolen goods, and something tumbled out of a bag and landed at Maren's feet. A gold watch.

Look at your watch.

Maren's feet stopped shuffling.

Look at your watch.

She peered at her wrist, and there was a fluffy pink bunny face with a whirling dial.

"I'm dreaming!" she yelled, but nobody heard her in the chaos. Maren's eyes snapped open, and the fantastical buildings transformed into gray, normal ones she recognized. It was Dalston, a city about an hour away from Rockpool Bay.

Maren sprinted for the little girl. The steamroller was impossibly close now, crunching up and over another cluster of café tables. Skidding to a stop beside the girl, Maren tried to untangle the balloon, but it was hopelessly knotted. She grabbed the string and tried to snap it—she even tried biting it—but it held fast, and it was too tight around the little girl's wrist to slip off. Still the steamroller-dog rolled closer. The girl wailed as it crushed the last of the tables.

Maren stepped between the girl and the sculpture and held up her hands. "Please stop! You're dreaming! Wake up, dog. Wake up!"

The steamroller-dog showed no sign of hearing. It didn't even have ears.

"Stop, stop, stop!" she yelled, her voice ragged with terror. At some point she must have started crying, because her cheeks were wet, but everything else was numb. She simply couldn't leave this girl to die, but she didn't know how to make it all stop. She had tried her hardest, but it wasn't enough. Everything turned to slow motion, and the city faded away. It was just Maren and the steamroller-dog and her imminent end.

And a strangely loud flock of ducks quacking overhead.

Something powdery fell onto Maren's head, fizzing slightly as it slid into her hair. A green powder that looked like electric neon pollen wafted down over the steamroller-dog, and it began to slow.

"QVAAAACK!" yelled one of the ducks.

Maren's head snapped up, and there was Henri, wings flapping, with a large saltshaker clenched in his claws.

"BONJOUR, BONJOUR!" he yelled. "ICH BIN EIN KLEINES ENTLEIN!"

Forty-Three

THE STEAMROLLER-DOG RUMBLED TO A stop, and Maren rushed over, climbed up onto its back, and ripped the dream bandage off.

"Not so fast!" Carmella strode out of the car dealership. Now that Maren was awake, the old woman's midnight robe was gone, and she wore a leopard-print jumpsuit. Before anyone could react, Carmella threw a handful of sleeping sand into the air and blew. The cloud billowed and grew, and Maren's eyes went gritty as she slid down the side of the sculpture. A roaring sound filled her ears as reality began to fade.

But the roaring wasn't in her head. It was coming from somewhere down the street. Maren tugged her shirt up over her nose and mouth, then tapped through half of a dance routine, trying to keep from slipping under. But it was impossible—the dusty grains stuck to her eyelashes, dragging them lower and lower.

"REVEIILE-TOI!" yelled Henri.

"There you are, sweetheart!" Lishta's voice rang out over the roar, but Maren was too far gone. She slumped against the steamroller-dog's side, unable to even wave to her grandmother, unable to understand anything about this situation or how she'd gotten here.

"Point it over here!" yelled Lishta, and the roaring intensified. A massive blast of wind hit Maren's face, and slowly the fog in her brain began to clear. More green powder filtered down, and with an enormous effort she wrenched one eye open, then the other.

Two women wielding leaf blowers stood before her. The pantyhose stretched over their faces made them look like bank robbers—but nice bank robbers, if that were possible. Maren's heart soared as she recognized Lishta and her mother under the nylon. Another stocking-clad face popped out from behind them, and it was Hallie. With a tiny scream, Maren leapt up and ran for them.

"Here, dearie, put this on!" Lishta tossed her a floppy stocking, and Maren yanked it over her head. "My goodness, we should have brought more!"

Maren's answer was drowned out by the roaring drone of

the leaf blowers as her family rushed forward, clearing away the silvery cloud as the ducks and Henri shook more green dust over everyone. The police officers and firefighters stopped dancing and stood blinking in the street. A woman from the jewelry store gasped and dashed inside her shop. "We've been robbed!" she screamed.

"So have we!" yelled a man from the watch store, and all of the police officers rushed over to help.

"Wait!" yelled Maren, pointing at Carmella, but everyone was still muddled from the sleeping sand, and several of the police officers were still doing the occasional dance move. Taking advantage of the distraction, Carmella pulled another fistful of sleeping sand from her pouch.

"Put. That. Down." Lishta strode forward, aiming her leaf blower straight at Carmella's face. The old woman's hair flew sideways, and all the dust in her hand splatted against the side of the car dealership. Quickly, she tugged her velvet pouch shut, then squinted at Lishta's stocking-covered face.

"The…lunch lady?" She let out an incredulous laugh.

Lishta glowered. "I'm not a lunch lady, and neither are my esteemed colleagues. We prefer the term food services professional."

The two old women circled each other warily, Lishta brandishing her leaf blower and Carmella her velvet bag.

Maren dashed over to Hallie, who was helping Henri and a couple of ducks to refill their saltshakers from a bucket full of green powder that smelled like mint and bacon and plastic.

"Is this waking antidote?" asked Maren.

"Yeah, we gave up on putting it in sachets," said Hallie. "It works much faster this way."

"What's that plasticky smell?" asked Maren.

"Powdered alarm clock." Hallie grinned, and so did Maren.

"How did you find us?"

"We were back in Rockpool Bay—on our way home from the police station, actually—when your friend Ivy called and said you were heading to Dalston," said Hallie. "We borrowed the leaf blowers from some friend of Gran-Gran's, and Mom drove like ninety miles an hour to get here."

"Are the campers all safe?" asked Maren.

Hallie nodded. "Everyone came back on the bus except for you and Amos. We got the police involved, and everyone's parents picked them up."

That was a relief, even though everything was still a huge mess. Maren grabbed two handfuls of dust and smeared it all over the steamroller-dog and rocket ship sculptures. George had bowled himself into an alley and gotten stuck, so she ran over and dusted him too, then pulled off his bandage with the sachets stuck to it. The firefighters freed the little girl and her balloon.

"That's the woman you want to arrest! She made you all sleepwalk!" Maren pointed at Carmella, but the firefighters stared at her in confusion. She shook a cloud of waking antidote at them, and they all coughed.

"It's not our job to arrest people," said a firefighter with a beard.

"I know that—" Maren was cut off by a frightened yelp.

"Get me out of here!" yelled the man who was still trapped inside the purple umbrella sculpture. The firefighters rushed over and pried him out, but the umbrella kept snapping and rolling and spinning. Henri and the ducks zoomed overhead like a fleet of bomber planes, coating it in green dust, and finally it settled down and closed.

"Everybody freeze!"

Maren whirled around, and there was Evan with his arm wrapped around Amos's neck and a gun pointed at his head. Everyone sucked in their breath, and even George's tentacles went still.

"Turn off those leaf blowers!" he yelled, and with a nervous look at each other, Lishta and Maren's mom cut their engines.

Carmella blew a silver cloud over the crowd, and

everyone's eyes drifted shut, except for Maren and her nylon-wearing family. "Put the leaf blowers down, and take off those ridiculous stockings," she snapped. "Birds, drop your saltshakers!"

Henri gave a furious screech, but his shaker clattered to the ground and all of the ducks followed his lead.

Maren edged close to her sister, who gave her a sad nod, and they both pulled off their stockings. She prayed that whatever happened, they'd be together. It seemed unlikely Carmella would let them go, now that they all knew who she was. It would be so easy for her to have them all sleepwalk onto the trucks and then make them...disappear.

There was a flash of movement behind Lisha, and Maren strained to see without turning her head and calling attention to it. Lishta pulled something from her pocket and passed it behind her back.

"Grammy, no!" Ivy came running up the street, tripping over flattened chairs and leaping over fallen traffic lights. "This has gotten so far out of control. You have to stop!"

"How nice of you to finally show up." Carmella glowered at her granddaughter, but Maren spotted a hint of sorrow in her eyes.

"I called for help," said Ivy, edging closer. "Because you need help. What you're doing isn't okay."

"I didn't see you complaining when I took you on that vacation to Iceland," said Carmella. "Or to Thailand or Paris. Where do you think all that money came from?"

Ivy sighed. "I didn't know."

"Who do you think bought your mother's house?" Carmella puffed out her bony chest.

"You?" Ivy glanced sideways for a flicker of an instant, but her grandmother was too busy gloating to notice.

"That's right, it was me," said Carmella. "I guess you and your mother will have to move out if you don't believe in buying things with stolen money, eh?"

Ivy took a sudden step forward, startling her grandmother, who grabbed Evan's arm and hauled him and Amos backward. The only thing between them and a clear path down the street was the unmoving purple umbrella.

"I don't care what you did in the past, Grammy," said Ivy, "but it's time to stop making bad choices."

The old woman's eyes flashed. "After everything I've done for you, you're going to lecture me on making bad choices?"

Ivy's gaze snagged on something behind her grandmother, but she quickly refocused. "You've been lying to me for weeks, but no, I'm not lecturing you. I'm asking you to make the right choice."

Carmella scoffed. "And I'm asking *you* to make a choice

too. Either you're with me or you're with them. There's no going back, darlin', so think carefully."

Ivy's face fell, and Maren's heart ached for her. Even though Ivy's grandmother was a diabolical criminal, this couldn't be easy.

Ivy took a slow breath and squeezed her hands into fists. "I'm with them."

Carmella shut her eyes and sighed. "Evan, bring the boy to the trucks."

"No," whispered Maren as Evan wrenched Amos around and the gun made contact with his skull. This was utterly terrible. She couldn't let them take Amos, but she couldn't move or he'd get shot.

With a sad smile at her granddaughter, Carmella pulled out a handful of sleeping sand and took a step backward.

SNAP.

The umbrella sculpture swallowed her up.

With a yelp, Evan lurched away, and a shadowy figure leapt out from behind the umbrella and knocked the gun out of his hand. Amos wrenched free, and the black-clad person shoved Evan just as the umbrella swung open again.

SNAP.

With a high-pitched scream, Evan disappeared inside too.

The mysterious figure pulled the stocking off her head, and silver hair tumbled out. Thalia Mandrake studied the bulging, twitching umbrella and patted its side. "Good job, my friend," she said. "Hold them tight."

Maren, Hallie, Lishta, and their mom all rushed forward to hug Amos, Thalia, and Ivy in a big jumble.

"You were all amazing!" said Hallie.

"Perfectly choreographed," said Maren's mom with a wink at her.

"But how did you get the umbrella to do that?" asked Maren.

Thalia held up a little metal tin. "Your grandmother passed me this whispering dust, and I gave some to it." She smiled over her shoulder. "The poor thing has had a rough day."

"I have too," said Amos, and Hallie dragged him into another hug that made his face turn the same color as the fire truck.

Lishta turned to Ivy and squeezed both of her hands. "Thank you for calling us, dearie, and for standing up to your grandmother. That was very brave of you."

Ivy swallowed hard. "It was the right thing to do."

"But not the easy thing," said Lishta. Everyone murmured their thanks to Ivy, but Maren knew it was hard for her to watch them be together as a family when she'd just abandoned her own. Where would Ivy live for the rest of the summer? Would her mother be able to leave her job in Chile? And what would happen to their house?

Henri snatched up his saltshaker, and he and the ducks soared over the sleepwalking shop workers and firefighters and police officers, coating them in powdery green. As everyone slowly woke and the world slid back into reality, Maren wrapped both arms around her mother's waist and held on tight. Finally, she was safe again.

Forty-Four

"MALADROITE!" YELLED HENRI, WHO WAS busy scattering safety pins all over the dream shop's shelves.

"Henri, that's not very kind," said Lishta. "Ivy is new at this, and she's doing her best."

Five months had passed since the ill-fated day in Dalston. Ivy's mother hadn't lost their house or her job, and she had finally agreed to let Ivy come stay with Maren and her family for winter break. Ivy had brought six batches of homemade chocolate chip cookies and a box of safety pins for Henri as an apology for her grandmother's actions, but everyone assured her she wasn't to blame and had been instrumental in saving the day.

"The bird is right," said Ivy, wiping up a puddle of elder-flower extract. "I *am* clumsy."

"You're doing a great job," said Maren. "You should see how much stuff I usually spill."

She helped Ivy finish up the dreams and sew their edges shut, and then they laid the sachets out in a line on the counter. Munching on a saltine cracker, Lishta wandered over and patted Ivy's shoulder.

"Go ahead, dearie."

Ivy took a breath and blew gently across the sachets, and they transformed from plain white to a rainbow spectrum of colors, starting with deep purple on the left and ending with brilliant crimson on the right.

"Spectacular!" Lishta and Maren clapped, and even Henri gave a begrudgingly impressed squawk. All week they'd been on a mission to figure out what exactly Ivy's magic did. So far, they'd learned she could change the color of magical things by blowing on them, and there was some element of sleepiness to them afterward. So, for example, any dreams she blew on didn't need dreamsalt anymore. Lishta was certain there was more to Ivy's magic, some thread that pulled it all together, and she insisted it was just a matter of time before they figured out what exactly it was.

"We should do a whole new line of rainbow dreams." Maren's head whirled with all the different possibilities.

"PUANT COMME UN VIEUX FROMAGE," yelled Henri.

"Did someone say cheese?" The door swung open and Thalia Mandrake strolled in, followed by Hallie and her mom. She set a shopping bag on the counter beside the dreams. "We found some delicious-looking Brie at the Green and Fresh and a baguette and salad to go with it for lunch."

Thalia had also decided to pay Maren's family a winter visit—she was spending six weeks living in a nearby apartment and studying Lishta's dream-making techniques to bring back to her own shop in Sedona. She said everyone swore Lishta's craft was the finest in the country, if not the world, and she was determined to put her own spin on it when she got home.

"I'm famished," said Lishta, dusting saltine crumbs off her hands and taking a couple of dirty jars over to the sink.

A gentle knock sounded on the door, and Artax, the cat, meowed.

"Please come in!" called Lishta.

The door swung open, and in walked a woman dressed all in black with short black hair. In her arms she carried a cardboard box. Hallie gasped and clutched Maren's arm.

"Oh. My. Sweet. Jamcrackers," she whispered, but Maren had no idea why her sister was freaking out.

"Can we help you?" she asked, putting on her kindest and most helpful smile.

"I hope it is *I* who can help *you*," said the woman, "after everything you've done for my creations."

"Huh?" Maren cast a quizzical look at her mother, who shrugged.

"Oh my goodness, Ms. Montclair, we are so honored to have you in our shop," gushed Hallie, rushing over to shake the artist's hand, which was difficult because she was still holding the box. "Can I get you some water? Tea? Coffee?"

"That's very kind, but no." Cleo Montclair set her box on the floor and beamed at everyone. "I've brought you all a thank-you gift for saving not only my precious sculptures, but also my reputation as an artist."

"It was no trouble at all," said Lishta, which was the biggest understatement in the universe.

Cleo opened the box and lifted out a miniature lumpy orange sphere with one eye, a wide mouth, and metal arms springing in all directions.

"Tiny George!" yelled Maren, and Cleo's black eyebrow lifted. "I—well actually, Ivy and I—may have named your sculpture George a while ago. I hope that's okay."

Cleo laughed. "This little friend belongs to you now, so you can name it anything you like."

"Oh my...you're joking...an actual...for us?" Hallie had completely lost the ability to form sentences.

"It's only very lightly magicked," said Cleo. "So it will move just a tiny bit and you won't have to worry about it... rolling away." She grimaced slightly.

"Thank you so, so, so, so much!" gushed Hallie, and Maren, her mother, and Lishta echoed her gratitude.

"Please, won't you join us for lunch?" asked Thalia, opening the shopping bag. "I've got enough food here to feed a small army."

"Did somebody say food?" Amos poked his head through the open door, and everyone laughed. Of course Amos wasn't going to miss a free meal.

Maren stood back and watched everyone rush around, pulling stools up to the counter and setting out plates and napkins. On the counter, Tiny George waved his springy appendages like he was dancing, feeding off the happy buzz of the crowded dream shop. Maren felt like dancing too, because her heart was filled to the brim with gratitude. For this day and this surprise. For dreams and magic. For new friendships and old ones.

And especially for her family.

Acknowledgments

To my agent, Kathleen Rushall, thank you for all of your support, and for your kindness and wise advice throughout the process of writing this book. And thank you to my editor, Annie Berger, for championing this project and helping me develop it into the (slightly bananas) story it was meant to be.

To Lynne Hartzer, Susan Barnett, Chelsey Moler Ford, and Cassie Gutman, thank you for your eagle-eyed copy edits and incredibly astute suggestions. Thank you also to Ashlyn Keil for all the publicity work and adorable dream-related ideas you've had.

A massive thank you to Jesse Sutanto and Grace Shim for reading drafts of this book and giving me invaluable feedback and encouragement. And to Margot Harrison and Marley

Teter, I'm so grateful for your friendship, for all your wise insights over the years, and for all the laughs we've had.

Thanks to Peter Patzak for helping me fix Henri's erratic German expressions, and to my husband, Ciaran, for checking over his French randomness. Any remaining errors in the text are fully my fault!

Thank you, Mom, for always being there for me and keeping me going. Alissa, I'm so glad that out of all the sisters in the world, I got you! Isla and Neil, reading my books to you and hearing your feedback is one of my favorite things in the world. And Ciaran, thank you for putting up with all my melodramatic "I need to write!" announcements and helping me actually do that.

Finally, thank you to my readers! I hope you've enjoyed taking this journey with Maren and her dreamy family.

About the Author

Nicole Lesperance grew up on Cape Cod and now lives near Boston with her husband, two kids, and two rambunctious black cats. She writes middle grade and young adult books. Visit her online at nicolelesperance.com.